D1414323

DEAD AGAIN

I heard a new sound, a sliding whisper. My gun was in the drawer in my bedroom. Was it even loaded?

I turned my head slowly, could see nothing behind me, nothing in front, no shadow. I made myself get up and move slowly to the edge of the room.

Then suddenly something was around my neck, pressing on my throat, something cold and round against my forehead.

"You're dead," said a voice. "You're dead."

The Cowboy Rides Away

Betsy Thornton

A DELL BOOK

Published by
Dell Publishing
a division of
Bantam Doubleday Dell Publishing Group, Inc.
1540 Broadway
New York, New York 10036

If you purchased this book without a cover you should be aware that this book is stolen property. It was reported as "unsold and destroyed" to the publisher and neither the author nor the publisher has received any payment for this "stripped book."

"My Adobe Hacienda" by Louise Massey and Lee Penny. Copyright © 1941 by Peer International Corporation. Copyright Renewed. International Copyright Secured.

Excerpts from *The Awful Rowing Toward God* by Anne Sexton. Copyright © 1975 by Loring Conant, Jr. Executor of the Estate of Anne Sexton. Reprinted by permission of Houghton Mifflin Co. All rights reserved.

"I've Seen That Look on Me (A Thousand Times)" by: Harlan Howard and Shirl Milete. Copyright © 1966 Sony Tree Publishing Co., Inc. (Renewed) All rights administered by Sony Music Publishing, 8 Music Square West, Nashville, TN 37203. All Rights Reserved. Used by Permission.

"The Cowboy Rides Away" by: Sonny Throckmorton and Casey Kelly. Copyright © 1983 Sony Cross Keys Publishing Co., Inc./Tightlist Music Inc. All rights on behalf of Sony Cross Keys Publishing Co., Inc. administered by Sony Music Publishing, 8 Music Square West, Nashville, TN 37203. All Rights Reserved. Used by Permission.

The author is grateful for permission to quote the lines from the lyrics of "Big Ball's in Cow Town," by Hoyle Nix, courtesy of Konawa Music Publishing Company.

Copyright © 1996 by Betsy Thornton

All rights reserved. No part of this book may be reproduced or transmitted in any form or by any means, electronic or mechanical, including photocopying, recording, or by any information storage and retrieval system, without the written permission of the Publisher, except where permitted by law. For information address: St. Martin's Press, 175 Fifth Avenue, New York, NY 10010.

The trademark Dell® is registered in the U.S. Patent and Trademark Office.

ISBN: 0-440-22327-X

Reprinted by arrangement with St. Martin's Press

Printed in the United States of America

Published simultaneously in Canada

May 1997

10 9 8 7 6 5 4 3 2 1

OPM

To my parents,
for their enduring support.

Thanks most of all to Elizabeth Atwood Taylor for her immeasurable help with every aspect of this book, and to Vicky Bijur, my agent, for making it all happen.

Thanks to Tom Glass of the Cochise County Attorney's office for his weapons expertise, to Stella Crowlie for giving me the tape that started it all, and to Patty Hill, Susan Mathews, Susan Perlman, and Toni Sodersten for all the Tuesday night respites.

PART ONE

Arizona

I

Out in the desert, in the middle of forty acres of scrub oak, mesquite, and yucca, the man aimed the Winchester pump .22 at the first of the empty Budweiser beer cans, twenty of them lined up on the red dirt across the wash. He pumped the rifle, centered along the bead, pulled the trigger, and the first can jumped. He pumped, centered, and fired again until he'd used up all fifteen shots, not missing a single can. He was thinking about women.

The repetitive action lulled part of his mind, putting it into a meditative state, and sometimes he could work things out better that way than if he concentrated on them purposely.

He paused to reload and saw a dark-haired woman, rich and glossy, wearing a pink bikini and a gold necklace, down on the beach in San Carlos. She was smiling, in love, and because of this, she was pretending to like the way he lived down there, his poverty and his ability to speak to the Mexicans, but he knew in fact she hated it, bred in her bones to hate it.

He rested the rifle butt on the ground for a moment and looked down into the dry wash, remembering how a couple of days ago it had filled up with runoff from the rains in the mountains, the water slithering like a snake down through the desert.

"But it's not even raining *here*!" the little girl had exclaimed, standing dangerously near the crumbling edge in her impractical black velvet shoes. They were the only shoes she'd brought, she'd forgotten to pack any more. He wished he could have bought her a pair of running shoes, but he didn't have the extra fifty dollars.

"It's a miracle," he'd told her. "Just a run-of-the-mill desert miracle."

Since the little girl had arrived he hadn't done much shooting, he didn't like to do it in front of her. She didn't approve of guns, and even though he'd done everything he could to teach her what he knew about life, about the desert, she didn't approve of him either.

Le Roi was what the little girl called him. He hadn't expected her to call him daddy, or father, but hadn't expected either that she would take his name and turn it into Le Roi. The king, in French. She was very intelligent and he was proud of that, but it had its dark side. Did she mean it as a joke or did she see something authoritative, controlling, in him? *Manipulative*—now he saw another woman screaming the word, a tall brown-haired woman, strong, stronger than he was in many ways.

Three Gambel quail scuttled out from the mesquite, in the distance a jackrabbit loped; the wildlife was coming out again now that he wasn't shooting. A true good old Valley boy would have taken a shot at all of them. When he'd first moved here and bought the house and forty acres from Mr. O'Hara, he'd gone out hunting with him a few times, to establish himself and to show respect.

But he didn't really like killing. After a while he'd found excuses. The last thing he'd killed had been his neighbor's dog, done it in a rage, unthinking, and that had scared him; since then he'd killed nothing. Nothing for four years. Did that make any difference? Probably not. He wondered what he'd be like now if he'd never killed. Gentler? Blessed? Kill. Middle English, deriving from the word *quell.*

He shot the rest of the beer cans and used the ten remaining shots on the ones that were already dead. He missed a couple.

Then he started back to his house, rubbing his upper arm. A .22 was a gentle rifle to use, but he thought maybe he had a little arthritis. The peacock screeched from a heap of beached tumbleweed, familiar, but for a second, stopping his heart.

The house was ahead of him, a small wooden structure with a good front porch to sit out on and watch the sun set; steer's skull hanging on the wall, corny, too Georgia O'Keefe. His blue pickup was parked by the staked tomatoes he'd put in at the side; behind wire fencing, some of the tomatoes ripening.

He went inside and put the rifle on the varnished pine table, missing the little girl's being there even though she hadn't been there long and he was always a little nervous around her. The cowboy boots, nearly new, that he'd bought for her at a yard sale in the Junction before she'd arrived, thinking, *all kids love cowboy boots,* stood on the floor, mocking him. They'd been way too small. Her rich stepfather could buy her running shoes any time he wanted, a hundred pairs of cowboy boots.

His house had never seemed so empty. He picked up the rifle from the pine table and began to reload it. *OK, he thought, I'm scared.*

2
___

It was summer in the high Arizona desert, monsoon
season, and I slept in my house in the little mountain town
of Dudley, dreaming of New York and my ex-husband,
Arnold, a handsome insecure boy of twenty-three. We
were married again, sleeping together, his legs intertwined
with mine, his arms tight around my waist. Every night for
five months of our marriage we had slept this way, and
whenever I tried to throw him off he held me that much
more tightly. Now I knew the truth: My whole life after
him, eighteen years, was the dream, we were still married
and I would never—

The phone shrilled and I jumped awake. Big Foot
leaped off the couch and landed on the coffee table, scat-
tering tapes and knocking over a mason jar of roses. For a
second, in the monsoon electric air, I could still feel
Arnold, like a phantom limb, imagined New York City just
outside, hypervigilant and dangerous. Then I picked up
the receiver.

"Hello?" Somewhere far away thunder grumbled, like

the trucks that had rumbled by my window back in the city.

"Hi there," said a voice. "Was that the monsoon or just you groaning? I'll be by in ten minutes."

"Bobbie? Wh—" I began, but she hung up.

My watch said 2:23 A.M. I'd fallen asleep on the couch. Every muscle, every joint, felt stiff and cramped, but at least, thank God, I wasn't still married to Arnold. Nor did I live in New York City, the French doors in the living room were open wide, not barricaded with bars and police locks. Ironic that it was a violent death that had landed me in Arizona—Hal's death—but I was not going to think of that now at 2:23 in the morning.

Water dripped steadily from the overturned jar onto the floor. I set it upright and shoved the wilted roses back in. Yuck, I should have thrown them out a week ago. I rescued the tapes—Clint Black, Dwight Yoakam, George Strait—wiping them on the rug. Then I groped my way to the bedroom.

My Victim Witness clothes were laid out on the wicker chair by the window: long purple cotton T-shirt, plain black pants because cops didn't like little ladies to wear jeans, my Keds—shoes were important, you had to be able to run in case you got a domestic violence call and the perpetrator decided to take a shot at the nice Victim Witness volunteer.

I'd never gone out on a call with Bobbie—Bobbie Jean Loper, married to Jim Loper, who was, I thought, a fireman, but Bobbie didn't let you in on her married life much. I was part-time paid staff at Victim Witness doing compensation claims, and I knew her from the volunteer training where she'd assisted, waiting to step forward with her eyewitness accounts after Lucinda, the coordinator, lectured on the stages of grief and death notifications, suicide lethality, and domestic violence.

The concepts of Victim Witness were new, ideas that victims had rights, that victimization created a whole series of needs and problems no one had thought to care about until back in '82 when the President's Task Force had analyzed the needs of victims and set forth recommendations.

"The only good thing Reagan ever did," I'd blurted out at the Victimology training, forgetting I was in Arizona.

Now, at least in Cochise County, Victim Witness volunteers offered twenty-four-hour crisis intervention, going out on calls with law enforcement whenever there were victims. Ruth and Annie had been there for me at the scene a year ago with their tote bags and goodwill when I saw Hal die, watched the spirit go out in his eyes.

"I guess I owe Victim Witness something," I'd told Lucinda when I decided to take the volunteer training. "They were there for me once."

"Uh-*hum*." Lucinda leaned forward in her chair; her wiry, prematurely salt-and-pepper hair framed her face roguishly, her green eyes were bright. Ruth and Annie had to have written it up on the C.C.I., the Client Contact Information form. *Client was offered three referrals to counselors, but refused them.*

I knew I was supposed to spill out the whole thing, not so much the details but how I *felt*, to counselor Lucinda. It was the healthy thing to do. "I'm not ready to talk about it," I said.

Now in the bathroom I stared at my pale pale face, dreaming still imprinted on it, dabbed on some blusher, eyeliner, felt the adrenaline kick in, making my hand shake, smudging the liner.

Bobbie was the star volunteer, following cases she'd gone out on all the way to court, where she sat with her victims, mute and seething and protective.

I hoped I wouldn't blow it.

I dumped a ton of cat food into Big Foot's dish and heard Bobbie's car lumbering up the last stretch of my hilly street. Not even ten minutes. I grabbed the ugly plaid tote bag stuffed with Client Contact Information forms, Resources and Referrals, alcohol swabs, latex gloves for cleaning up death scenes, radio, and pager, and started out the door.

"It's a death notification," said Bobbie, backing too fast out of the driveway and almost hitting the streetlight. Her face, with its Bugs Bunny overbite, was cute; she was so little, she sat on a pillow to see over the steering wheel, but she was wiry and strong and her energy filled up the car.

"Where?" I asked.

"Out in the Valley."

That would be Sulphur Springs Valley, some sixty miles of Route 666, bordered on one side by the Swisshelm and Pedregosa Mountains, on the other by the Mules and Dragoons, and emptying at the south end into Mexico. A vast and biblical-looking plain of red dirt and mesquite, a corridor for drug dealers and illegal aliens.

I braced myself as, heavy footed on the accelerator, Bobbie ran the stop sign at the bottom of my hill. The streets of Old Dudley were dead quiet, streetlights shining on shacks painted San Francisco quaint, on shacks painted not at all.

Her little hillbilly face contorted in a grimace. "Hippie dippie land," she said, then looked over at me and added, "No offense." She lived over in New Dudley where the real locals lived.

Here I was, a New York liberal—New Left for a while in the sixties—in a job aligned with the prosecution, riding down the road with a redneck in the dead of night, cops at the end of the journey. Part of me was in love with the whole thing—the newness, the unexplored territory. Another part watched—suspicious, withholding, reticent to assign responsibility to criminals, possibly even criminal myself. Think of the lies I'd told the police about the circumstances surrounding Hal's death. But that was over and done with, case closed.

I thought of Lucinda lecturing on the stages of grief from

Elisabeth Kübler-Ross. All neat and defined. Shock/Denial, Anger, Depression, Bargaining, Acceptance.

"Have a banana," said the redneck.

"Thanks." I took one out of the Safeway plastic bag next to the pager on the dash and unpeeled it. Foods with potassium were good for stress: lettuce, kiwi fruit, orange juice, but the only one anyone ever remembered was bananas. Bananas were a Victim Witness joke, volunteers tearing off to help victims, holding bananas aloft as they drove.

Face intent, Bobbie ran the stop sign on Subway Street, whizzed past art galleries and stores that sold hip second-hand clothing and junk masquerading as collectibles, and ran the stop sign at Main.

"Dispatcher didn't have many details," she said. "Just the address." The white Honda swerved as we exited Old Dudley onto the highway. Bobbie whooped, loving it—at heart an adrenaline-junkie cop. "Hold on."

Actually I loved it too. Here we were two women, Bobbie just forty and me past, in some ways as emotionally flighty as teenagers. Somehow I'd never dreamed myself past maybe thirty, so I had to make my life up as it went along.

We rounded the curve by the pit that divided Old Dudley from New Dudley: once a copper mine, now an immense terraced environmentally incorrect hole in the earth, a vast blackness that concealed brilliant poisonous pools of water left from the leaching process.

We passed the sign saying SCENIC VIEW and I threw my banana peel out of the car. Despite the potassium, I was still nervous.

"We're going to one of those milepost addresses," Bobbie said after we passed the pit. "Probably be a bitch to find and the radio doesn't work a damn in that part of the Valley, but there'll be cop-car lights. Ed Masters and my brother."

I missed a breath, breathed deeper to catch up. We had

reached the traffic circle and I feigned intense interest in
the empty road leading off to my right, the one that went
to the Safeway and then Hereford and Palominas. I waited
awhile. We roared down the winding road through the tail
end of the Mule Mountains and took a sharp left at Double
Adobe. Suddenly you could feel the Valley, feel the broad
plain endless all around you, feel how far away the stars
were in the vast black sky.

I said in a voice that sounded overrehearsed, "I thought
Kyle was a detective."

"He is."

"So why would he be coming in on something like
this?"

Bobbie accelerated to seventy on the straight stretch,
roaring past a 45 MPH sign peppered with bullet holes,
headlights picking out the bodies of small animals. "I
didn't say it was a heart attack or anything, I just said
death notification. Probably something's funny."

"Funny? Like what?"

"Well, nobody that died in their sleep."

The desert air smelled damp and herbaceous. It must
have rained, one of those quick monsoon storms that
dumped a bucket of water, then moved on.

Bobbie glanced at me. "Kyle's got four kids." Her voice
was knowing. "I never did like Laurie, she's a little wimp,
but he's got those kids or I'd say go for it."

My face burned and I was glad of the dark. "I'm not that
kind," I protested.

"If I thought you were, I wouldn't have said it." She
laughed. "By the way, I got the dead guy's name. No one I
know, so I forgot to mention it. No one you know either,
Chloe. You don't know anybody."

Everything was suddenly quiet in my heart, the way it is
when you hear about a plane crash close to somewhere
you have once lived.

"So what's his name?" I asked finally.

"Harris. Leroy Harris."

Not even close. No one I knew would have a name like Leroy.

Dreaming of Arnold had awakened something, and as we sped down the road, time seemed to hurtle backwards to a deeper past: Marrying Arnold so young had just been an experiment that failed, an attempt to lead a life like my parents had.

Now I thought of a childhood of Monopoly games and canasta, tents staked out in the backyard, nature walks and late to church. My professor parents, being mushy in the kitchen after thirty, forty years of marriage, erudite and slightly bewildered by the world as it was now. My two brothers, James, now dead, Danny, the youngest, living in a Buddhist colony in Vermont. And me, the only daughter, born into the last functional family in America, arriving late to loss, grief, and emotional complexity and still trying to figure out how to handle it.

All around, the desert was dark and the night sky dotted with stars, like that connect-the-dots game kids play, but without the numbers.

3

A Cochise County sheriff's deputy's car, red and blue lights flashing, and a white compact were parked at the end of the dirt road in front of a small house. The compact would be Kyle's, it was the kind of unmarked car all the detectives drove. White, I guess, because they were the good guys.

The lights washed over the frame house, painting it red, then blue—it was just boards shedding splinters and flakes of dingy paint. But the dirt yard was neat, no trash lying about, no rusted cars. A blue pickup was parked to one side, bumper sticker half peeling off that said RODEO, COCHISE COUNTY FAIRGROUNDS.

We got out. The rain had released the smell of creosote and damp earth. Over my head there were so many stars, they seemed to blot out the sky; far away on the horizon was the little rim of lights from Douglas, and beyond them, Mexico.

Somewhere a windmill creaked, crickets chirped; there was a whir and a rustle, and a big bird, trailing long glistening blue-green feathers, strutted into the light. It opened its mouth and made a sound like a huge rusty gate being opened.

"A *peacock*," I said.

"Bug control," said Bobbie, already striding competently up the porch steps. "Also they kill rattlers."

Lights were on inside and the porch light too, battered by powdery gypsy moths and a surreal green stick bug. A steer's bleached skull hung on a nail on the wall over an old brown velvet couch.

Bobbie opened the screen door and it creaked, bits of torn screen sticking out. The inner door was already open. We walked into a dining room where four chairs were pushed into a varnished pine table. A rocking chair had a sheep pelt slung over the back; a pair of cowboy boots, run-down at the heels and muddy, leaned into each other on the floor, and beside them a smaller pair, a child's pair, hardly worn, stood straight and stiff.

The air was full of the thick sweet smell of whiskey and something else, coppery, metallic.

Two cops stood in the archway on the left that led to what must be the living room; one of them was Ed Masters in his tan deputy's uniform, a hefty slab of beef, medium rare coloring. The other, blond and lean in plaid shirt, jeans, and running shoes, was Kyle Barnett. He wore the baseball cap that said POINT BLANK on it that he'd told me once had come free with his Point Blank bulletproof vest and he'd grown a beard since I'd last seen him, but it was such a neatly trimmed straight-arrow beard, it hardly changed his appearance.

He turned his head, but didn't really take us in. His gray eyes blazed dark with concentration. He said fiercely, "Don't come any farther!"

Startled, we stopped, rooted on the wide pine floorboards.

Ed stood on one foot, then the other. "Uh, I don't think you guys were supposed to walk in," he said. "Right in the middle of the crime scene—except it ain't a crime, it's a suicide plain and simple. Legal in the state of Arizona."

"Let's wait till the investigation's complete. Medical examiner's the one who calls it," said Kyle.

If Ed was some kind of big sloppy dog, Kyle was a cat, sleek, short-haired, and all wound up. You wanted to unwind him slowly, see what you came up with.

He took off his baseball cap and put it back on. Suddenly he blinked as if he'd just noticed us. "Bobbie Jean. Chloe." I hadn't seen him in a couple of months, but it could have been centuries, his eyes skimmed off me as if encountering slippery ice. "Sorry. I didn't mean to yell."

"Sure it's suicide," blustered Ed. "The note's right there on the table. And you ladies got to tell the next of kin."

He walked heavily over to the pine table, and next to a pile of papers I saw an empty fifth of Jim Beam sitting on a thin slip of paper. Ed leaned over and read out loud,

"The last good-bye's the hardest one to say. This is where the cowboy rides away."

"Well, for heaven's sake," said Bobbie. "That's beautiful."

"George Strait," I said. "It's from a George Strait song." I looked at Kyle.

"That's right," he said. "It is." He glanced at me for a second, then down at the floor. "What Ed just read is classified, OK? Now, you guys get out of here. You don't need to see this."

"And why not?" I said, like an idiot; maybe needing to impress Bobbie, impress Kyle, wanting to get his attention. "It'll help with the notification. We can take it."

Kyle looked at me directly, challengingly, then stepped back from the archway, and I saw a man on the couch, not far away, only a few feet, bloody head back, wearing a brown plaid shirt, jeans, stocking feet, a rifle half off his lap. Blood spattered the faded red- and green-striped Mexican blanket that covered the couch. Rorschach spatters of blood and something else on the wall behind.

Half the top of his head was simply missing. What was left was black with blood. I willed myself not to flinch or something worse, to see it through until the horror diminished, aware of Kyle and Bobbie watching me. I made my eyes travel down, forced myself to look at his face.

I couldn't belive it. "Randall!" I gasped.

Then I was a balloon collapsing with the air rushing out, fighting to stay on my feet. Oddly, I seemed to see my mother's face, smiling at me as she read Winnie the Pooh, "Huff, huff, a horrible heffalump," she said. Black spots floated in the air, everything turned sepia, and then Kyle grabbed my arm.

4

Blood washed over me again and again.

Dimly I heard Kyle's voice. "Who lives down that way?"

"Frank Gresham," said another voice, who?

"Couldn't ask for a worse neighbor, could you?" Kyle again. "They fighting about anything?"

"I'm sure they was," said Ed. "Can't think of anyone that's not fighting with Frank Gresham."

"Chloe?" Bobbie was saying. "Chloe?"

I opened my eyes. The blood was only the cop car lights. I was on the porch looking out at the cars and the desert. Moths were hitting the porch light above my head, clicking at the glass. Bobbie sat beside me on the brown velvet couch, and Kyle and Ed, alert as a couple of beagles, stood a few feet away.

"Chloe, are you OK?" Bobbie held a glass of water in her hand.

"Yes," I said. "I just had my eyes closed." All I could remember was Kyle, leading me out to the porch. "What happened?"

"You almost fainted. Here, drink this."

I took the glass and drank the water all the way down, but my mouth still felt parched.

"Did you know him?" asked Bobbie curiously. "You called him Randall."

Then I remembered. "God," I said. "He looked just like someone I knew. . . ." Kyle and Ed weren't talking anymore. They were listening. "But . . . it *can't* be. . . ." My mind was numb; I couldn't think clearly.

"Randall," said Bobbie again. "Who's that?"

I felt embarrassed that I'd nearly fainted on my first really tough call-out, not to mention that Kyle was there watching. I closed my eyes, but in the darkness behind my lids I could see the blood again. I opened them.

Kyle was hunkered down in front of me, hands resting on his knees. This close I could see the prickles of his beard, the delicate bluish skin around his oddly innocent eyes. It had been two whole months since I'd seen him last, when he'd come to my office to talk to me about a young rape victim who he thought should get counseling. He'd looked surprised to see me even though I was sitting there in my own office, then he'd smiled like he was about to tell some big cosmic joke. "How's the resident liberal?"

But he wasn't smiling now; the look he gave me was cool, focused, and impersonal. "Who's Randall?"

I hesitated. "A friend. Randall Hartman. Back east when I was in college, a freshman." Suddenly I had the odd thought that it hadn't been Arnold in my dream, but Randall. I'd married Arnold on the rebound from Randall. And now Randall had come, in dream disguise, as if to tell me something.

Bobbie, Kyle, and Ed were all looking at me expectantly. I shook my head. "That was more than twenty years ago."

Kyle blinked. I could see him thinking *twenty years ago.* Doubt settled in the empty night air, settled on everyone's face, especially Bobbie's. If I didn't shape up fast, she'd never go on a call-out with me again. I doubted too, but some memories were coming back—*there was a way to know for sure.*

"Guy's name is Leroy Harris," said Ed Masters. "Been here ten years. Course, you ain't been here near that long yourself, Chloe. What, a year or two? Wasn't you some kind of investigator back in New York City?"

"Financial investigations," I said. "Nothing like this."

Kyle stood up. "You sit back for a minute, then we'll go inside, you and me, take another look at the guy." He flashed me a quick smile, patronizing, reducing me from someone in on the job to a victim.

I stood up defiantly. "It's nothing. I just feel a little queasy, is all. I don't think bananas agree with me, Bobbie."

"Look," said Kyle, "people react when they see something like what you saw. Even cops. OK?" He smiled again, more like the smile I was used to. "At least you didn't throw up."

"Hear, hear," said Bobbie.

"Let's go," I said to Kyle.

I walked into the house, the new volunteer who maybe wasn't going to work out, maybe carrying too much excess baggage in the emotion department. I could feel Kyle behind me, being a cop, smart, dedicated. They had the greatest respect for him over at the county attorney's. I did too.

Twenty years. It wasn't going to be Randall. Randall evoked different loyalties from the ones I'd taken on now. I watched my feet advancing, so I wouldn't see the man again until I reached him. When I did, the metallic smell was even stronger: the copper smell of blood. I looked down and something shifted in my mind. This was a movie, the man an extra, well made up. I saw a determined chin, long elegant nose, forehead veiled with blood; tried to see Leroy Harris, a stranger, because it was absurd to think otherwise, but Leroy Harris wasn't who I saw.

I glanced down and there on his left wrist, exposed below the cuff of his plaid flannel shirt, was the long half-moon scar. The top of a sardine can had cut him almost to the bone, he'd told me, back when he was a kid. With one finger I'd traced that scar as we lay in bed together in the Earl Hotel in Greenwich Village. Before he left me forever to go off to save the world with his leftist politics.

Suddenly the distancing mechanism was gone, and I was awake in a nightmare wherein that which was hidden reveals a face and the face is death, waiting for you. My knees started to tremble.

Randall and I had been a whole lot more than friends, and here he was dead in the desert, dead with someone else's name. Even in death there was still the gambler in his face, which had so attracted me once, the outlaw. Dead in the country of the enemy. Or at least it had been, back then. He would have had a reason, and I ought to know that reason before I told anyone who he was. A man alien to here, bound to be misunderstood, and I hadn't told on Hal either. Mistakes Hal had made long ago had led to his death years later. Why should he be remembered for those mistakes? *So I hadn't told on Hal to anyone and the secret kept him safe.*

Shaky and confused, I turned away towards Kyle, I thought for comfort, but what I felt was anger. Angry at him for being a cop at this moment, but more angry at him about something else I didn't want to think about.

We're all outlaws, Kyle, some of us just don't admit it. The survivors, the victims, were there any who would be harmed by my telling? There had been with Hal. I needed to know.

"It must have been the . . . the blood and all," I said. "It doesn't even look that much like him."

The peacock strutted in the dirt yard with magisterial authority. I was feeling better now, guilty about lying but like I could handle it. It had been a lie from instinct, not intellect, and instinct took time to explain itself. You had to trust it. Had to.

Kyle put one hand on the porch railing and stood looking out at the lights over in Douglas. Then he turned back towards us. "Must of bought this place from old man O'Hara, part of that big ranch he had before he started to break it up. It was Mrs. O'Hara called the sheriff's dispatch. Heard the gunshot she thought round eleven and been stewing about it. One forty-five was when she called."

"Never thought I'd see the day," said Ed, "an O'Hara would call the cops."

"Kyle," said Bobbie suddenly. "What were you doing, coming out so soon on a routine call?"

"Cause at two o'clock Fern Wilson called *me*," Kyle said. "She'd been trying to call Leroy and got worried, so I came out as a favor. See, he's got a daughter, Didi, she's spending the night at Fern and Homer's in the Junction. Thirteen years old. Fern knows something's up. We better get you over there."

5

Bobbie's car bumped down the narrow dirt road, rutted from the rain, Kyle ahead of us. Lights approached, blinding, then the medical examiner's van inched past.

I thought of the tiny cowboy boots, new and stiff just inside the house. *Randall had a child.*

What had happened for him to die this way—a suicide? It didn't seem like something he'd do. But what did I know—I hadn't seen him in twenty years.

Kyle's right signal light blinked as we followed him onto the paved highway.

"I hope you don't mind my asking," said Bobbie, "but was there ever anything . . . *actual* going on between you and my brother?"

"No," I said firmly. "Absolutely not. We used to talk a lot. But we don't anymore."

"How come?"

A jackrabbit froze in the light at the edge of the road. Over the mountains in the distance lightning lit up the sky, but the clouds were past us, racing towards Douglas and the border. Suddenly I felt adrift, floating in darkness. "I don't know," I lied.

"I was just kidding about the, um, go for it. He's my brother and he's such a good guy. He's also got four, I said *four*, kids."

"I *know* he has four kids," I said.

"Four kids," Bobbie repeated, but she wasn't thinking about her nieces and nephews anymore. "Suicide's extra tough on kids."

"How do we play this? I mean for the little girl?"

"As straight as we can. Gunshot to the head. Winchester pump .22, a rifle," she added matter-of-factly. "We say we don't know exactly the circumstances, it's still being investigated. But he left a note and it looks like suicide."

"Ouch," I said.

"You can't lie. People deserve the truth, even it if makes the person who tells it uncomfortable."

I nodded. My lips felt numb. "What about Fern? You know her?"

"Knew her when I was in junior high—she was older, my brother's age. Always got picked for things, Rodeo Princess, stuff like that. Real pretty. I'll tell Fern."

Kyle's blinker went on again, signaling left; he turned and we followed.

"Never thought she'd end up living all her life in the Junction," Bobbie went on. "Seemed like some rich guy would spot her and take her to his mansion on a hill. People used to joke Homer was the only man in the Valley who'd get a girl pregnant just so she'd marry him." She laughed. "He was a lot older, but you know, he was a real good dancer. The really sad part, their boy, well, he died, but she's got two daughters."

Ahead was the Junction, a cluster of buildings along both sides of the road, closed in, dark, harboring secrets. At the corner by the Valley Co-operative Feed Store we followed Kyle onto a darker street. Halfway down he stopped at a cinder-block house, just before, because cops never parked directly in front. It was painted white, set back from the road. We pulled in behind him. Zinnias bloomed in the headlights along a chain-link fence, dogs barked up and down the street. We got out of the car into night air that smelled of horses, clutching our tote bags.

Ordinary things jumped out at me, poignant with meaning; a calendar with horses grazing, a yellow chrome and Formica table, pink and purple African violets on the windowsill.

Fern Wilson wore a long plaid man's bathrobe, a pink lace-trimmed nightgown peeking out. Her husband was in jeans, blue striped pajama top. Bobbie told them straight out, just the bare bones, as we stood in their tidy kitchen.

"*No.*" Fern backed away, her nightgown swirling, tripping her up till her legs hit a chair and she sat down abruptly, her large blue eyes searching Bobbie's. She wore her hair Valley style, long and helped-along blond, permed into waves with a little cluster of extra curls perched unconnected on top, but her face was dead-on beautiful, any style would have worked. "Leroy wouldn't *do* that." She looked at her husband.

Homer had a big square lantern jaw and a gold molar, his face as homely as his wife's was beautiful. He went over and stood beside her, one big hand squeezing her shoulder.

"*God*damn, you know it must of been an accident." He reached up nervously with the other hand and smoothed back the ghost of hair that had long ago fallen out. "Leroy could shoot that gun pretty good, but he didn't have a speck of ordinary sense. Oh, he was smart enough. . . ."

"Educated smart, but trying not to be," Fern broke in, in a rush. Her hand, red and worn, belying her beautiful face, reached for Homer's. "He tried real hard to fit in."

"But folks round here don't shoot themselves with their own guns," said Homer firmly. "At least not often."

"Maybe not by accident," said Kyle, "but hell, they do it

all the time on purpose and you know it, Homer. Like Bobbie said, he left a note."

Fern bit her lip. "He said *why*?" Her voice trembled, panicky.

"Not so's you'd notice," said Kyle. "But a suicide note—you want the next of kin seeing it first."

Fern said fiercely, "You're going to let his *daughter* see it? Kyle Barnett, she's not but thirteen. She hardly knew her daddy. He's been here ten years and this is the first time she ever come out to visit."

Kyle looked down, turning his baseball cap round and round in his hands. Then he shrugged and started towards the door. "I got to go get back to the scene, so you all work it out between you how to tell the little girl. I'll be back another time, talk to you folks some more, OK?"

We watched him go. His walk was tense, he'd hated doing this, and I wondered if he even knew it. Not introspective.

Fern blurted out, "She's been here three weeks. In another week she'd of been gone."

"Just a *week*?" Bobbie clicked her tongue. "He could of waited. Some daddy, that Leroy."

Some daddy was right. Unbelievable.

"Didi, that's her name?" Bobbie asked Fern.

"Short for Diandra Dawn." Fern's voice was calmer now. "Diandra Dawn Steinberg. Guess her mother remarried."

Bobbie blinked. The foreign-sounding name reverberated in the kitchen.

"You're going to tell her *everything*?" Fern asked.

"Got to," said Bobbie.

"All of them are out back, in the tepee," said Homer. "Didi, and Violet and Jody. Violet's her age."

"This is the worst thing." Fern got up abruptly and went to a Mr. Coffee pot. Coffee wasn't great for people under stress, but neither Bobbie nor I said anything. "This is just the worst. Like to let her sleep a little longer, poor little thing. So far away from her mother back east."

Back east. Where I'd come from not so long ago. Bobbie's eyes glommed on to mine.

Fern went on, "I don't know a thing about her folks, could you people find out? . . . And there's Leroy's girl- friend too. Starry."

From out back we could hear voices, high and excited, then footsteps coming to the door. A tangle of little girls fell into the kitchen: two miniature Ferns with long blond hair and topknots, in matching yellow nighties, and behind them a dark one.

The taller blonde, almost her mother's size, said, "Mom, a police car just drove away down the street. We watched to see if it would go to Tommy Roger's and arrest him again for drinking."

The little one pushed her aside. "We was *scared* 'cause of all the stories Didi told us. She told us the story about the mashed-up man that comes up the stairs, and the hand under the bed. Mom, if you got a strawberry mark on your ankle in the morning, that means he *got* you."

Fern said, "Okay, you two, why don't you come into the living room with me."

Homer's pale blue Valley eyes veered around the room, seeking an escape. "Gosh darn," he said. "We got to get us some *coffee*."

Bobbie and I looked at the third child.

Dark thick curly hair, cut short in the best haircut I'd seen since I moved to Arizona. Little gold studs in her ears. Long elegant nose. She was wearing a black T-shirt, the kind you wear with leggings, silk-screened in orange and red letters HARD ROCK CAFE, NEW YORK CITY. Just on the verge of not being a little girl anymore, but she stared right back at us, poised and arrogant.

She looked just like her father.

"Hard Rock Cafe," Bobbie said under breath. "*New York City.*" And she gave me a little shove.

6

I sat on the back porch steps with Randall's child. Did she know that he was using a false name?

"My name's Chloe Newcomb," I told her matter-of-factly. "I'm from New York City like your T-shirt. Is that where you're from?"

"I live out on the Island," she said in a grown-up, slightly affected voice. "But I go into the city a lot. I mean I used to, but . . ." Her voice trailed off.

"Well, Didi, I work with a program here called Victim Witness." I paused. "I'm sorry to tell you your father's dead. Killed with a shotgun. The investigation's not complete, but we're pretty sure it was a suicide. He left a note."

There was a long pause as she looked at me, her eyes very round. "He . . . he said . . ." she stammered involuntarily.

"What? He said what?"

She shrugged and sat motionless for a moment, then pulled the long T-shirt down over her knees and rested her forehead on them. From now on she'd be monitoring, defenses up.

Head still down, she asked in a small voice, "What did the note say?"

Fern hadn't wanted me to tell her, but why not? Bobbie had said it was best to tell the truth, so I took a breath, recited, "The last good-bye's the hardest one to say, this is where the cowboy rides away."

"Oh!" She sat up straight. "The *cowboy* song." Her voice was plaintive, wobbly. "I always played it—on the jukebox at the Horseshoe Cafe." She sniffed.

Why, Randall? If she was going to be leaving in a week. It didn't make sense. You didn't get over these things; how well I knew, from personal experience. Just when you thought you had, that videotape in your head would start to run again and you couldn't stop it.

The night air smelled rich and fecund. I stared out to where Fern and Homer's backyard vanished into the dark of the desert. There were some sheds and a barn at the edge, an old car on blocks nearby. The tepee where the girls had been was off to the right. Behind a line of fencing, a large dark creature, a horse, snorted.

Didi made a noise through her nose just like the horse. "Beauty," she called forlornly. "Hey, Beauty."

Lightning flickered far away behind the mountains.

She said suddenly, "V-Violet was going to teach me how to ride."

And then her father went and killed himself and wrecked her plans. But I knew it was just a way of dealing with it. And I still thought of things I might have done with Hal, had he not gone and got himself killed. Things I never said, things . . .

Didi bit her lower lip. "A *shotgun*?"

"I'm sorry," I said, startled that she had caught me on that small detail. "A rifle, actually."

"Le Roi," she said. She didn't pronounce his name like everyone else, more like anglicized French. "Le Roi's rifle?"

"He owned one?"

She nodded. "A Winchester pump .22. They all have guns around here; Homer has four and they go out and shoot jackrabbits and make jackrabbit burgers. Guns are *so* dangerous. I *told* Le Roi that, but he wouldn't listen."

Denial. We sat in silence.

She took a long breath, huffed it out. "Well, I'm not going to cry. Sorry to disappoint you."

But I understood that pride that refuses to cry in front of strangers. "I'm not disappointed. Whatever you want to do is OK by me."

"That's what counselors say, but they don't mean it. Roxanne sees them all the time, and all her friends. For fine-tuning. Fine-tuning their psyches. I had to see one this year. *Boring.* She was fat. A lot of them are."

I stifled a smile. It sounded like her mother wouldn't need any referrals to counselors. I referred my compensation clients to them all the time; me, the compensation advocate who refused to see a counselor. "Didi, we're going to need to reach your mother."

Didi stood up, ignoring what I'd just said. "Want to meet Beauty?"

I followed her across the crabgrass and around the tepee. The horse came towards us, its head graceful. Didi put her hand above its velvety nose. "Pretty Brown Beauty," she said. Her voice was heartbroken. "Poor Pretty Beauty."

"Didi," I said, trying again. "Your mother?"

"Roxanne. And Harry's my—my *step*father. And we *can't* reach them. They're in Europe going to unknown French churches. Alchemical churches. Roxanne read *Mont-Saint-Michel* by Henry Adams and was drawn deeper and deeper. I could be with them, but Roxanne said I had to be with Le Roi. She said it was very very important."

She stroked the horse's nose sadly. "He didn't have any idea about being a father. I could tell he'd been practicing things to say to me, he even had those cowboy boots waiting for me, that he got at a yard sale. They were for some little tiny kid, like all kids are the same size."

"Umm," I said, not prepared for the pity that engulfed me, pity for Randall, trying hard to be a father. But then why . . . ? I'll protect you, Randall, I thought, at least till I know what was going on.

Didi went on, "Do you know what he gave me to *eat*?"

"What?"

"Peacock's eggs. I told Roxanne and she practically swooned on the telephone, she thought it was so romantic."

"That's a good way to remember him, Didi," I said. "The peacock eggs."

"They weren't bad if you didn't *think* about it." But she looked skeptical, then her lip quivered.

"We need to reach your mother, Didi."

"She won't call till Tuesday. She . . . she just called. She does it twice a week. I have to wait by the phone at three o'clock at Le Roi's."

"What about your other relatives? Your father was from New York?"

"Chicago," she said.

No. New York City, born and raised there.

Didi went on. "Anyway, Le Roi doesn't have a single relative in the whole world, they're all dead. So are Roxanne's and Harry's. I can only talk to Roxanne."

Three people and not a single living relative between them?

"I'll tell you something else," said Didi.

"What's that?"

"He didn't kill himself and that's that."

I shivered, the night air suddenly cold. The house door banged shut and Fern and Bobbie walked across the grass towards us, Fern in her plaid bathrobe, Bobbie in a pale pink sweater and khakis, their faces not smiling but pleasant. Roxanne wasn't like them, you could bet on it, but she'd sent her child out here, to pleasant people who all had guns and ate jackrabbits. It must have felt like sending her daughter off to Mars or Venus.

Fern went over to Didi and put an arm around her shoulders. "You OK, honey? You're going to sleep in Jody and Violet's room, and Jody has to sleep on the couch. Boy, is she mad. You can stay with us just as long as you're here. We're real happy to have you."

Didi looked at her earnestly. "Could we call up Shawn?"

Fern's wide mouth set in a thin line. "We'll talk about it in the morning."

Bobbie looked up at the lightening sky. "Close to morning now," she said.

Bobbie fiddled with the radio. "Victim Witness," she said. "We're on our way home." She shook it. "Damn radio. It never works."

Purple verbena and desert marigold lined the road edge. Mourning doves cooed and I saw a bright oriole fly up out of the mesquite. The rains that had come in the last two weeks had covered the desert with a watercolor wash of grasses, pale green and pink and gold. Beautiful but it struck me as heartless, without pity.

"Did she open up to you?" Bobbie asked.

"Kind of."

"Poor little kid. No other relatives, so we wait for her mom to call, I guess." She sighed. "Fern said she'd clean up, after law enforcement's done, so Diandra won't have to go back there with her daddy's brains splattered all over the walls. One of us should be with Didi when her mom calls. Let her in on local resources, and all that."

The growing light revealed wrinkles around Bobbie's forty-year-old eyes, and bluish circles underneath. Chicken pox had left a tiny crater on her chin.

"All those people renovating over in your part of town," she added. "We've been real busy at the hardware store."

"My compensation job's part-time," I said. "You know that. I can take care of it."

"Fern said Leroy told her before Didi got out here that Didi's mom said she was kind of a handful. Skipping school, stuff like that. Fern says she's been real good here, though." She veered to avoid a rabbit. "But we better keep an eye on her."

Randall's daughter, a rebel. It seemed appropriate. "Didn't Fern say something about a girlfriend?"

"She's out of town and not expected back till Wednesday. Camping, so she might not hear. Fern said she'd take care of it, have a friend tell her. Starry, and her last name's Noel, isn't that a pretty name. Or is it just tacky?"

We reached the curve around the pit. R.V.s were already parked by the scenic pullover for the giant ugly hole in the earth, and a few joggers ran industriously around the rim.

"Who's Shawn?" I asked suddenly.

"Didi's boyfriend. He's sixteen and Fern says it's a real teenage romance. She says Leroy watched them real careful."

In Old Dudley we passed the Lyric Theater, now a real estate office. The cafe next door sold cappuccino and espresso and displayed local artists' work on the walls. The whole of Old Dudley trying hard to be someplace else. Bobbie drove past the Copper Queen Hotel, with its red-tiled roof and balconies, the umbrellas up on the terrace, but it was too early for the tourists to be sitting out, and up the hill past the little miners' shacks renovated by urban escapees who didn't count in her world, to the steep grade that led up to my house.

She downshifted. "Something doesn't feel right about this whole thing," she said. "I don't know. . . ."

"I agree," I said fervently.

"We're volunteers," recited Bobbie. "Victim Witness volunteers do not want to appear in court. We have nothing to do with investigations. We're there to listen to feelings, not facts. We're there for the victims and that's it."

"Right," I said.

7

My house dozed in the morning light, frame, white paint needing to be scraped, primed. . . . I didn't want to think about it. The driveway was empty, my car in Brody's shop. A plate of green corn tamales was on the ground in front of the back door, with a note stuck on the plastic wrap. *Chloe, hope all well, Lourdes.* My neighbor, whose husband worked nights while she monitored the neighborhood.

Numbly I carried the tamales inside and put them in the refrigerator. The cat dish was full, but Big Foot had knocked down the bag of Purina from the top of the refrigerator and gnawed through the bottom. Star-shaped pellets littered the floor, next to a small puddle of kitty vomit. Exhausted by his night's work, he lay prone, a heavy mass of striped fur, on the kitchen counter.

I was exhausted too. The house had been partially renovated by Hal, who'd torn out the walls between the kitchen, dining room, and living room, leaving only the three tiny bedrooms intact. He'd put in skylights and

French doors, but had willed me the house and died
before getting to major repairs.

Hal had been the lover of my brother James. James,
owner of hotels on Boardwalk and Park Place, all the rail-
roads. James the good brother, always smartest in his class,
dater of studious neutral girls in high school whom he
brought home to meet the family. They got along well in
our house, fell right in with the family jokes, pulled weeds
alongside my mother in the asparagus patch out back. But
they never worked out.

Danny, the youngest, had been the bad boy, the rebel,
who'd spent time in prison for drugs way back in the early
seventies, now being a Buddhist up in Vermont, a survivor.
But James had been dead now for four years, dead of AIDS.
He'd met Hal after he was diagnosed, so maybe not lovers
in the strictest sense, but a lover, Hal had been nevertheless, caring for him to the end. Hal had come to the funeral
and sat with my parents, stiffened with unfamiliar grief.
Hal, the counselor, had known how to handle them, how
to listen, let them talk about James; grief was a place he
knew well. It made sense, Hal leaving me his house; I was
family.

Light shimmered around me, stripping away familiarity,
and with sudden clarity I saw the cracked windows in the
French doors, the stain in the ceiling where the roof
leaked. A house in Arizona, me a New Yorker, moored in
an alien state, but surely no worse than New York City had
been becoming when I left for good, thinking this house
was some kind of message from Hal, something I needed
to learn. I could almost see his face in front of me, his
beautiful and androgynous face, mysterious—like all good
teachers, not telling, letting you find out for yourself.

But Hal's death was what I remembered the most, it still
had the power to come back to me as vividly as the night it
had happened—what I had feared would happen for Didi
too; the memory of our conversation in the Wilsons' backyard. I thought of Lucinda's lecture on Death Notifica-

tions. *They're very important,* she'd said, *because people never forget them.* A videotape replaying the same scene over and over. Mine played less now than it used to, but I never knew when the tape would start.

Not now, I thought, not *now.*

Shock/Denial, Anger, Depression, Bargaining, Acceptance. Stages of grief. Where was I now? What sense did it make, chipping at the walls of other people's grief when I didn't know where I was myself?

I walked outside to the front porch, which needed to be torn out and replaced. Wild morning glories flowered deep purple and pink on the railing, but in the garden only the marigolds and evening primrose had survived the hot days of June. Now that the monsoons had come, green young weeds were pushing up everywhere.

All that rampant life and truth was too much for me. I went back inside to my bedroom, closed the curtains, lay down on the bed, and finally allowed myself to think about Randall.

Randall Hartman and I were sitting on a lumpy bed, covered with a white chenille bedspread, on the seventh floor of the Earl Hotel, just off Washington Square in the Village. We'd spent two nights there, smoking dope and making love and looking out at the Empire State Building, which was perfectly framed in the window.

I was packed, my overnight Pan Am bag sitting on the floor.

Randall didn't have to pack, he lived in the city now, in an apartment he hadn't offered to take me to. I had to go back to college in the Midwest. There was nothing back there for me, just this preppy kid called Arnold, so persistent I'd gone out with him a couple of times. I thought Randall and I had had a wonderful time, except Randall had just finished telling me we shouldn't see each other anymore.

I was suffocating, holding my breath with the need not

to cry. I couldn't swallow—it was as if my tears had all gone to my throat, threatening to drown me. Last year, Randall's senior year, my freshman, I'd followed him around until he noticed me, in my little flowered skirt, my Pappagallo shoes, my Kappa Alpha Theta pledge pin. He'd looked at my pledge pin with utter contempt, though surely Thetas were the best on campus; they had all the *blondes*.

What did he care about blondes? He'd grown up in New York City, gone to Ethical Culture School, his mother did something with the U.N., his father owned a bourgeois business, which Randall held in utter contempt too.

In no time at all I was transformed from being the future darling bride of a Sigma Chi or an S.A.E., to someone whose hair was long and straight, who wore jeans all the time, who threw away her pledge pin. I followed him to Antioch to the S.D.S. convention and looked hopefully around for F.B.I. agents rumored to be there.

I sat and listened to him make speeches at rallies, walked with picketers in front of the Student Union building carrying a sign saying STOP THE WAR, and I sat with him and his sidekick, big blond Charlie Pomeroy, in the townie bars where he loved to go to meet the *people*. It was a good thing Charlie was there, because Randall didn't want to talk to me at the bars, I wasn't the people. He had a thing about the people, where are the people, where have the people gone, always there was something preventing them from being the people.

Back then, he wore blue chambray work shirts, work boots, jeans jackets studded with buttons announcing his various political allegiances. Patiently he would argue his points, while redneck townies shook their fists in his face, and then bought him a beer. He was charming and warm and anxious to meet them, anxious to know the working class.

When we made love he was passionate, but detached as if formulating some new speech, arguing a point. It was enough for me just to look at him, at his curly black hair, his gallant swagger, the way his smile focused on who he was talking to. It wasn't his words, though he thought it was, that made people like him, it was his absolute focus, his concentration on them.

I'd only known him for a few months before he graduated. I really didn't know him very well.

That didn't stop me, as I sat on the bed at the Earl Hotel, about to go back to college, to prison, from feeling as though I were being robbed of my destiny, to follow this man into whatever extremes of political action he decided to take, and to remain loyal to him always. We were made for each other; I even thought back then, in the idiocy of love, that we were just alike. I loved him and I loved New York City, too. I wanted to stay there, move into his mysterious apartment, print up pamphlets, go to protests; I would dress however he wanted me to, look however he wanted me to look, cook for him, clean for him, wash out his socks at night.

Later, after I married Arnold on the rebound, clingy Arnold, I understood: I must have seemed like a giant chain manacled to his ankle.

Randall and I stood outside the Earl Hotel. I was supposed to go over to Fifth Avenue, get a taxi to the Port Authority bus terminal. I couldn't afford to fly. It was April and I could see Washington Square Park, the fountain, the Arc de Triomphe–style memorial to Garibaldi. All the trees were newly green.

Randall raised his hand—he wasn't even going to help me get a taxi—and saluted me. "Well, *ciao*," he said.

I stood there holding my Pan Am bag, till he was down about a block, then I followed him. The only way I could cope with this was to believe it wasn't really going to happen, to believe he would change his mind, if not now, then soon. I was already making plans to come back to the city, come to his apartment and stand there at his door. He would have to let me in, wouldn't he? I didn't know where his apartment was. But I knew it was here in the Village. So I followed him.

Randall swaggered in his work boots, his jeans jacket, in pursuit of the working class as I pursued him, through Washington Square Park, past the N.Y.U. students sitting on the edge of the fountain, with their guitars, their long long hair. A girl with a thick black mane of it stood in the center of the fountain wearing a dress made from an Indian bedspread, splashing water all over herself, until the bedspread became transparent. People cheered, couples caressed each other on the grass. I didn't know it, but I was walking through my own future, walking through the place I would live in for years after I got out of college.

Over to one side, a black man declaimed to a crowd and I followed Randall.

"Spare change?" asked a young girl with a purple headband and bells around her ankles.

I fumbled in my purse and found some quarters I'd been saving to tip the taxi driver.

When I looked up again Randall had vanished.

While some annoying female survivor in me whispered, *Well, there's always Arnold*.

Years later when I moved to New York, and after my brief marriage, became a financial investigator, I tried to find him a couple of times, through my connections, even looked up his father's name in the phone book, Jacob Hartman, called the number, said I was an old college friend.

"He's not in the city," his mother had said, voice tight, unwelcoming. "He's traveling." And she hung up. Things Randall had said about his mother reverberated. *She's so principled, she can be pretty unforgiving.* Unforgiving about what?

Then Jacob Hartman's name was gone from the book, and I'd never seen or heard from Randall again.

*   *   *

I lay there trying to grieve for Randall, but I'd done my grieving years ago. It was an explanation I was after, not reasons but explanations for a life that had not once but twice intersected mine. It seemed to me so much of what I did centered around aimlessness and chance. Randall had been the most directed person I'd ever met. And in the end he'd chosen . . . suicide.

It didn't seem like him, but he'd had twenty years to change, to turn inward; what had he seen when he finally turned his attention to himself that had made him want to die? What was he doing, being a man called Leroy Harris, living out in the desert on forty acres? Had it been a mistake, pretending not to recognize him?

Finally I got up, went to the kitchen, and cleaned up Big Foot's messes. When I got over that, I ate the tamales, ate them without salsa even, unfolding the corn-husk wrappers, scraping off the *masa* that still clung to the husks with my teeth. The taste of the green new corn was almost wicked, like eating the tender flesh of newborn babies.

All day long the Valley where Randall had died haunted me, its fields golden in the morning sunshine. Rough and stranded in time and heartless enough to make a man take his own life, but fascinating, too, and interesting like a man can be when you fall in love from a distance.

Late in the afternoon they had a band down in City Park, reggae, foreign music, and I turned on my cassette player and put in *George Strait's Greatest Hits, Volume 2*, playing it loud to blot out the blur of the other music. Waiting till they got to Randall's song. George Strait sang it with a slow sad beat that loped along like a horse.

> "My heart is sinking like the setting sun
> Setting on the things I wish I'd done
> It's time to say good-bye to yesterday
> This is where the cowboy rides away."

8

Back behind the courthouse they were beginning to unload the prisoners from the county van; Monday was law and motion day, the day of arraignments and hearings and sentencings. In the brilliant Arizona sunshine the line of men, generic in their orange jumpsuits, hands and feet cuffed and chained, looked unkempt and brutally exposed.

"Every damn one of 'em's guilty," said Kyle Barnett.

We stood by the window in a hall of the courthouse, near the county sheriff's offices. The sun coming in shone on his face. His features were finely molded; a Kentucky boy originally, pure-blooded Anglo. The bluish skin under his eyes was darker now. Those innocent eyes, some cops have them, the innocence of unswerving dedication.

"And one in ten will get the time he deserves," he went on. "*Maybe.*"

I *tsk-tsk*ed, baiting him to get a response. "No faith in the jury system?"

"Shit. Most of 'em will get pled out."

This was standard talk, but Kyle was angry today, a spot of red on each cheekbone. I could feel his anger, intimate as a caress. I stood there and took it.

"I don't buy it," he said suddenly.

"What?"

"His daughter was supposed to leave in a *week*. He can't wait that long before he does it?"

"Yes," I agreed. "It's odd."

"Course, by the time I found that out, they'd already been at the scene tromping around, messing up the evidence."

"The evidence?"

"Didi and her dad went into the Junction that day," he said doggedly, shifting mental gears. "They bought some groceries—milk, bread, and peanut butter. They didn't go to the liquor store, though, or to a bar. They didn't buy a bottle of Jim Beam."

"Well, he might have already had it."

"Didi doesn't think so."

"You talked to her? How's she doing?"

"She's a cool little kid. Told me right off her daddy didn't kill himself."

"She told me that, too."

"She tell you anything else?"

"Nothing useful but she's protected by confidentiality if she had," I said, true blue. "I'd need her permission to repeat anything."

"Well, she didn't talk much to me, unfortunately. She was real closed in and Fern was hovering around, being protective." His anger had suddenly gone, we were just talking now the way we used to.

The way we'd talked back that day when he'd called me the resident liberal. He'd sat on the vinyl couch in my office and we'd talked about the rape victim and I'd promised to call her parents, see if they were interested in compensation. "You could mail them a form anyway," he'd said.

And then—I put my hand on the wall beside me as if to steady myself and focused back on what we were talking about. "Leroy could have gone out, after she went to Fern's," I said, "and bought a bottle."

"Yeah," said Kyle. "Could be."

"Except you already checked the likely stores and he didn't."

"He had to have gotten it somewhere."

"Maybe he'd hidden it," I said, "so Didi wouldn't think he was a drinker."

"Hell, far as I can tell, he wasn't."

I waited.

"The bottom line is," he said, "when there's one thing that doesn't make sense, there's usually more when you start looking. They found plenty of prints in the bedroom, bathroom, kitchen, for instance, but not too many in the dining room or living room. The front door was open when we got there, just the screen door was shut. No prints on the front door."

I looked at him in surprise. "*None?* On the front door?"

"Guess no one had been in and out the door for a long time." He snorted. "Guess they used the window."

"Back door?"

"There isn't one."

The last of the prisoners had gone in. On the steps outside a couple of deputy public defenders, in suits with jackets that stretched too tight over the shoulder blades, waved their arms and argued.

"Leroy had a longtime feud going on with his neighbor," he said. "Frank Gresham. Didi's got a crush on his kid, Shawn. And vice versa. Seems like Frank went over to Leroy's last week and told him to keep his daughter away from Shawn."

"Oh?"

"So I talked to Frank, he said he hadn't seen Leroy since that happened. Says Saturday night he was home, sound asleep, and never heard a thing except maybe some thunder when the storm went over. Shawn was there, too, and he didn't hear anything either."

"I'm going to be talking to Didi's mother," I said. "I'm the one she's going to hear the details from. Maybe they weren't close anymore, but she's going to want to know what happened, how to handle it with Didi. So what was it, Kyle? What should I tell her?"

"Tell her the investigation's not complete. We're waiting on the medical examiner's report." He sighed. "And that we got a note and right now it looks like suicide."

"But off the record, you don't think it is?"

"Look, even if I should figure out someone did it, the chances of putting a case together that the prosecution will buy, much less getting an indictment . . ." He shrugged in frustration.

The anger was back. The distance between us shortened.

"That kid will never get over this," he said. "Never."

I looked right into his pale gray eyes, opaque now, but somewhere behind them was a man I knew. He knew it and he knew I knew it. Except sometimes I wasn't sure anymore that I did.

I walked back to the county attorney's offices, filled with a feeling of hyped-up power that seemed to be useless and without meaning, but which often came to me after talking with Kyle. *"I taught you how to cheat,"* I sang in my head from a 1985 George Strait album, a Harlan Howard song, *"You're doin' fine. . . ."*

Back in my office, things were quiet. I was the compensation advocate, dealing with compensation claims from victims of violent crimes, covering counseling, medical/dental, living expenses, burial, but not loss of property. Lucinda, who coordinated the program and supervised the volunteers, was on a two-week vacation and no trials were coming up for clients, no witnesses sitting in my office; no rape victims crying, no molested children, childhood shattered, and their heartbroken mothers, no homicide victim's relatives praying the guy got death.

That was the part I found compelling, not the paperwork, compensation part, but that paid enough to live on, if I stayed here in this run-down, partially renovated ex-mining town in Arizona, considering my house was all paid for.

Had someone killed Randall? It was hard to imagine a killer coming up with a note like that, because it fit the Randall I knew to a T; I could almost hear him reciting it with a flourish.

On my desk was the pink African violet that one of my clients, Jolene, had given me. Gratitude for the help with her medical bills and some counseling after her handsome boyfriend had tried to slit her throat. Also she needed to get rid of the plant because she was leaving town—a new boyfriend, this one even handsomer.

Jolene, Jolene, I thought.

I went through the mail, then took a file folder, punched holes on the top of both sides, punched holes in the claim form that had come in in my absence, punched holes in the medical bills included with the claim since the woman had had her arm broken by her husband, clamped the claim and the medical bills into the file folder with metal strips that folded over, labeled the file folder, and assigned her a number.

Brody stood at the front of my car, the hood up, absent-mindedly wiping his hands on his jeans. My car was a nondescript gray 1982 Dodge Omni, in keeping with my bare-bones financial situation. The windows didn't wind down too well anymore, only half the doors opened, the heater hadn't heated in two years. Nevertheless, it kept running except for minor repairs.

I took it for granted, just as I did Brody. He was one of the first people I met when I came here, while Hal was still alive. I'd been seeing him ever since, more than a year, two or three times a week until lately. He liked movies like *Top Gun*, I liked movies like *Blue Velvet*, but he was as safe and reliable and comfortable as a good marriage. There wasn't a speck of drama in his bones or pain or angst. I guess if he was in the back of my mind a lot, he was never in the front.

He slammed down the hood. His accessories—key rings and the tape measure that always dangled on the ready from his belt—clanked together. He was building an addition onto the back of his shop, and sawdust lingered in his red hair. One thumb had a deep cut on it that looked as if it was permanent. He wore his skydiving T-shirt, the black one with the skull on it and the words BLUE SKY, BLACK DEATH.

"What was wrong with it?" I asked.

"You don't want to know."

"Brody, honestly, quit treating me like an idiot."

"It was the solenoid and the condenser—they were scrambled and I had to jack up the manifold."

"That sounds terrible," I said.

Brody chuckled. "It was."

"Do you want cash or dinner?"

"Might as well be dinner," said Brody. "You can't afford what it would cost."

I went over, kissed his neck, without really noticing what I was doing. "I'll make pork chops with apple cider for dinner. Soon. For dessert, Jell-O and Cool Whip. Don't rednecks love Cool Whip?"

"They just love food. With ketchup."

I got in the car and turned on the stereo, already primed with a tape, and George Strait started right up. No one else in the whole world could sing about an old country boy's hillbilly heart breaking in two with the grace that he did.

I leaned out the window.

"You know," said Brody, "you used to be so crazy about heavy metal. Guns N' Roses. What happened to that?"

"I like cowboys now," I said.

9

"Here comes Shawn," said Didi.

Just like on the Saturday morning movies on TV when I was a little girl—parents sleeping in, kids hypnotized in front of the tube—the cowboy was silhouetted against the sky, holding the reins, keeping the horse moving at a leisurely pace as he tacked towards us across the desert.

He shimmered in the heat like a mirage, everything a cowboy should be, boots and jeans and jeans jacket and the biggest cowboy hat I'd ever seen. A black hat with a crown rising high as a magician's hat in a fairy tale.

Didi stood beside me in her father's front yard, stock-still, head cocked, key to the door in her hand. Her clothes didn't belong in the desert—the Hard Rock T-shirt and black tights and little sling-back black velvet shoes. The only thing Western about her was the silver and leather concha belt slung low and elegant on her hips.

According to my watch, the phone should ring in about

five minutes and we weren't inside, we were out here watching the cowboy.

"Didi," I said, "when it rings do you want me to answer it?"

"I will," she said authoritatively. "Could you stay outside please, until I let you know?"

But she didn't move. The cowboy came within a few feet of us, not a cowboy like from the movies, aged in real time, pouched and wrinkly, but a very young cowboy with a square handsome face, his eyes green as a tomcat's, not yet faded by the Valley sun. Honey-colored hair poked out below the side brim of the big hat.

"Hi," he said with a becoming shyness.

"Hi." Didi tossed her head, her voice bored, but her eyes were bright.

He patted the horse's mane. "Fern wouldn't let me talk to you when I called. How come?" The horse raised its head, gave a little whinny.

Didi acted as if she hadn't heard him. "Hi, Prancer," she said in a gentle voice.

He glanced at me, not really seeing me, and away. "Can we talk for a minute?" he asked Didi.

"N-not right *now*."

He dismounted, took the reins, and led the horse over to the wire fence where there were staked tomatoes, some of them ripe on the vine and no one to eat them. The blue pickup was still parked to one side, its paint faded and scraped, but there was no sign of the peacock. Shawn tied the reins to the fence post. The horse began to nibble at the weeds that grew around the fence.

The phone rang.

Didi was up the steps and unlocking the door in a flash, banging the screen door behind her.

It was hot out here, so hot, sweat dried instantly. My Indian cotton sundress didn't help, exposing my shoulders to the sun. Already they felt burned. I took off a huarache and shook out dirt from the dusty yard.

Shawn looked at me now, a poor substitute. "What's going on?"

"That's her mother calling. Didi has to tell her mother what happened. Give her a break."

He gave me a stricken look. "I just want to help. I'll do anything. I never *met* a girl so unusual as her."

With his scuffed turned-up boot, Shawn kicked at nothing on the ground. He looked at the closed front door for a while. Then suddenly he looked back at me. "You think he *did* shoot himself?"

I didn't know what to say.

After a while Didi came out of the house, biting her lip. "Roxanne wants to talk to you."

Inside the house already felt abandoned, hotter even than outdoors because the windows had been closed. The varnish on the pine table was blurred by dust. Through a door I could see a stove that needed wiping, heard a fly buzzing disconsolately. The cowboy had thrown me, I wasn't prepared for Roxanne.

I set down the ugly plaid tote bag, pulled out my resource books, already folded back, thank God, to Death Assistance. I sat down on a straight-backed pine chair at the table. Through the window I could see Prancer's shiny head, reaching beyond the fence for grass, and beyond that, the blue pickup. I couldn't see Shawn and Didi. *We better keep an eye on her,* Bobbie had said.

I picked up the receiver. "Hello? Mrs. Steinberg?"

"Who's this?" said a woman's voice, sharp and full of authority. A woman Randall had married?

"Mrs. Steinberg, my name is Chloe Newcomb. . . ."

"*What?*" said the woman. "You must be kidding. Is this a joke?"

Was what a joke? "Didn't Didi tell you? I'm a Victim Witness volunteer out here in Arizona. We're here to, um, help victims."

"Oh," she said. "Please. Call me Roxanne. I'm *sorry*. A ghost walked over my grave. . . . I'm stunned. Appalled. *Suicide?*"

Her voice had a snooty ring to it, familiar, it resembled a voice I used sometimes, what an ex-boyfriend called my "sorority girl" voice.

"The investigation isn't complete," I said, dutifully, a representative of the county attorney's office, trying to use Kyle's exact words. "There's still the medical examiner's report, but it appears to be a suicide, there was a note. Didn't Didi—"

"We're in St. Pierre-d'Ax, that's in France. We'll fly back today, tonight, as soon as we *can*. I don't even know where the nearest airport is. I want Didi *home*. Two days at the most. We've had problems with her, you know. Just ordinary adolescent things, but until you experience it, you can't . . ." She stopped, took a breath. "God. No, Didi didn't. What did it say?"

"The note?"

"Of *course*, the note."

I took a deep breath. "The last good-bye's the hardest one to say," I recited. "This is where the cowboy rides away."

"That's it?"

"That's it."

"Say it again, would you?"

I did.

"My God." She paused. "Is that *typical*." Her voice mingled grief and exasperation; yes, Randall was the kind to put just those notes in the voices of women. "Is that ever ever typical."

"Roxanne," I said. "I have information to give you. There's the burial, things like that. Didi says there aren't any other relatives."

"God," said Roxanne in a worried voice. "Oh, God."

"What?" I asked urgently.

She didn't answer.

"Let me give you some numbers to call, listings. Mortuaries."

"Harry, give me a pen. Harry! Hold on."

I waited. The phone had a long cord, so I carried it over the fireplace in the next room; even without looking at the couch, I sensed that the red and green Mexican blanket was gone. Books were lined up below a bleached steer's head—paperback junk Westerns with names like *Fastest Draw*, *Riders of the Silences*, *The Gentle Desperado*, *Ghost Rider*—all stamped on the ends COCHISE COUNTY LIBRARY. Then one that wasn't junk nor a library book—*Deadwood*. I loved that book, *we could have talked about it.*

"OK," said Roxanne. "I'm ready."

I went back to the table and read off the names of mortuaries, then gave her Fern's number and the Victim Witness number as well.

"My daughter doesn't think it's a suicide," she said. "Why is that?"

"It's a process called denial, probably," I said. "When—"

"Oh, never *mind*." She hung up.

I went to the door, hoping Shawn hadn't swung Didi up onto Prancer and galloped across the desert with her— clear to Douglas and across the line into Mexico where they'd live happily ever after in a little adobe hacienda, Didi plump with child, pummeling tortillas on a flat rock while Shawn hoed the corn.

No, they were still there, holding hands, Didi on tiptoe yearning towards Shawn's face, her sling-back velvet shoes slipping off her heels, his scuffed cowboy boots planted firmly on the ground as he leaned towards her.

I hurried out.

"OK, Didi," I said briskly, the chaperone, the duenna, the eighth-grade sub. "We have to get back to Fern's."

Shawn looked at me pleadingly. "We were thinking, we

could all drive into the Junction, get a soda. I'll ride
Prancer home and you can pick me up on the road."

They both stared at me with adolescent intensity, their
entire future together encompassed in the small span of
maybe forty-eight hours if they were lucky. "Oh, OK," I
said. "I'll have to call Fern."

10

Shawn and Didi sat silent in the backseat, hands tightly locked, Shawn's face blank, Didi's tense and brooding as I drove into the Junction. The hot sun glinted off the windshields of the pickups parked in front of the Valley Feed Store on the corner, bleached the color from the rosebushes around the Baptist church. I parked in front of the Horseshoe Cafe and we all got out.

Shawn held the cafe door open and we entered, the air inside not much cooler than out. Voices murmured, cutlery clanked on cheap dishes. Suddenly behind the counter a little wiry woman with a tight gray perm stopped what she was doing and posed motionless with a dishcloth. A cowboy sitting on a chrome and red vinyl stool held a fork suspended at his mouth. Two old men near the front, in weathered denims, feed-store caps, eyeballed us, a mother hushed her children. Silence fell over the place that was palpable.

Shawn took off his hat. "How you folks this afternoon? Art. Mr. Blakely, Marge?"

"How're you, Shawn?" said the woman at the counter, coming to life, face motherly now. "And the little one. I'm sure sorry, honey. How you doing?"

Didi exploded suddenly. "We're not doing good at all," she said. Her face was set and angry.

"*Didi,*" said Shawn, "ain't you got no manners?" A smile, half exasperation, half pride, flickered across his face.

Didi ignored him. "He didn't do it," she said, addressing the cafe at large. "He didn't do it and everybody here knows it. Somebody did it to him and everyone's sitting around pretending they didn't. Somebody *shot* Le Roi. Murdered him. They'd just better turn themselves in, because I'm going to see to it they get caught anyway."

I put my hand on Didi's shoulder. "Come on," I said. "Let's go."

She pushed my hand away. "They're going to get caught because I'm going to tell the police everything I know. Everything. I'm going to—"

Shawn took both Didi's arms and pulled her back out the door. I followed.

"Goddamn." Shawn whooshed out a long breath. "I can't believe you did that. I just plain can't believe it."

We were sitting in my car in front of the cafe. It was incredibly hot. Drying sweat tickled my upper lip. Hands shaking, I fumbled in my purse for my keys, but they slipped through my fingers like fish in a stream. I turned in my seat to face Shawn and Didi. "You OK?" I asked her.

"They all just sat there," she said indignantly, "and stared at us."

"Well, of course they was staring," said Shawn. "Wouldn't you? What the hell were you talking about anyway? *What* is all this you're gonna tell the cops? You don't know shit."

"So what? Can't you see?" said Didi. "It was a trick. If they think I know who did it . . ."

"You're the smartest girl I ever met," said Shawn, "and

also the dumbest. If they think you know who did it, they'll go after *you*."

Didi took his hand. "I'm not afraid." But her voice quavered.

A woman came out the door of the cafe, wearing skintight acid-wash jeans that showed off a rounded, almost pear-shaped body and thin legs. Her hair was cut in jagged strips and bleached to pure white, her blue eyes were ringed with mascara, her breasts close to falling out from a skimpy halter top.

Shawn leaned out the window. "Rose!" he said.

She came over to the window, pulled out a pack of Kools from her halter, and lit up. A rose was tattooed on her upper biceps. "Shawn . . . hi, honey. Me and Lance saw the whole thing. We was waving from the back, but you guys were busy. . . . My car's broke down. Can we get a ride to my place, me and Lance? His pickup's there. He's paying inside."

Didi's face was suddenly brighter. "If Chloe thinks it's OK. She works with Victim Witness. You don't mind, do you, Chloe?"

"I don't mind. Get in," I said.

"You got to get rid of that Eldorado, Rose," said Shawn. "It's junk."

"Just as soon as I win the lottery, Shawn." She got in the front seat and looked back at Didi. "I'm real real sorry about your dad, honey."

The black mascara made her eyes seem incredibly blue and piercing. She reminded me of some of my clients: tough, knowing, and pausing briefly to file a claim with my office before moving on to the next disaster.

"Not a soul in this town thinks Leroy killed himself," she commented to me.

But there was still the note, like an indigestible fact no one could swallow.

Rose turned half around to look at Didi. "But the rest of it, honey, you shouldn't of said all that. If you know anything, you tell the police right now and then get out of town."

"It wasn't true," said Shawn in disgust. "She don't know a thing."

A cowboy came out of the restaurant, tall and skinny, walking slightly pigeon-toed in his boots. He had a tough weathered face, squinty Roy Rogers eyes. His hat was the color of mud and his clothes looked like he'd slept in them.

"Here's Lance," said Rose.

We drove off down the main street of the Junction. Heat quivered off the blacktop, making false oases ahead of us. Every window in my car was down, but it made no difference, not with five bodies inside. I'd bought the Omni back east, years ago, and air-conditioning had seemed frivolous.

Lance said, "Rosie Rosebud, we ought to stop, pick up a six-pack."

"I got most of one at home," said Rose. "And I got to go to work later anyway, I'm the eight-o'clock shift."

"Look at that!" said Shawn suddenly. "That silver Ford Bronco, behind us. Ain't it pretty. Damn, I'd sure like to have a vehicle like that."

In the rearview mirror I could see the Ford Bronco cruising slowly along, late model, tinted windows, air-conditioned certainly; it carried a cool separate world inside.

"Can't think who'd own it," said Lance. "Only yuppie in the whole Valley. I didn't think we had a one."

"Passing through," said Rose. "You know," she said to me, "I was thinking, you being Victim Witness, I'm a friend of Leroy's girlfriend, Starry, and I promised Fern Wilson I'd tell her about Leroy, but now it turns out I got to be in Tucson. Maybe you could do it."

"I guess I could," I said. "Where does she live?"

"Just down that blacktop road past the Baptist church.

You keep going till it turns to dirt, then it's the second house on the left, tan. She's due back Wednesday around five."

"Starry wasn't his girlfriend anymore," said Didi. "They had a fight."

"Yeah," said Lance. "Leroy stopped by to see Rose, when—last week? That when he told you, Rose?"

"Lance, you got to quit your spying." To me she said, "I don't know if it counted. Some fights count and some don't. Anyway, someone needs to tell her *right*."

"I can do it," I said. "What's she like?"

"A little crazy," said Rose matter-of-factly. "Turn here on Ocotillo. It's down a little ways."

I turned left on a dirt road and the silver Bronco sped up, going away down the highway.

Shawn craned his neck to look after it. "Damn. There it goes. Didi, you should get on your rich stepdad to get himself one. I'd give anything . . ."

"A little crazy?" I said to Rose.

"You'll do fine," she said. "You even kind of talk like her. Stop right up here, that first trailer."

The trailer was rooted in an excess of oleander bushes, an old mud-colored pickup in front, dirt yard, clothesline strung across it.

"We sure thank you," Rose said to me, then added to Didi, "You be careful now. Don't go anyplace alone. You take that big, good-looking Shawn with you."

"We should of stopped," said Lance regretfully as he got out. "Not even a whole six-pack till eight o'clock."

II

"Didi, you did tell Detective Barnett everything, didn't you?"

We'd dropped off Shawn and were headed back to Fern's.

She was in the front seat now, one hand picking nervously at a cuticle. "He reminded me of Mr. Suby, that policeman. The principal at my school. I kept thinking he was going to give me detention." She giggled. "But I answered all his questions. Even when he asked me about Frank, I told him Frank hated Le Roi."

"Why did he hate Leroy?"

" 'Cause five years ago Le Roi shot Frank's dog."

"He shot Frank's *dog*?"

"Frank shot Le Roi's cat *first*. It was a beautiful special cat. And it wasn't a good dog, Shawn told me it killed all his mother's chickens. She got so mad she left, moved away to another state. And Le Roi told me he was really sorry he killed Frank's dog. He said it *haunted* him. And I know why you're asking me all this."

I stared at her. "You do?"

"Yes. Because you're an investigator, like Detective Barnett. Bobbie told Fern that's what you did back in New York."

"Not like Detective Barnett. I investigated people's finances. That's different."

"Oh." She sounded disappointed. "Detective Barnett told me if I thought of anything else to call him. But I wasn't sure what he meant."

"He meant pretty much anything out of the ordinary you could think of. Even if it doesn't seem relevant, it never hurts to mention things, just in case."

"Well, I did think of something that happened. But it was two weeks ago."

"Tell me," I said, "and we can decide whether or not to tell Detective Barnett."

"Someone, I don't know who, came to see Le Roi, it was very late at night. I didn't hear a car, but I heard Le Roi go out on the porch and talk to someone, and after a while they went down the steps. The next day Le Roi was upset and he started a fight with Starry on purpose."

"Is she easy to start a fight with?"

"She never said much to me. I was just there a week when she quit coming over." She shrugged. "It's not much to tell."

"It's enough. Tell him."

"OK." She stopped picking at her cuticle and began biting her nails.

I turned down Homer and Fern's street and pulled over before I got to the house. Then I reached into my purse and took out one of my cards, found a pen, wrote in my home phone number, and handed the card to Didi. "Call me anytime," I said, starting up the car again, "if you want to talk some more."

"Should I . . ." Didi began, and then stopped as we approached the house. Fern and Homer were standing out in the yard, looking our way. "Uh-oh," she said. "They look pretty mad." But her voice was resigned; I could tell this was nothing new for her.

We got out and walked up the driveway. They watched us, Homer rigid, arms folded on his chest, Fern's hand clutching her throat.

She started toward us. In the daylight her features were a little worn, buffed by time, but gentle as velvet. Her blue eyes, set in hollows in her face, were faintly rimmed in pink. She looked like she was going to cry. "Didi, I can't believe what you did. Saying all that in front of Art and Mr. Blakely. Marge." Her voice quivered on the verge of tears. "How could you put yourself in danger like that?"

"Fern," said Homer. "Now, you calm down. You'll give yourself one of your sick headaches."

Didi rubbed her nose and stood on one foot. She looked about ten. "But we just left there. How'd you know?"

"How'd I know? My phone wouldn't stop ringing with all the people wanted to tell me. Mr. Blakely is Homer's great-uncle and Art works for Homer sometimes and Marge's related to Lance Eubanks that used to be married to my niece Hazel. . . ." Fern stopped helplessly.

"It's just so *incestuous* around here," said Didi.

For a moment Fern looked shocked, then she composed herself. She walked over to Didi and gave her a hug. "I'm sorry, honey, but we've been so worried. And your mother called an hour ago. We're taking you to Tucson, to the airport, first thing in the morning." She looked over at me. "I made a nice dinner, because Didi's leaving. Chicken enchiladas. My family's favorite. Won't you stay?"

"I'd love to," I said.

Homer looked at me, jaw working. "What'd she mean? About knowing who killed Leroy? Was it true?"

I shook my head. "But I'd like to call Detective Barnett. Didi has something she'd like to tell him."

After dinner, Homer unfolded some chrome and webbing chairs and we sat out in the backyard to watch the sunset and wait for Kyle. Just as I'd sat out with my family on warm summer evenings on lusher grass, when I was a child. You never get back those long-ago summers, except in snippets—children's voices shouting, a car going by with the radio playing an old song; year after year you wait for them, but they always elude you.

The sepia light played in the yucca and mesquite in the desert, and Brown Beauty shook her head and pawed the ground in her corral. Jody and Violet and Didi climbed the fence and Violet got on bareback and let Didi lead her around, while Jody ran in little circles, waving her arms.

"Best to get that little girl back to her mama as soon as possible," said Homer, breaking the spell. "What happened at Marge's has got me on edge."

Fern looked at me regretfully. "I shouldn't have said it was OK to take those two into town. I was feeling sorry for Shawn, his mother left about five years ago. I don't blame her leaving Frank, but she left him too. Now he's going to see her face in every girl that comes along. Sure way to get your heart broken."

"Do you really believe Didi's in danger?" I asked.

Homer said matter-of-factly, "Well, I've got my shotgun loaded, just in case."

Fern touched a gold cross around her neck. "Death. That's what I do believe in. I hope the Lord forgives me saying it. I never heard of so much untimely death as we have around here. About twice a year someone shoots someone 'cause of drinking and actually manages to kill them. Not three months ago, drunk, Lance Eubanks' uncle shot Stan Kilmer in the leg, but he lived."

Then he started across the grass towards the little girls. I could still feel the touch on my hand. Maybe there was nothing between us a wild night of love couldn't take care of, but I wished I could have watched him on some crisp October night in the country, carrying a ball down a football field, and cheered him on.

12

The houses got sparser then the blacktop turned to dirt. All these dirt roads, I should check the air in my tires sometime. Brody always nagged me about that. But even though I owed him a dinner, Brody was far away in my mind, keys and tape measure clanking, receding fast, not about to entangle me like an Arnold-octopus. Poor Arnold, he'd probably learned to be normal by now. Or maybe his experience with me had made him fearful to commit ever again.

But what was my excuse anyway? My parents had a solid marriage. Delighted with my precocious reading habits, they never should have let me read *Madame Bovary*, *Anna Karenina*, *Colette*, at an early age. I wasn't academic like my parents, I read things for the story, swallowed them down whole, without learning a damn thing.

The second house down the dirt road was cinder block, painted tan. There was no car parked anywhere. I drove into the empty driveway and parked where it widened at the back of the house so when Starry returned she'd have room. The sun was still hot at five o'clock, but the leaves of a massive cottonwood that dominated the backyard trembled as the heat slowly released them.

Victim Witness volunteers weren't supposed to go alone on something like a death notification. People were in a state of shock, disoriented, and the anger could come fast on the heels of denial. Make sure everyone in the house was accounted for, check for guns, especially in bedrooms. In Arizona everyone had a gun and bedrooms were where they kept them.

Bobbie was working, but there were volunteers on call. Maybe Ruth, or Annie. All I had to do was check the schedule. But I was asking questions, the kind of questions that weren't supposed to concern volunteers. And Starry was a single woman, what could she do? I was nervous about breaking the rules but not worried, not scared. And Lucinda was out of town; if I did the paperwork on Client Contact Information right, maybe no one would notice.

Under the cottonwood was an iron porch chair from the thirties, painted blue, a book lying facedown on the ground beside it as if someone had just set it down and gone inside. Or as if someone had sat for hours under the tree, reading, then let the book slide to the ground, mind suddenly empty, eyes drawn farther and farther into the desert clear to the Chiricahua Mountains.

I opened my door and sat sideways on the seat. Cicadas sang, peaked to a crescendo, started again. The nearest house was a ways away, the desert closer. Neat bronze rows of marigolds lined the steps up to the back door; white petunias bloomed determinedly in two galvanized buckets on either side. I knew almost nothing about Starry, including her punctuality, but I'd be able to hear her car coming before she saw mine. It only took a few seconds to walk over and pick up the book.

It was a paperback, thin and old and wrinkled from having been rained on. Anne Sexton, *That Awful Rowing Towards God*, open to a poem, words circled:

> *It is difficult for one woman*
> *To act out a whole play.*

I thumbed through, lines circled everywhere, poems plundered for phrases—*"When it is night the cows lie down but the moon, that big bull, stands up."*

A car engine sputtered down the dirt road. I set the book down hastily.

A woman in jeans and a black tank top got out of the blue Volkswagen bug, then leaned in and pulled out a backpack. She was tall, almost six feet, and slender, but her arms were strong, muscles well defined. Her brown hair was thick and fine, streaked with gray, pulled back into a long braid. Ostentatiously preoccupied with getting her stuff out of the car, she didn't acknowledge my presence.

I felt like a door-to-door salesperson, confronting a busy housewife, unwanted, soon to be gotten rid of.

She took everything out of the car and then she looked over at me. "Yes?" she said.

My heart was thudding with what I had to tell her, my little speech with no cop, no fellow volunteer, to take up the slack.

"Starry Noel?"

She didn't deny it.

I said, "I'm Chloe Newcomb, from the Victim Witness Program."

She stared at me, tucking strands of hair into her braid. Her face was sunburnt. "And . . . ?"

"It's about Leroy. . . ." Get it out, I thought, you're supposed to do it straight out, then let them digest. There wasn't any other way. No way to give them hope when there wasn't any. But this was harder than with Didi. "He's dead. He . . . shot himself. Though the investigation isn't completed. Saturday. Saturday night."

She stared at me as if she hadn't really taken in what I

said, her eyes a pale cold blue, her face hostile. "And what does that have to do with *you*?"

"I'm a volunteer. Victim Witness does notifications like this, because people find us easier than the cops. Look, I'm sorry. They didn't want you to just find out, they wanted to have Rose tell you, but she's in Tucson."

"They," she said.

"I can tell you resources, people to talk to, counselors. If you can't afford a counselor, I might be able to get you Victim Compensation to pay for counseling." I was supposed to be silent, let her respond, instead I was going too fast, getting ahead of myself, but she made me nervous.

Starry smiled coldly. "If you can't afford a lawyer, one will be appointed for you." She glared at me, her face still hostile. "They knew he was someone different."

"They?"

She ignored me, picked up her backpack and sleeping bag, and carried them over to the back steps. I followed at a distance. She dropped everything suddenly and closed her eyes. *"God."*

The cicadas, silent for a while, began to hum again.

Starry opened her eyes and looked at me accusingly. "What about Didi? Did they do it in front of her?"

"Didi was at Fern's when it happened. Who's they?"

Starry shook her head. She looked up at me. "You're not local, are you? Don't tell me. You live in Old Dudley. Where'd you come from?"

"New York City."

"New York City," she said, taking the words and making them a phrase from a poem maybe, longing in her voice, and bitterness. "Well, come inside, I might have some ice tea if it hasn't gone scummy."

In Starry's living room an old copy of *Our Bodies, Our Selves* lay on a thrift store coffee table painted white. Everything had been painted white, the floor, the walls, the ceiling, the bookcases. There were even spots of white paint on the blue batik bedspread that covered the couch.

"We broke up before I left," she said, sitting down in a white-painted rocking chair. She seemed to have forgotten the iced tea. "That's why I left. I like to camp out anyway, where you can't see anyone else or talk to them. Then it makes sense that you can't. He gave himself away to people, that way he could adapt better, he could have girl-friends and play games that men play. I never could. I guess I can't cope the way he could. All I had was him, like it or not, like in Sartre's *No Exit*. But people aren't reading Sartre anymore, are they?"

"Maybe some people are."

She shook her head. "Not in fashion. It's all fashion in this country. Even what people say are their deepest beliefs just turn out to be fashion. So you can't attach yourself to anything or the world will just grind you up and spit you out like yesterday."

Under the sunburn, Starry's face was ashen, but she sat in the white-painted rocking chair, back very straight, resisting the chair's invitation to lean back and rock.

"He wrote me a letter. I knew what it was going to say because it wasn't the first time, but I read it anyway. I could see him writing it, turning the phrases. Histrionics. Then I sealed it back up so he wouldn't know I'd read it. I took it to his house, when he was out, and left it on the table. It's *hot* in here."

She got up and went around opening windows, slam-ming them all the way up. Then she sat back down. "Well, let's go over this, like two sensible people." She looked anything but sensible, her face rigid with control. "The note. Did anyone actually see the note? Or did they just plant the rumor?"

"I saw the note," I said. I recited the words.

Starry began to rock in the rocking chair, silent for a minute. "Well," she said finally. "I guess that's settled."

"What?"

"Those are the same words he wrote in the letter. A postscript. His very own handwriting. Clever. People vanish and everyone wonders what happens to them, they must be someplace, we're not in *Argentina*. But they're just dead, folks. Cut out from the letter."

"What?"

"It was a thin strip of paper, wasn't it?"

"Yes, it was," I said, uneasily.

"Right. They just cut them out, the postscript in the letter he wrote me."

That was it. I felt dizzy. But there were other explanations, too, even if I didn't believe them myself. "Maybe *he* cut them out, Starry. But you need to tell law enforcement about this."

Her face was like stone.

"They," I asked again. "Who, exactly?"

"God," said Starry. "I'm so lonely and they come around, peep in my window when I'm taking a bath, watch me out in my backyard, 'What's she planting now, it'll never *grow*,' they ride down over the mountains, with their shotguns, headed for my house."

"*Who?*" I asked.

She gave me a scornful look. "The vigilantes."

Suddenly she shot up from the rocking chair, so violently it rocked hectically on its own. "They don't stop in and chat like real people, they sneak around and watch." She paced the room, holding her hands to her eyes like binoculars. "Watch and wait. Waiting for you to give in, to give up." She came up close and aimed the binoculars at me. "You're one of them, aren't you?"

"I'm here from the Victim Witness Program. I'm just a volunteer." I didn't know what to do. She sounded crazy, but in another context, everything she said made a kind of terrible sense. "You only knew Leroy for *two years*?" I asked suddenly.

She lowered the binoculars and closed her eyes.

"Starry," I said urgently, "let me give you a name, see if

it means anything to you." It made my heart thud again just knowing what I was going to say. "Randall," I said. "Randall Hartman."

She opened her eyes. Suddenly she looked different, saner, as if what had happened before were only a charade. "Get out," she said between her teeth. In her cold blue eyes I could see fear forming like little ice crystals.

I reached into my purse and took out one of my cards: CHLOE NEWCOMB. COCHISE COUNTY ATTORNEY'S VICTIM WITNESS PROGRAM. VICTIM COMPENSATION ADVOCATE. I handed it to her. "Call me if you change your mind and want to talk."

She tore it up slowly, staring at me.

Maybe it was time to go.

13

It was dusk when I drove away from Starry's, almost seven, getting dark here in the only state that didn't have daylight savings. My foot kept trembling on the accelerator. How would the killer know about the letter? Someone who knew Starry would have to know her pretty well to know about the letter, wouldn't they? Rose, had Rose . . . Of course, they might just know Randall. Know the letter had been returned.

I had to tell Kyle about this. Did Didi know about the letter? I didn't have her phone or address. But Fern would.

Even before I reached her house I heard the music, blaring out full volume. I pulled up in front and parked. Every light in the house was on. Were they having a party? I got out of my car and started down the driveway past the chain link fence and the row of zinnias. Backed by horns and strings, someone with a baritone like honey was singing:

> *"Just for a tender while*
> *I kissed a smile upon her face. . . ."*

It was eerie, out of time, but just right for walking under the stars on a balmy night in the desert. And how well I knew the song, though I couldn't recall when I'd heard it; it seemed to have existed in my unconscious, waiting to be brought forth. Music maybe in their youth my parents had danced to some romantic night, eyes closed, swaying together, a nice change from Benny Goodman.

> *"It was fiesta and we were so gay*
> *South of the border, down Mexico way."*

I went round to the side of the kitchen door and knocked, but no one answered. The door was half glass and inside looked like a stage set. The calendar with its scene of grazing horses hung half-tilted on the wall, dates circled in red. The counters were empty, the Formica table wiped clean, bare except for the shotgun lying there on the edge as banal as a piece of fruit in a still life.

I knocked again, louder. "Fern!" I called.

The song had changed, fast fiddles.

> *"Big Ball's in cow town,*
> *We'll all go down."*

Suddenly Homer appeared through a door on the left, face very red, the feed-store cap low on his forehead as if he'd jammed it on hurriedly and got it wrong. He did a few dance steps, lifting one arm to accommodate an imaginary partner. He looked over, saw me at the door, stopped, waved.

> *"Big ball's in cow town,*
> *We'll dance around."*

"Hi, there!" he shouted over the music, coming to the door and opening it. Fern's neat house smelled like a bar. "Come on in! Just in time for a little Bob Wills! You like Bob Wills?!"

"Sure!" I said.

"Song before this was Tommy Duncan singin'! He's the best!"

"Where's Fern?!"

"Just me!" he said. "Me and all them Texas Playboys."

By now I realized he was extremely drunk. The shotgun made me nervous. I walked over and stood between him and the table. "Did Didi get off OK?"

"Sure she did. We been gone all day, getting her on the plane, and then the girls wanted to go to a mall. Got back here and Fern took them over to her mother's! First night we could be alone with just our own little girls and she goes to her mother's!" He grinned inappropriately. "Maybe I should turn down the music!"

"Yes!"

He left. I picked up the shotgun and put it on the counter, pushed back where it wasn't so noticeable. The music sank down to a whisper, a whimper.

When Homer came back he was different, his walk slowed, his demeanor subdued as if the music alone had been giving him life. He blinked, looking bewildered. "What was it you wanted?"

"I wanted to talk to Didi and I was wondering if you had a phone number for her."

"Well, sure, I think so. Where'd Fernie put that?" He turned, lurching a little, and stopped. "*Damn*. What's my shotgun doin' on the counter like that?"

He picked it up.

I said, backing off, "Well, never mind about the phone number, I can call Fern later."

He held the gun loosely, pointing at the floor, looking down at it. "Can't see a damn gun now without thinking about Leroy. Fern was awful close to Leroy, did you know that? They was always talking. Talking and talking."

"Fern's a very nice person," I said.

He said sadly, "I sure miss that Western swing. When Fernie and I met she was a rock and roller, but I taught her all the old steps. Fernie used to love to dance. Back when I was a well driller. Did you know that?"

"Know what?" I asked.

But he wasn't really talking to me. "Well, I was. A well driller, but people don't farm like they used to. All I am now is a damn pump man." His face was so vulnerable, he looked like a giant ugly little boy. "She's pining so for Leroy, don't even see me no more. Guess she can't love a pump man like she can a well driller."

He swung the gun up, pointing it at the ceiling. "Sometimes she'd be over there at Leroy's talking and talking, she told me that was all it was and she's a Christian woman, but I'd be sitting back here at home, those damn thoughts going round in my head like big fat bumblebees. How long can you talk and talk without nothing happening? And everyone's saying it wasn't him that did it, someone shot him. And you know why?" He peered at me, his eyes bloodshot.

"No," I said breathlessly, a good reason dawning. "Why?"

" 'Cause they can't imagine doin' it. But hell, it's easy, you just put the gun in your mouth and pull the damn trigger. You aim right, you don't feel nothing." He stared down at the gun.

Everything in my Victim Witness training told me to leave, get away as fast as I could when there was a weapon involved no matter what my feelings. I was supposed to help out, not get myself killed. Volunteers getting killed was against Victim Witness policy. But I stayed.

"Homer," I said. "Take it easy. Put the gun down." I was amazed at how calm my voice was.

Instead he turned away and walked through the door

into the living room. I followed him, praying he wouldn't shoot himself right there in front of me. But he was putting the gun into a rack over the mantel. Record albums, old ones, collector's items probably, littered the beige wall-to-wall carpeting.

When he saw me behind him, he grinned. "Scared you, didn't I? Don't worry, it ain't the kind of thing I do, I just go along and see it all to the bitter end."

He went over to the record player and turned up the music loud. "The bitter end!" he yelled.

He turned his back on me and began to dance. Tommy Duncan was singing again.

> *"In my adobe hacienda*
> *There's a touch of Mexico."*

Drunk as a skunk, Homer danced light and graceful on his toes, elbows akimbo; he was beautiful. He didn't ask me to dance, he already had a partner.

> *"Cactus lovelier than orchids*
> *Blooming in the patio."*

14

"*Big Ball's in cow town, we'll all go down,*" I sang under my breath as I drove back to Old Dudley. Thunder was rumbling in the distance, the stars blotted out, the monsoons returning maybe. Whatever had happened to Leroy Harris was a story, a tale to be told late at night, when the wind was blowing.

A love story maybe, with a classic ending? Full of renunciation and longing? Or fulfillment ending in tragedy? Homer, who owned four guns, standing by watching, unable to take it any longer, and Fern's eyes red rimmed from tears. *He said why?* Panicky in her own kitchen when we told her. Tears kept coming to my own eyes and I blinked them back.

Still it was a tale I'd like to have told someone—Brody? But I owed him a dinner and I didn't feel like cooking. Anyway my life was going all to hell, the private, ordinary part that kept me sane. Running to Circle K to stock up was a bad sign, so I drove to Safeway.

The store was nearly empty this time of night; its

checkout personnel bored at the registers in a vast land of
even white light, all the dark corners illuminated. In pro-
duce I selected a cantaloupe, nectarines, and started down
the aisles.

Normal, I wanted things normal. Normal meant Jell-O,
raspberry Jell-O, like James, our hero, used to make for me
and Danny, weekends when our parents were going out.
Just plain Jell-O, which James cut into little squares that
looked like jewels. Shimmering Ruby Jell-O, he called it.
We piled on great mounds of Cool Whip. I grabbed three
Jell-Os, then headed for the frozen foods to stock up on
diet dinners.

I put six Budget Gourmet Lights into my cart. The chilly
aisle, the bland slick floors, the music playing from some
unseen source, filled me with a sense of unreality, or
maybe it was a delayed reaction to my visits with Starry and
Homer.

Still trying for normal, I was reaching for the Cool Whip
when I realized it was Grace Slick singing on the PA
system, "Go Ask Alice," right there in Safeway.

Grace's cool knowing voice. Jimi Hendrix, Country Joe
and the Fish, a girl in the fountain at Washington Square
in a dress made from a bedspread. Randall and I wandering
around the Village, stoned, God, I could even smell that
odd burnt-coffee smell by Cooper Union—and it wasn't
even Randall I missed, but myself, so green, so receptive,
so hopeful.

I had my songs like Homer had his. How could they
have this piece of my best, brimming with loss, playing so
banally in the frozen food section of Safeway?

Suddenly, in the present, a man came round the corner
and smiled. He wore a black cowboy hat, black cowboy
shirt with silver studs, jeans. His boots made muted competent clicks on the floor as he dodged a cooler of marked-
down Weight Watchers and came right up to where I
stood.

He had chestnut eyes, *good looking*, and his look at me

was more than just casual, maybe coming on to me right there in the Safeway.

"Takes you back, doesn't it?" he said, opening the freezer door beside me. A breath of cold air rushed out.

"What?" I asked, startled. I dropped the Cool Whip into my cart.

"The song," he said. He closed the freezer door without taking anything out. He didn't even have a cart.

"The song," I repeated, avoiding his chestnut eyes, moving away, putting several feet between us. "Sure, I guess."

"You know, I can still remember . . ." he began chattily.

If my nerves hadn't been frayed by other people's emotions, if I hadn't been feeling so vulnerable, I might have flirted a little. But right now everything seemed dangerous. I turned my back and headed for the nearest checker.

I didn't want to be like my victims, my victims of violent crimes, I wasn't like *Jolene*, who would have been sure his presence there signaled some kind of destiny she had to succumb to. *He said just what I was thinking* would be her last thought before she lost her will entirely.

I piled my stuff on the rubber runway, glancing over my shoulder as I paid. I didn't see him anywhere. He probably called women *darlin'* too. I don't know why I find that sexy, I never used to.

Out in the parking lot the cars were sparse. My Dodge Omni was parked several spaces from the entrance, and there were plenty of parking places closer, but someone had parked a silver Ford Bronco right next to it. Just like the one, clear down to the tinted windows, that Shawn had yearned for as we drove down the main street of the Junction.

The misplaced yuppie just passing through? There weren't too many yuppies in Dudley either.

I got in my car and drove over where it was dark, down by the video store. It was closed for the night, a big poster in the window for *One False Move*. A couple of minutes

later, the cowboy with the chestnut eyes came out of
Safeway. It didn't look like he'd bought a thing. He got in
the Bronco and drove off.

Signifying what? Probably nothing. Raindrops splatted
on my windshield as I drove round the curve by the pit. I
pushed in a tape and turned it up loud.

Tourists scattered in front of the Copper Queen, a man
mouthed words I couldn't hear over the music; George
Strait, singing a song to Lefty Frizzell, laying each word
down just the way it should go, all about Lefty playing to
no one in the cold rain at the fair in Dallas.

The words had nothing to do with Kyle but reminded
me of him just the same. Then I realized what it was—that
sense I had of his isolation. He didn't need to know Leroy
Harris' true identity, but I could call him the minute I got
home and tell him about Starry's letter. I wanted to help
him with all the details just so long as I could continue to
keep the Big Secret. Surely this last had some cosmic appli-
cation to love in general.

I pulled into the carport, let the song finish, and turned
off the engine. In the sudden quiet my phone was ringing.

I opened the car door, ran inside, and caught it at a half
ring.

"Hello?"

"Chloe. It's Roxanne Steinberg. You knew him, didn't
you?"

"What?"

"Is this Chloe?"

"Yes."

"You gave Didi your card. I thought it was my imagina-
tion until I saw the card. Your name. You knew him, didn't
you? He mentioned your name. We need to talk. I can't
get away, but I'll pay your way to New York. How soon can
you leave?"

PART TWO

Back East

15

The house was on a narrow country road somewhere on the way to Mattituck, an imposing three-story white frame with green shutters, a hedge of privet all along the front and the driveway. It needed a paint job just enough to make it look like old money. I wondered where the money came from; it looked like more money than just a judge's salary. His or hers?

I turned the rental car in to the long driveway, drove to the turnaround, and stopped.

Didi and a blond girl were nearby, but they didn't look over at me. Beyond was a big three-car garage, and a gray BMW, a red pickup, and a battered gray station wagon were scattered haphazardly on the blacktop. Both girls wore white shorts and pastel polo shirts and held badminton rackets. The blond girl carried a portable CD player.

"I don't want to listen to Garth Brooks again," she was saying, swinging her racket. She had good cheekbones, a

spiffy bob, and pearls in her ears. "I want to hear Green
Day."

"Garth," said Didi in a bossy voice. She swung her
racket too, more aggressively than the blond girl. "I *need* to
hear Garth." She glanced over at me, saw me.

"Chloe!" she exclaimed in surprise. "I was looking for
your junky gray car." She started towards me.

A woman leaned out of one of the many windows of an
enclosed sun porch. Her sleek black hair was glossy in the
sun, and she wore a white top, cut in deep at the arm-
holes, showing off rounded perfect shoulders lightly
tanned. "Didi," she said. "Don't be *rude*. Go play with
Jennifer."

Didi rolled her eyes, stood there for a moment, then
turned back. "Come on," she said to Jennifer.

"I don't care what you say," Jennifer complained as they
walked off. "Arizona sucks."

The woman looked at me appraisingly. "You must be
Chloe. I'm Roxanne Steinberg." She pointed to her left.
"There's the door, it's open. Someone's here," she added
as if in warning.

I went up three steps and into the sun porch. It was full
of antique wicker furniture, flowery glazed chintz cushions.
A long table stood at one end, and on the table were three
flower arrangements. A blond man in a bright blue shirt,
wheat-colored pants, and loafers without socks stood in
front of them, his back to me.

"I don't know," he said. "I like what you've done with
the copper and those subtle subtle pinks, but the blue and
yellow is truly elegant. It makes you *understand* how much
blue there is in euphorbia."

"Hold on, Teddy," said Roxanne.

He turned then, stared at me. Under blond bushy eyebrows, his eyes were the exact blue of his shirt. "And who
is this?"

"Chloe," said Roxanne. "A friend of a friend all the way

from Arizona." Her voice was glib, social, and I could tell she really didn't want to introduce us.

By the pool under a white Italian market umbrella Roxanne and I sat on striped canvas chairs. Beyond a hedge of salmon-colored roses, Garth Brooks was singing plaintively about such teenage problems as adultery and people lining up at the bars, looking for love.

Everything was so impossibly green, the sun so mild, I had to struggle to maintain my focus. "You said he talked about me?"

"Not *really*." Roxanne stretched her legs out to get the sun. She wore white sandals with jewels on them. "It was a joke. He never said anything personal about you."

I felt relieved and disappointed all at once. "What was the joke?"

Her face softened. "I seduced Leroy Harris in San Carlos, Mexico. Got him into my room and made advances. Well, you have to give them a push to get them going, don't you? 'I don't know,' he said to me, 'we'll have to see what Chloe Newcomb says about this.' "

"*What?*"

"I guess it was the old-fashioned name. I stored it in the back of my mind because he was so secretive, so mysterious, and that first time I'd caught him off guard."

She touched her hair with the back of her hand rather theatrically, pushing back the glossy wing of it. "I knew Leroy wasn't his real name. He told me that, but he said he couldn't tell me more for my own protection."

In the pool a wasp floated, busily drowning. She got up, knelt by the pool in her cream linen shorts, and put her arm in the water. She let the wasp crawl onto her arm, then she flipped it off onto the cement border and stepped on it.

"I'd gone down to San Carlos with a friend, flew to Hermosillo and rented a car. There's a Club Med with a big cactus garden, fantastic banana trees, but we rented little rooms on the beach. I wanted to go native like a peasant because I was engaged to this stuffy rich guy and it was my last chance to be . . . myself."

She paused and looked at me significantly. "You know what I mean."

I looked at the bright expensive water in the pool, felt the big expensive house behind me. "Sure," I said.

"I thought he was Mexican at first, he was tanned so dark. The Mexican boys were beautiful, so poetic." Her voice was rapt, engrossed, as if she'd been waiting for years to tell this great story and now at last she could. "But you know," she added more prosaically, "when they don't speak English very well, you feel too—too *carnal*."

She reached down into a straw bag, took out a pair of red-rimmed sunglasses, and put them on.

"What was he doing in San Carlos?"

"He had no visible means of support. My friend and I thought *marijuana*. It was the draft, he'd evaded the draft. That's how it started and he was wanted, a fugitive because of it, and then I think there was marijuana involved that compounded things. But I mean the war was over and lots of people had worked out the political stuff by then. I told him something could probably be worked out, I knew people, but he didn't want to discuss it." She looked exasperated. "Pure ego."

Poor Randall, exiled from the very country he'd wanted to save.

"Anyway, my friend left and I stayed four months. Totally, utterly in love. I wanted to stay with him there forever, but . . ." She sighed.

I didn't believe that this woman with the perfect haircut and the good clothes would have been happy for long living with some draft evader down in Mexico. I thought the whole episode was like some romantic icon she could take out and look at from time to time. And now it had blown up in her face.

"Anyway, when I came back to New York I was pregnant, though Leroy didn't know that. The man I was engaged to couldn't handle it. But what was I going to do, kill *Leroy's* baby? I would have married him too, I was ready to settle down and be a mother. So I married Harry instead. I'd known him for years and he always was in love with me. He didn't exactly not mind, but he coped."

Poor Harry, cast not as mysterious hero but as day-to-day coper.

"His real name was Randall," I said. "Randall Hartman. I was in love with him when I was eighteen. He was into New Left politics and he was born and raised in New York City. I never met his parents, but their names are Helen and Jacob Hartman and they don't live in the city anymore. His mother worked for causes and his father owned an air-conditioning factory."

"An air-conditioning factory," said Roxanne faintly. I could tell this was a blow, but she rallied. "Well. Harry's family got rich on pickles. But not for a *very* long time." She paused. "Leroy's parents must be dead now, at least he told me they were." Suddenly she looked dubious.

"If Randall didn't know you were pregnant, how . . ."

"When Didi was two I had a fit of insanity and sent him a picture of her, with a little note, saying this is what you've wrought. I had my return address on it, not on the envelope but inside. I mean, I didn't want it coming back. But I never heard from him. Not for a long time. Not for eleven years."

"Then he showed up? He got your note after eleven *years*?"

"Not that long. He wasn't living in San Carlos anymore, but he stopped in there a few months after it arrived and someone had saved it for him. Stuck in a drawer, and they almost forgot to give it to him. Destiny."

"So he showed up," I prompted.

She sighed. "The judge was in Albany. It was around ten at night and he knocked at my kitchen door. Stood there with a haircut and cowboy boots. A new name, a new life.

He even had photographs of Arizona, of his house, the way the land looked."

Her eyes were far away. "He told me he'd come to the realization that the only thing he'd done in life that was enduring was to create this one child with me. He said he wanted her to come visit him."

She paused. "Didi's playing bad girl, but she's devastated. I foresee months, maybe years, of therapy if I can even get her to go." Her voice broke, she was being herself now. "She's so brave and . . . spirited, I don't want her to lose that. I trusted him. If I thought he'd actually killed himself while she was visiting . . ." Tears came to her eyes. "*I let her go.*"

"Some things have come up, it looks like he didn't kill himself, but proving it might be hard or impossible." And I explained.

"What about this investigator? Did you tell him who Leroy really was?"

I shook my head.

"When he showed up I begged him to tell me his real name and he wouldn't. 'I'm Leroy Harris,' he said, 'and that's who I want to live and die as—Leroy Harris.' Let's keep it that way. Besides, he was a wanted man; I don't want Didi to know that about her father." Roxanne looked blank for a minute.

Didi had been right about the exile part, but he hadn't been a king after all.

"Well," Roxanne continued, "the bottom line is I'm here in New York. You're there and Didi says you've done investigations in New York. So how about investigating this? I'll pay you. When my parents died I inherited some money and I've always kept it separate. Why not? Harry's money would have swallowed it up. Steinberg money," she said, with a significant look that was lost on me. "The police's hands are tied in so many ways, I know that, living with a judge. And I don't want Harry to know anything about all this. He'd think it was . . . unhealthy."

I hesitated. "I don't want to do anything under false pretenses. I'm not licensed in the state of Arizona. And I don't think Victim Witness volunteers are supposed to—"

She raised her hand to stop me, then dabbed at her eyes. "You knew him, you loved him, but what I want to say, is, do it for Didi. So she can heal. I'll pay you under the table. God, do whatever you have to, I'll spend every penny I have if necessary, it's carte blanche."

I was easily persuaded. "No," I said bravely. "You don't have to pay for my time, just my expenses. I'll do it for Didi, for Randall. I need to make a phone call and then I want to talk to her. I might have to ask her . . . some grown-up stuff."

Roxanne sighed. "She's a big girl now."

16

The last time I'd seen Didi in Arizona she'd been talking to Kyle. I resisted the urge to ask her what they'd talked about, just to hear the sound of his voice in her answer. It seemed to me I was getting worse about him, or maybe I was just lost from catching a plane and coming here so fast and I needed to find myself.

"I should be there," said Didi in exasperation. "Back in Arizona. I could help you—Shawn could too, he's very resourceful and he's already promised to help me in any way he can. Roxanne's so *unreasonable*."

We were sitting on the sun porch, the flower arrangements stiff and still behind us. On a glass and wicker table were photographs of Didi and Roxanne and Harry. Harry wore glasses and favored flannel shirts for casual wear, and looked young for a judge and nice like those guys you didn't go for in high school.

"That's between you and her," I said tactfully. "But you can help me a lot right here just by answering some questions. I want you to think hard. Leroy wrote Starry a letter, did you know about it?"

She made a face. "Yes and then she returned it. We came home one day, Starry has a key, and there was this letter on the table. I said, oh, someone came and left a letter for Starry. He took it out of the envelope, then looked exasperated and left it lying there."

"For anyone to see?"

"Well, who would see it? Fern? She wouldn't read someone else's mail. Neither would I." She blushed. "Well, not at Le Roi's. I was a better person with Le Roi."

"When was the last time you saw it? Think. Did Leroy throw it away?"

"I . . . I think it just stayed there. He'd keep stuff on the table, then after a while he'd throw it away or put it on his desk. I . . . I just can't remember."

"That visitor who came at night? Did you hear the voice at all? Did it have to be a man or could it have been a woman?"

"It could have been *anybody*. Man or a woman." She closed her eyes tight. "Oh, God," she said. "Oh, *no*."

She opened her eyes, got up, began to pace around the sunroom. She said, her back to me, "I know what you're thinking."

"You tell me," I said.

"Le Roi had another . . . another girlfriend and she gave him an ultimatum, so he broke it off with Starry. Roxanne's friends that aren't married are always giving men ultimatums. You have to," she added earnestly. "But how could he have another girlfriend? Like *who*?"

"Yes. Like who?"

She picked up a pillow printed with fat cabbage roses and tossed it in the air and caught it. Then she sat down, hugging the pillow. "Obviously it would be someone I never met. The only women we really saw except for Starry were Rose and . . . and *Fern*, for heaven's sake."

"Let's start with Rose."

"They just kidded around. I mean I know Rose was in
. . . in jail for a little while and she's probably an alcoholic,
and her boyfriends are crazy and she smokes too much,
but you can really *trust* Rose. She always listens and she
doesn't tell you what to do. She's a good person."

There was a silence. Didi dropped the pillow on the
floor and stared restlessly ahead as if she could hardly wait
to grow up and be a good person like Rose.

"Rose was in jail?" I said. "Why?"

"I don't know," said Didi. "Now you're being
judgmental."

"You don't know how things connect," I said, "until
you have the whole picture. I'm not even saying he had a
girlfriend, we're just exploring things."

Didi looked stricken. "You are saying it, you are. And it
can't be, not Rose, not *Fern*. Le Roi and Fern just used to
talk a lot. Homer didn't like to talk about certain things
and there was no one Fern could go to."

"What certain things didn't Homer like to talk about?"

"Fern's little boy. He fell down an abandoned mine
shaft and drowned before they could get him out. Violet
doesn't know much about it 'cause she wasn't born yet.
He was four years old. It must have been terrible. It was on
a picnic, Homer was there too. Violet told me Fern still has
dreams where she's leaning over the shaft and she sees him
down there in the water, but she can't reach him."

I had dreams like that too, surreal dreams wherein
time spins backwards and lets you fail all over again. I
shuddered.

Through the many windows was hedge, and beyond
that the pool and the white Italian umbrella and the safe
manicured lawn. A fly buzzed futilely on the glass pane,
trying to get out to that world.

Suddenly I wanted to be out there too. I was beginning
to hate it in here. "Didi, you guys were out sleeping in the
tepee that night. What were Fern and Homer doing?"

"Watching TV."

"So they didn't go anywhere."

"Homer went out to get some beer, that's all. About eleven. He always does that. They never seem to have enough beer. We heard his car and Violet said, 'Beer run' and we all laughed." Didi giggled, then stopped abruptly. "Why do you want to know . . . ?"

"To keep you on your toes," I said. I felt sick. "How long was he gone?"

Didi looked white. "I don't know exactly because we were telling ghost stories and screaming, so we didn't hear him come back. His car was there when I looked out later."

"How much later?"

"I don't *know*."

"Didi, I'm sure the police have checked all this already." Had they? A beer run was perfectly plausible from what I'd seen of Homer. "I just need to get all the information I can. OK? Let's go back to earlier in the day that Saturday."

"Le Roi and I went to the Horseshoe Cafe and had lunch, got some groceries, and then we came home. Violet called me up to come spend the night and then Fern drove over to get me. I heard her car when I was in the bedroom reading, so I looked out the window and Le Roi was giving her something and then—"

"Wait," I said. "Leroy gave her something?"

"Some kind of envelope, you know the big orange ones?"

"Manila," I said. "A manila envelope."

"I guess. I didn't see it when I got in the car."

"Go on."

"I got my stuff together and came into the other room and Le Roi was at the table loading his gun."

I stared at her. "He was loading his gun?"

She flushed. "It didn't mean . . ." She looked exhausted. Loading his gun. She'd even seen him loading his gun.

"And," Didi said suddenly, "at the restaurant, at the Horseshoe Cafe, he said, 'If anything should happen to

me, Didi, don't worry, I'll be in touch.' " Her face was
tense, stubborn. "That's what he said. He'd be in touch."

She blinked back tears. "I need to be alone." She got up
and went to the door that led outside. She put her hand on
the knob, looked back at me, and smiled with a fierce
brightness. "That's what he said, so I'm waiting."

17

The phone call I'd made at Roxanne's had been to Logan, an old boyfriend from my days in New York. He lived out on the Island.

"Good to see you again." Logan smiled, bringing his face close to mine, putting his hand on the back of my neck, and I could smell the ocean smell of sweat, sexy but I was detached, ever so chilly.

"Back off, Logan," I said.

He backed off.

He used to be a cop, but he was retired now on permanent disability, though he could do just about anything he'd always done, except he couldn't be a cop. He did some part-time P.I. work, mostly on his computer.

Logan's eyes were warm and snappy and he looked in pretty good shape, but I could see the empty beer cans in the trash in one corner of the kitchen by the dishwasher that had once belonged to his grandmother that he'd fixed good as new. Sometimes he went to AA, but it looked like not recently.

"Did you find out anything?" I asked him.

"Course I did."

"What?"

He grinned arrogantly, superman, and walked to the refrigerator. There was just the slightest favoring of one leg over the other, the right over the left. He opened the refrigerator, took out a Budweiser, offered it to me.

I shook my head.

"Got some O.J., milk."

"I'm fine." The kitchen walls didn't use to be yellow. I wondered who'd picked out the color.

He popped the top and sat down at the kitchen table, so I sat too. I'd spent many Sunday mornings here reading the paper; the mornings Logan wasn't too hung over were good mornings.

He swigged several swallows of beer, as if he'd been out in a hot field all day, and wiped his mouth. "Jacob Hartman had a small stroke in 1978, sold his air-conditioning plant in Queens and moved to Chesapeake Bay, Maryland. Drum Point, to be exact." He pushed over a piece of paper with an address on it.

"Alive," I said.

"Not dead. Alive if not totally well on Chesapeake Bay. At least as of eleven o'clock this morning when I checked it out." Logan tilted the chair back and put his feet on the table. "Him and his wife, both alive."

Had Randall told Roxanne the truth about *anything*?

Logan finished his beer, crushed the can, and threw it towards the corner, missing the bag. "Also there's nothing on a Randall Hartman that I could find, no outstanding warrants. Marijuana stuff could be misdemeanors—and shit like that would be long gone."

He stood up and got himself another Budweiser.

"He's not in trouble anymore if he ever was," I said. "He's dead." And I told him a good bit of the story.

"Course," said Logan, "crime scene's all shot to hell. You might try to get ahold of the medical examiner's report. Look for things like nitrate residue on the hands, all that. He'd have checked if he's competent. Don't count on competence. What kind of guy they got investigating it?"

I felt my face getting pink and I got up and went to the refrigerator. "He's good." I scanned take-out cartons of Chinese food, milk, O.J., and two six-packs. "But if the medical examiner's ruled suicide, he can only do so much." I closed the refrigerator door.

"What, you got some kind of crush on this guy, you got to hide your face when you talk about him?"

"Logan, honestly," I said, sitting down again. I sighed. "He's married."

"Who cares about that, nowadays?"

"Four kids."

"Maybe a little fling then."

I looked at him, but I was thinking once again about the day Kyle had come into the office. *"You could mail them a claim form anyway,"* he'd said, *"or I could give them one,"* and I'd said, *"I just ran out, let me go back into the supply room and get a stack."* It was just off my office, he'd followed me, and stood at the door.

"Logan," I said now. "I'd hate that. That's what I like about him, he's not the kind of man who would cheat on his wife."

"Then what kind of man is he?"

"He's . . . he's a man of . . . *honor*." I felt my face getting pink again.

Logan tilted his chair back some more, staring up at the ceiling, contemplating this until I could feel the old-fashioned word bouncing off the walls back at me.

"The most dangerous kind," he said finally. He assumed a serious look. "What you should do is get married, Chloe."

"I tried that once," I said. Suddenly I had a little vision of Arnold, tanned and healthy looking at the country club his parents belonged to, swinging a tennis racket exuberantly and missing the ball.

"What? When you were just a kid? Those kind don't count."

"Life's more exciting when you're not," I said, "and who are you to talk?"

Logan grinned. "You still like that music, you know, the stuff you were always so hot for? Old Neil Young songs, Joni Mitchell."

"I haven't listened to them in years," I said, and added, to change the subject, "What about Charlie Pomeroy?"

"I'm waiting on a phone call."

Charlie should remember me, his companion in the townie bars, the one I talked to as we watched Randall charm the locals. He was blond, thin-skinned, face always chapped in the cold, never quite able to get warm. He hadn't been a bad companion either. I knew more about him—his fascist parents, his old girlfriends—than I did about Randall. And he'd been witty in a kind of loser way. But I hadn't kept in touch. How much we neglect in our pursuit of what we think we want.

"The thing about these rural communities," Logan went on, taking out another beer, popping the top, continuing to do the very thing I'd left him about, right in front of my eyes, unrepentant. Why, I might have married *him*, or did I choose him because he was an alcoholic? "Everyone's connected, they all stand together and protect each other. Such a convenient resolution, sui—"

The phone rang.

There was a phone in the kitchen, but he went into the other room. I stared at his yellow walls, waiting and thinking how I'd gone through months of withdrawal with this guy.

Finally he came back into the room. "Charlie Pomeroy's dead—been dead for a while."

"*Dead?*" I bit my lip. "Are you sure?"

He sat down. "Course," he said. "That was your *alma mater*. I did like you suggested, checked on alumni records—he died in a skiing accident in 1975 in Stowe, Vermont. He a good friend of yours?"

"He should have been," I said. "We were both kind of . . . entranced with this guy. With Randall. I guess I never paid attention."

I had a sudden memory of Charlie and me, in the middle of winter, following Randall down a dark alley where some redneck had arranged to meet him so they could discuss the role of the U.S. government in suppressing certain information in regards to the measurable real victory taking place in the war between North and South Vietnam, or that was how Randall had put it.

Randall, Charlie, and I had argued on the corner at the mouth of the alleyway for several minutes. Charlie had been shivering as usual. "It's not worth it," I said, "endangering yourself. He's not your friend, Randall, can't you see that?"

"I *have* to go," Randall argued. "To show good faith. To set up a dialogue."

Charlie's teeth chattered and I nodded. We were the lesser committed, the not quite as worthy, and we respected what Randall was trying to do. But the redneck had never shown up. Scared off, no doubt, at the sight of Randall's two friends, holding piles of pamphlets and clippings from *The New Republic*, *The Realist*, and *Ramparts*.

Suddenly I felt very sad. Charlie had come from a well-to-do conservative family. "Stowe," I said. "Skiing. He probably wasn't even voting Democrat by then."

"I voted for Bush last time around," said Logan. "Hey, he's always had a keen understanding of law enforcement needs."

I stood up. "I'm leaving, Logan," I said. "Bill me for your services, OK?"

"Leaving?" He stood too, took my hand. " 'Cause I voted for Bush?"

I kissed him on the cheek, on the neck, like kissing the

ocean, and I had a sudden clear recollection of the last time we'd made love, which was kind of like drowning, going under for the third time but you didn't care at all, since some things were more important than life. Or so I had thought at the time.

"No," I said, "not 'cause you voted for Bush."

18

I turned off the highway onto a small paved road, then in a few minutes turned again onto one still smaller and unpaved. To my right were tall stands of pine and tulip trees, interspersed with patches of marshy land and fields of orange day lilies. Beyond them were the calm waters of Chesapeake Bay, a couple of motorboats *putt-putt*ing across. I could smell salt in the hot and heavy air.

I saw the mailbox with HARTMAN on it before I saw the house, hidden behind young pines, a white Volvo parked in the driveway. I stopped on the edge of the road, got out, and walked to the house down the drive, slippery with pine needles. Blue jays argued raucously in the trees, cicadas hummed to climax, started again. The house was wood, stained dark brown, all jutting angles and big windows, with wooden verandas and red geraniums blooming in big pots.

I went up steep wooden steps. Where the veranda changed to a deck was a door. I knocked. I took a deep breath to still my heart, which, as usual, was pounding. Death notification and me without my tote bag.

After a while a woman opened the door, but she didn't open the screen. The light was behind her, but I could see she was tall and wore a long red muumuu-type garment and heavy African-looking beads.

"Mrs. Hartman," I said. "Helen Hartman?"

"Yes?" She opened the screen door and now I could see her. Her hair was pulled back, neatly, taming a tangle of ringlets so like Randall's, like Didi's, but entirely gray. She had his nose too, and what I can only describe as his presence.

"I hope you're here about the petition," she said. "The situation is absolutely appalling. They sprayed again just last week." Her voice was resonant, professional in the way it was placed, as if she'd spent some time doing public speaking.

"No. My name's Chloe Newcomb. I'm an old friend of your son's. Randall?"

Her hand flew up, touching the African beads one by one. Emotions flitted over her face in succession, reluctance, anger, sadness. "When did you see him last?" she asked me, her voice cautious.

It was too soon. I couldn't stand there and just tell her. "The last time I talked to him," I said, lying by omission, "was back in New York, right after he graduated from college. We were friends in college. Please, Mrs. Hartman," I said, "I really need to talk to you."

Minutes seemed to tick past. Blue jays screamed, boats *putt-putt*ed. Even with that, I distinctly heard pine needles dropping on the wooden veranda.

"Well," she said. "All right. Come in. And you can call me Helen."

I came into a kitchen, all wooden counters, neat wooden cupboards. A table was in one corner and a computer on it. Beside the computer were stacks of envelopes.

There was a thumping and a bumping behind Helen

and she turned. A man in a wheelchair came barreling through a door. He waved his arms and made unintelligible noises.

"Jacob!" she said.

He looked up at her from his wheelchair. He must have been powerfully built, once, but now unexercised excess flesh hung from his forearms where his short-sleeved gray shirt ended. He had thick black brows and deep lines around his mouth, and his face was full of yearning.

"This is my husband," she said to me. "Jacob, this is Chloe Newcomb."

He made more unintelligible noises.

Helen sighed. "Jacob, go into the living room, please; we'll join you there."

Jacob hesitated, then wheeled backward reluctantly, vanishing through the door.

Helen took my arm and looked at me intently, her voice urgent again, low enough to be a whisper had it not been so resonant. "He's lost his speech, as you can see. And the use of one leg, but his mind is perfectly good. I really don't know why you're here. Whatever you have to say, I beg you to listen to me. He'd like to hear about Randall, he *needs* to hear about him at this time in his life. Talk to him about Randall, when you knew him in college. But please, only pleasant memories."

I followed her into the living room. There were two leather couches facing each other over a chrome and glass coffee table. Windows filled one entire wall, looking out onto the Bay. Books lined the room, and a gallery of photographs, pictures of a young and polished Helen shaking hands with various politicians, some of whom I recognized. A chipper boyish John Lindsay, a fresh, less droopy-eyed Mario Cuomo.

Only pleasant memories.

I sat down on one of the leather couches and Helen sat across from me, her hands folded in front of her, her back straight, like a queen deigning to listen to a subject. Jacob wheeled his chair to the edge of the chrome table.

"Jacob," said Helen, "Chloe went to college with Randall. Isn't that interesting?"

He rolled his wheelchair closer to me, and plucked at my arm earnestly. "Auuam . . ." he said.

"Were you good friends?" asked Helen.

"We, uh, dated," I said under Helen's watchful eyes. I searched my memory. "I . . ." I felt myself blushing. "I was very much in love with him. He was so full of confidence and *fun*. We used to go on bike rides. Randall always insisted he knew where we were going, so we got lost a lot."

Jacob's eyes searched my face.

"Um, one time," I said, "we packed a lunch, apples and cheese and bread, and we rode our bikes out to an old quarry. Then it started to rain, and we had to ride back in the rain and we got lost. Randall's hair got curlier and curlier and it stuck up from his head so high, we joked he would attract all the lightning."

Jacob nodded his head up and down. He pointed to Helen's hair.

"Randall's hair was just like mine," said Helen.

Was, she'd said.

She looked at me brightly. "And then what happened?" she prompted.

"Finally we had to stop at a farmhouse and the people let us in. An elderly couple. We sat in their living room and the old woman pulled out patchwork quilts that her grandmother had made. Randall was just fascinated. He said there's whole lives in those quilts, a whole sense of history and time, you can feel it just by looking at them."

He'd really cared about the old woman and her quilts, it wasn't just rhetoric and power and wanting to control, those bugaboos of the New Left. He'd always been different that way. People felt this and responded to him.

Hustling rich women in Mexico. What had happened? He'd turned that natural gift into a weapon.

I came back to the living room in Chesapeake Bay, confused. Out on the Bay a sailboat floated by like a big white butterfly. Helen and Jacob were looking at me, waiting.

"They really loved him, those two old people," I said.

There was a silence.

Then, "That was a beautiful story," said Helen approvingly. "Thank you for sharing that with us."

I hadn't thought about it in years, pulled out from my subconscious intact for the occasion. Though nothing in the story had been intimate, I felt vulnerable, as if I had removed a piece of my flesh and handed it to these two strangers.

Jacob was scribbling on a notepad, his face strained with the effort, the pen flopping in his hand.

Helen looked at him worriedly. "Jacob can't take too much excitement," she said to me, "so we rarely have people to visit, mostly I correspond. I'm afraid I need to ask you to go now."

Jacob nodded violently, pushing the notepad towards her. She read it and shook her head at him. He became more agitated, kicking at the footrest of his wheelchair.

She turned to me, her face guarded, a warning in it. "He wants me to ask if you know," she said reluctantly.

"Know what?"

"About Randall." She looked at me so intently, I felt hypnotized. *"The plane crash."*

"No," I said, "I didn't know."

"Randall was killed in a plane crash eighteen years ago." Her eyes held mine.

Of course, it was a lie, and somehow I could see that she knew it. I faked surprise, pain, for Jacob's benefit.

"Well." Helen let out a long breath and got to her feet. "I'll see you out."

* * *

We walked together onto the deck and down the steps. We walked over the slippery pine needles. When we were away from the house and almost to my car, she said, "Jacob never had a chance to say good-bye to him properly. They fought the whole time. He's pretended not to care for years, but now that death has given him a warning . . ."

"Mrs. Hartman," I said, "Randall wasn't killed in a plane crash."

Her face was closed, rigid.

"He's dead," I said bluntly. "He killed himself or was killed last Saturday in Arizona."

Her hand went back to the beads, fingering them, but her face still was expressionless.

"He was using another name, Leroy, Leroy Harris. Why? Do you know?"

"I don't have any idea what you're talking about," she said.

"Helen, it's really important—"

"*Stop* it," she said. "I know what important is, he was my *son*. What you're saying is nonsense." She turned away. "Utter nonsense. Harassment."

I stood my ground.

She turned back to look at me, eyes blazing. "And if you're not gone by the time I get to the house, I'm calling the police."

The hell you will, lady, I thought. I fumbled in my purse, for one of my cards, my Chloe Newcomb, Victim Compensation Advocate, Cochise County Attorney cards, and thrust it at her. *The hell you will.* But I hurried to my car and started it up anyway.

PART THREE

Arizona

19

No one was following her—it was easy to tell because there was nowhere to hide in the long desert distances. All the way to Kansas Settlement the Volkswagen was making funny noises somewhere under the hood, but she didn't know enough about cars to tell if it was serious.

She'd planned to learn about cars, take a class or get a good mechanic to teach her, she'd kept putting it off because it wasn't much good if you didn't have the tools. She knew how to change the oil and the tires, but tools— they were things to carry along, to not forget, to weigh you down. How lightly I've traveled all these years, she thought sadly.

The road ended ahead and she turned left towards the Coronado National Forest. Ever since she'd left the house she'd been thinking of long-ago times; one of her mother's barbecues when she'd invited those cowboys who'd worked on the dude ranch in Jackson Hole, Wyoming, where they'd gone one summer. The cowboys were in Chicago, for some obscure reason, no one had asked or cared, and they were supposed to mingle with the guests, like props.

At the Chiricahua National Monument sign she took a left turn, and then another, and parked the car off the road under a big pine tree and got out her gear, thinking about those cowboys, how they'd lost their glamour at the party, had seemed smaller and stupid, more like, well, like servants, was how she'd thought then. Not now. She understood things now, really had her life down; she could carry everything she needed for several days without being so loaded up she couldn't enjoy the hiking. Class was an utterly meaningless concept once you turned to survival.

Blue jays screamed at each other over her head. The air smelled cool and piney. Making that scene at the Watering Hole had been stupid; no matter who was responsible, they'd be thinking she knew more than she did. Bait, she thought. I made myself bait. All those years of running and now I've walked right into it. Maybe I can't stand the waiting, maybe I need it to happen.

But still she was safest in the mountains. If they came, it would be at night, she was certain of that. She had a gun in her pack, and when she slept it would be beside her. All these years, she slept like a warrior, always prepared.

I never did any of it, after all, she thought, never married, had children, used all the stuff I'd have inherited from her. I never did any of it. She slung on her backpack and began to walk, down the creek bed, for a while, stepping from stone to stone.

The creek had water in it this time of year, and the trees met overhead and rustled in the breeze. The creek, the land, belonged to something abstract. She thought, in the old days, I have could settled down, lived here forever if I pleased, oh, just to live *somewhere* forever.

She exited the creek where the mountain started to climb; if she climbed steadily, she would be near the top by dark. The trail was wide at the beginning, but it narrowed considerably as the view widened. Someone had said years ago when it happened . . . never mind. *Now death will always be at your back.*

But it wasn't at her back at all, but at her front in broad daylight as she rounded a rock, near the top; a creature. She drew in her breath, stopped abruptly. An image, a hallucination blocked her path. it was so *unreal*, not a *person*, garish, red and orange and white.

"*What do you want?*" she said out loud, still trying to match what she was seeing with something that fit. She turned to run but the creature lunged at her.

And then she was struggling, silently, even though screams would have been her best bet, struggling but losing; at a disadvantage with her pack, with not screaming because she'd learned so long ago not to make noise and attract attention.

Then she did scream as she lost her footing on the edge. She screamed as she fell, but briefly. She hit the rocks twenty feet below and lay there, not dead, but maybe mortally injured. The fall had at least temporarily saved her life. No one could get to her here.

She reached round her waist for the water bottles she carried, still intact. She was at the edge of a little cave, which could shelter her, if she needed shelter. Still survival oriented, she thought, and for what?

No one could get to her here. No one. So why not just give up.

As she faded out, she kept thinking of that phrase her mother always liked, her mother who'd grown up not poor but not quite rich, among very rich people. The phrase symbolized the utter uselessness of what she had learned as a child, the tools her mother had given her to cope with. "*If you can't be rich, then you'd better be amusing.*"

20

Storm clouds were massing over the Mule Mountains. The air cooled as I drove slowly up Mule Pass in that magic interval between day and night. The mountains were covered with scrub oak, walnut trees, and juniper, and it must have been raining in my absence, because little waterfalls trickled down among the rocks everywhere. I climbed to the Divide and coasted down through Mule Tunnel and into Dudley.

It seemed like I'd been gone for years.

A little wind was coming up and it was cool, so cool. Sweet peas grew in the drainage ditches, and fennel; its licorice smell filled the air that rushed through my open car window. Red and pink roses bloomed in vacant lots, and valerian and prickle poppy. Cottonwoods and Chinese elms and cancer trees shaded the wood-frame old-fashioned houses where people sat out on their porches. Kids skateboarded down the canyon and couples strolled.

But I felt as detached as if I were looking at a scene

in a glass bubble; one shake and snow would fall and cover it up.

Helen Hartman, so cold and angry, haunted me. Had Randall failed to write all those years, the errant unforgiven prodigal son? We'd all been struggling to break free of our parents back then, yet he'd called her faithfully once a week, going off secretively to do it, closing the door behind him. Even *then* he'd called her.

I hadn't liked her, so it had been easy for me to tell her right out what I had to say. Walked away leaving her holding my card like a bomb. Right now I regretted that deeply. What if she called my office when I wasn't there, demanding further information? And no one would know what she was talking about.

I had lost a brother; Helen's attitude was inexplicable, holding some old grudge. I would never get James back, she would never get another son. How could she not grieve, or had she done it, for some reason, long ago?

I stopped at the Circle K. Clusters of teenagers in baggy long shorts and skateboards flirted and strutted by the ice machine. The weight of my past was dissipating with the details of Randall, Charlie—*Stowe*, he must have been cold when he died. Had he been skiing with a girl-friend, friends, family? I thought of his thin skin. Unanchored, I could feel the seeds of death in the summer night around me.

Thunder rumbled outside as I stood in line with a quart of milk. In front of me a big man in a fluorescent pink baseball cap and paint-stained shorts was buying three six-packs. A haggard woman in long layered skirts and purple top embroidered with tiny mirrors like hippies used to wear came up to me, a guitar slung over her shoulder. She looked at me, her eyes searching my face but not really seeing me.

"Jesus loves you," she said.

For a second I could see bits of my own past in each

little mirror and my future in her aging wrinkled face. "He loves you *too*," I said.

In my absence, Big Foot had attacked the *flotaki* rug my mother had got for me in Greece when she and my father had gone there on research. They were always getting grants for stuff like that. Bits of the rug lay scattered about the floor. He looked at me without interest, his heart given away to Lourdes, no doubt, who'd been feeding him. The house smelled musty, full of mold, with a hint of cat pee. A tiny spider had spun a web between the coffeepot and the gas burner, and in the sink a scorpion lay as if waiting for my return.

I called Kyle right away, at the county sheriff's, but he was off. I wanted to know how the investigation was progressing, needed to see if Starry had told him about the letter—and, least pleasant of all, check on Homer's beer run, but on the last I would wait. I didn't want to call him at home.

Then I called Roxanne. I was working for free, but she was spending a fortune in plane tickets and one night in a motel. I'd talked to her from Logan's and told her Randall's parents were alive and how she could reach them. But she'd wanted me to meet them, check them out. The news had put a damper on her social skills.

"You didn't tell her about Didi?" she asked now.

"That's up to you."

"God," said Roxanne. "All the lefties I know have made up with their parents. How could she be like that?"

"I have no idea."

She faltered. "Maybe there's a lot he didn't tell me."

"Well, at least he didn't blow up a bank or anything. If he had, there'd be a warrant out. The ball's in your court, Roxanne, if you want to tell Helen Hartman she has a grandchild."

"And tell Didi she has extra grandparents. Oh, dear . . ." Her voice went away.

"The P.I.'s going to be billing me," I said to bring her back. "I'll send it on to you."

"Anything you need. Carte blanche," she said. "That's what I told you." She hardly heard me, worrying about whether or not to tell Didi.

We hung up.

I sat down on the couch. All I had was useless knowledge and no answers. Tapes were jumbled on the coffee table, stacked on the floor, but I didn't put one in the machine. I couldn't shake the sense that things were profoundly wrong, that something I did not want to know lay in wait for me, and that whatever it was would do nothing but wreak more tragedy out in the Junction.

I sat on the couch for a long time, watching it get dark outside, the light sepia for a while from the cloud cover. Big Foot forgave me and came to lie heavy on my feet where they were tucked up on the couch. In the fading light doves cooed in the trees outside as if that alone could call love to them.

Then I fell asleep to New York time, lying on the couch, as the thunder started up in earnest.

It rained all night.

21

In my office the next morning I wrote general demands on the county for the bills that had come in on approved claims; a counselor bill for a rape victim and one for a molested child and a hospital bill for a man who'd been assaulted behind a bar. The demands would go to the Finance Department and they would issue checks that would come back to me. I mailed out a couple of checks Finance had sent me, including one to Jolene's counselor, for the last two sessions before Jolene left. Jolene who had given me the pink African violet and run off with a new man before completing counseling.

I was wearing work clothes, little heels and stockings and a black straight skirt with a red silk blouse buttoned at the neck. I made four trips to the lounge for coffee, my walk brisk and efficient, but who was I kidding? After a while I just sat and stared at the calendar. It was still on July and September was approaching, but I didn't get up and change it.

Outside the Chinese elms, the cottonwoods, were drip-ping and the sky was gray and swollen with rain.

I needed a break.

It wasn't busy. I decided I could take a little time off now if I worked double time right before the board meet-ing, which wasn't for three weeks. I called the sheriff's office, but Kyle was out somewhere. I left a message for him to call me. A few times I got up and went out into the receptionist's area to look out the back windows, just in case I might see him, my man of honor, shoulders hunched against the rain going into the sheriff's offices.

Then the phone rang and it was Fern. "I just wanted to let you know something," she said, "you being with Victim Witness."

"What's that?"

"Well, Lance Eubanks who used to be married to my niece Hazel, he's been hanging around Rose Davison. . . ."

"Lance," I said. "I know who you mean."

"Anyway, Thursday night he was in the Watering Hole where Rose works and he said Starry Noel was in there acting real crazy."

"Real crazy?"

"Talking about how somebody had killed Leroy. Saying she knew who it was and they'd better come and get her before she told. Just like Didi did, but she's a grown woman. And she wasn't even drinking. I mean maybe the police should come and give her protection."

"I don't know," I said. "Victim Witness isn't in the law enforcement business. Maybe you could call Kyle direct."

"I did that, but he said she was downright rude to him and he doesn't think she'd welcome the attention, but I said, well, she's crazy, everybody knows it, and she needs to be protected from herself. I thought you might put in a word."

"I'll tell you what. I spoke with Roxanne Steinberg and she wants me to check on a few things at Leroy's, so I'm coming out to the Junction. I can stop and see Starry,

how's that? I'll see her on my own, not as Victim Witness."
I thought I should make that clear.

"That's good, someone should, Victim Witness or not."

"And I'll need to get the key to Leroy's from you."

"It's hid under a rock over by that first tomato plant.
Thought that'd be better than right by the door." She
added plaintively, "You know, I told Didi's mother I'd look
after things. Homer went and got those peacocks, the cock
and the hen; *she* wouldn't want them. And he took the
pickup to the garage. I was just over there yesterday,
cleaning."

I thanked her and hung up, not asking her about what it
was that Leroy had handed to her or about the beer run. I
would have to do that in person.

Cleaning. That would make the second time it had been
cleaned since Leroy's death. There probably wouldn't be
any signs of Randall at all if this kept up, the women of the
Junction industriously scrubbing away all traces.

In the desert the cream-colored flowers of the yuccas
bloomed waxy and funereal under a gray luminous sky as
small storms swept down the length of the desolate Valley.
The mountains were shrouded in clouds like mountains in
a Japanese print and the washes were running, swollen like
white-water rivers, carrying sticks and stones and uprooted
plants. Rain pelted the red dirt, each splash a little fountain
as I drove down the road to Leroy's, to Randall's, to search
his house, not knowing what I was looking for.

Years ago Randall and I had walked in the rain around
the Village holding hands, looking in the windows of the
antiques stores around Union Square, laughing at the
dusty gilded cupids, the fringed lampshades, the absurd
eighteenth-century chairs; the past and its lessons were
nothing to us, we had escaped entirely. Hardly anyone had
been on the street, a whole city hiding out from the rain,
except for us, who owned it. I wore a trench coat and a
flowered minidress and we'd ducked into a basement

restaurant off Washington Square and eaten lamb stew with homemade bread for lunch.

Maybe what I was really looking for was that day.

I got my flashlight out of the glove compartment, ducked out of the car, and found the key under the pungent leaves of a tomato plant. Inside the rain fell gently on the roof, numbing sound and making the place like a cocoon. The table shone with Fern's cleaning, the four rush-bottomed chairs neatly pushed in, the phone where I had left it. I picked up the receiver. Dead.

I went to the bedroom first, there was only one. Randall must have slept on the couch when Didi visited. There was one window, double hung, with plain white curtains; an outdated calendar of some mythical Mexican god in vivid colors on the wall, the kind they gave away at Mexican curio stores; a beautiful quilt on the bed, a pattern called Kansas Troubles, tiny triangles forming the jagged pattern that resembled a rooster's comb.

Did Randall see it and think of our long-ago visit to the farmhouse?

I opened the two top drawers of the chest, empty except for a crumpled boarding pass for Didi's flight from New York. The bottom two held flannel and cotton shirts, boxer shorts, jeans, socks, all in ordinary masculine drab colors.

I got down on my knees and shone the flashlight under the bed and under the dresser. Fern hadn't really cleaned in the bedroom, probably just made sure the bed was neat. I imagined her making it up. Regretful as she smoothed sheets she had never lain on? Or never would again?

Dust balls under the dresser and more dust balls and a balled-up man's sock under the bed. There was a rectangular area free of dust under the bed, which could have been where Didi's suitcase had been stored.

The closet had clothes pushed towards the back, red plaid wool Pendleton jacket, a jeans jacket. I searched the pockets of the jackets, found a glittery rock, a shell casing from a .22, two pennies. I shone the flashlight on the closet floor. Nothing. So many people had been here before me.

Twenty years had been here before me. I felt like a spurned lover, reduced to voyeur status and sneaking into an ex's house to go through the mail and check the sheets. I sat on the bed and closed my eyes. *Randall,* I thought, just in case it might work, *if you're out there, give me a sign.*

I sat there for two or three minutes and then, suddenly, a shadow passed before my closed eyes. Tiny hairs prickled on the back of my neck. I opened my eyes. There was nothing there.

I got up and left the room, not looking back.

In the living room the Westerns lined the mantel, overdue at the library, the couch had dark stains on it that made me shudder. Against the wall was an old rolltop desk. Bills lay scattered inside. I opened drawers, found blank envelopes, stamps, paper clips—looked for letters, found none. I shone the flashlight behind the desk, in the space where it met the wall, in case something had fallen off the top . . . and bingo, a white square, just out of reach of my hand. I pushed the desk out slightly, leaned down and got it.

Then I heard the noise, a low chuckle deep in the throat. I looked up.

A man stood at the door, he might have been there for some time, a half smile on his face, watching me.

22

Dirty blue shirt, dirty jeans, cowboy hat, rubber wading boots, and that ubiquitous Valley accessory, a shotgun. His big-boned face would have been handsome had it had any charm at all. The shadow. He'd probably been sneaking around by the window in the bedroom.

"Goin' through his desk, huh?" He held the gun pointed at me, though I knew it was not good etiquette, any gun owner could tell you that. He smiled knowingly.

"Frank," I said. "You're Frank Gresham, aren't you?"

"What's it to you?" He jerked the gun.

I backed away. His smile widened.

"As a matter of fact," I said, in the most authoritative voice I could muster, "this house belongs to his heirs now and I have their permission to be here. What are *you* doing here?"

"Bein' neighborly." He jerked the gun again.

"Could you lower that," I said, "if you don't mind?"

"And maybe I do." His hard green eyes skimmed off

mine, so flat, not really seeing—more sensing like some wild animal. "Scared?" he sneered.

"No," I lied. I hadn't heard anyone pull up outside. But he had on those waders, he must have walked over, waded through the washes. No one would know from the highway that Frank Gresham, meanest man in the Valley, was inside the house with me.

As if reading my mind, he said, "What the hell, out here, nobody around, nobody'd hear the gun go off if I shoot."

"You'd be that stupid?"

"Somebody was. Back then. Nobody to hear that shot either, right? I told Kyle Barnett that."

"What shot?"

"You know the one." He tensed.

"Well, you're wrong about that," I said. "Mrs. O'Hara heard it. She called the police."

He lowered the gun for the first time. "Son of a bitch! That what they told you?"

"That's what *happened*," I said.

"Damn cops."

He went and sat down heavily on the couch. This gave me a clear path to the door, but he'd have plenty of time to raise the gun. "We don't need them out here in the Valley, we can settle things ourselves. And they know better too, they're local boys, most of 'em. I'd still have my wife living here with me if it wasn't for the damn cops and Leroy."

"Leroy?"

"Sure, he's the one told her about the law. What business this country got making laws about what goes on between a man and his wife? Putting the lives of ordinary citizens in the hands of goddamn *lawyers*, is what they're doin'. Destroying all our *traditions*." He blinked, for a moment looking sad and confused.

Then he went on, "Leroy filled her head with stuff like restraining orders. Shit. She run over here and they'd talk and I"—he spat violently on the floor—"I don't know what all."

"You must have been pretty mad," I said, paraphrasing in my best Victim Witness manner.

"Told Shawn a million times, you miss your ma, blame it on Leroy." His voice turned pious. "What the hell has happened to the *family* in this country? Hell, she'd a taken Shawn, too, if I hadn't told her right out, she did that, I'd track her down and kill them both."

"And you would have?"

"Shit." He ran his hand, nails grimy with dirt, across his face, staring over my shoulder at I don't know what all. "I loved her too." A look of surprise came over his face. "Hell, maybe I would of."

He looked at me, his eyes unfocused now, blurry. "But don't you believe it. Mrs. O'Hara never made no call. Number one, she wouldn't. She's a traditional woman, all the O'Haras are. More likely they'd a come over with a gun themselves to check things out. And number two, she's been up at Casa Grande visiting her daughter for more'n two weeks now."

"Did you tell Kyle Barnett that?"

"Hell no. Why should I make his job easier for him? He don't believe a damn thing I say anyway, probably thinks I done it."

There was no way I was going to let Frank Gresham shoot me before I checked this last piece of information. I stood up. "I'm leaving," I said, "and you have to leave too, so I can lock up."

"The hell you—" He stopped, head cocked, listening. "What the . . . That's my damn truck."

He got up clumsily and tramped to the door, went out. I came quickly behind him, key in hand. Way down on the highway I saw a green truck speeding by, maybe seventy miles an hour.

He said, "Son of a bitch—there it goes. Shawn knows he can't take it without askin'." He began to run, heavy footed in his waders, then stopped, as the truck vanished into the horizon.

Hurriedly I turned the key and took a run too, got to my car and got inside and locked those doors as well. My flashlight was back on the desk and I hadn't put the key under the rock. . . .

"That boy's getting clear out of *control*," Frank yelled, loud enough to be heard through the closed car windows. "Don't do a damn thing I say anymore." His face was red, strained with frustration, and could you blame him? Wives running off, children disobeying—his whole damn world going nontraditional.

I drove off, as I drove looking down at the paper still clutched in my hand, the one I'd retrieved from behind the desk: a flyer for an auction, tools mostly, dated two years ago.

The sun had broken through the clouds that had scurried down the Valley just in the time I'd been in the house. You could almost feel the desert greedily trying to suck up the moisture. I headed towards Starry's, thinking about the fact that someone had called the law about the gunshot at Leroy Harris' house, someone who was not who she said she was. A woman.

Like Starry, who told everyone in the Watering Hole she knew who did it? Had she been there when it happened, maybe come to give Leroy a piece of her mind and seen the killer leaving? Then why not just tell the police instead of putting herself in danger? Because she saw the police as one more enemy. The *vigilantes*.

I drove through the Junction on the damp streets and turned down the blacktop to her house. The dirt road was muddy but already drying up, passable. Starry's car wasn't in the driveway, but just in case I parked and went up the steps between the marigolds, and knocked on her back door. Water dripped from the eaves of the house, the blue metal porch chair from the thirties lay on its side under the cottonwood. I knocked again, but no one came.

I didn't think she had a phone. So if she'd made the

call, it would have to have been from somewhere else. I
conjured up a new scenario. Maybe it had been Leroy's
she'd called from, after she killed him. Called, then set
down the receiver, wiped it off, wiped off all the prints on
the front door, all her crazy scenes afterwards nothing but
cover-ups.

Back home I called the Cochise County sheriff's again
and asked for Kyle Barnett.

"He's out today," someone told me. "Want to talk to
another officer?"

"No, thanks," I said. "This is Chloe Newcomb—he'll
know who that is. I've already left one message, but now
I'm home. Could you have him get in touch when he has a
chance?"

"Will do," said the woman.

Earning my money, I called Roxanne.

"Just tell me what you have to say," she said furtively. "I
may not be alone long."

If this kept on, poor Harry would think she had a lover. I
said that I'd been told that the person who supposedly had
called the cops about the gunshots maybe hadn't, and
didn't go into the Frank Gresham part. For what?

"So it was a woman, though?"

"It seems like it."

"I know there's a woman involved in this somewhere,"
said Roxanne fervently. "They could never stay away from
him. Do you think he broke someone's heart?"

Breaking someone's heart did put you at high risk statis-
tically to be murdered. "I don't know anything," I said.
"I'll keep in touch."

Then I called nice, solid, reliable Brody, whom I owed a
dinner to for fixing my car, and owed maybe more than
that, and asked him out on a date. I didn't feel good about
it, but my mind was so set on this course of solving Randall's murder that I didn't have time to feel bad either.

23

In his plaintive, rusty voice, Clint Black was singing about living it risky, women and whiskey.

Rose came down the aisle behind the bar in the Watering Hole; stepping in time to the music, gold chains glittering around her neck, jeans so tight you knew she'd had to take a deep breath to get into them. When she got to Brody and me she reached one ringed hand up and adjusted the strap on her black lace camisole. With the other hand she poured a shot of Jim Beam into a glass and pushed it in front of me. It was my third.

I was wearing black jeans and one of those white fringed Western shirts that had suddenly appeared at the Wal-Mart, and I thought I fit right in. I didn't hang out much in bars, and when I did it was usually one glass of red wine, nursed through the evening. But the minute Brody and I walked in I'd made a decision—tonight I was going to *drink*. I don't know why, maybe just a need to merge with the natives, maybe just looking for that edge on secrets any kind of drug can sometimes give you.

Rose held the whiskey bottle poised high. "How 'bout you?" she asked Brody.

"I'll have another ginger ale," he said.

Poor Brody, a recovering alcoholic dragged to a bar and forced to spend the night drinking ginger ale. "But cars, Brody," I'd said to him on the phone. He was a real car nut. "You know everyone in the Junction has an old car sitting in their backyard. And they'll be drunk and you'll be sober. You could get a *deal*." Guiltily I touched his arm now, my hand lingering there with false reassurance.

"You *still* quit drinkin'!" exclaimed the man next to him who'd been introduced as Killer. "Good Lord."

"Five years, two months," Brody said.

I swallowed the Jim Beam in a couple of gulps, the way I'd seen drinking men do in the Dudley bars.

Rose watched me with interest.

"So it must of been close to six years ago that I met old Brody here," said Killer. He had dull blue eyes, a battered nose, a handlebar mustache, and wore a cap that said KING ROPE, SHERIDAN, WYOMING. He winked at me and nudged Brody. "Remember? You bought that old sky blue Chevy Starliner I had in my backyard. I believe you was drinkin' hard then."

"Explains why I bought it," said Brody gloomily.

I sighed.

The bar was long and the decor sparse, as if the whole place existed for one purpose and one purpose alone. Except in a room to my left was a pool table and a few couples were dancing in a little area at the end, moving to the music, arms around each other's waists, swaying, to Clint Black singing about how you lived and never really learned.

"Yep. Must of been still drinking," said Brody, "to buy that old junker. Well, now I got Chloe here doing my drinking for me."

He poked me surreptitiously.

Rose sashayed back down the bar. At one end, next to

the cigarette machine, Lance Eubanks was spread over two barstools, cowboy hat pushed back, Roy Rogers eyes monitoring her progress. The Watering Hole was filling up.

Brody was to one side of me, Killer standing behind, and to the other side a man sat, dead quiet, drinking steadily. Jackalope antlers hung on the wall. The spotty mirror over the bar was sepia; hand-lettered signs mentioned pickled eggs, and half-price drinks on ladies' night. Another said:

> *SEVILLE DERDAGO*
> *ATOZIN BUZZIZ INNARO*
> *NOJO DEMARNT TRUKS*
> *SUMMIT COSIN SUMMIT DUKS.*

Rose was back with the Jim Beam bottle. "You ready for another one?" she said skeptically.

"Sure," I said recklessly.

Rose filled my shot glass. Her arm with the tattoo was more muscular than you would expect from her sexy getup, she could double as a bouncer. Why had she been in jail?

"Is Starry in town?" I asked her. "I stopped by her house earlier, but her car wasn't there."

Rose set down the Jim Beam bottle, looked around, then leaned on her elbows and said in a low voice, "She went camping. She was due back today, but she could of decided to stay longer. It might be a good idea for her to stay away."

I took a long sip of Jim Beam. "What happened exactly when you talked to . . ." I began, but her expression said *don't ask*.

She watched me drink half the Jim Beam. "Now, you might go just a little easy," she said. "Though I don't see why when that gentleman down there's paying for it."

"He is?" I stared down a row of sepia faces. "Which gentleman?"

"The one in the getup," said Rose.

I leaned to look down the bar where it curved, past the pickled pigs' feet. There, a lock of chestnut hair falling over his forehead, wearing a blue Western jacket, with a deeper blue yoke, white shirt, and bolo with a large chunk of turquoise holding the ties together, was the man I'd seen in Safeway. The one who drove the silver Ford Bronco.

My heart might have stopped for a moment had alcohol not dulled my reflexes. "Oh?" I said.

"Told me his name was Doc," said Rose. "He was too cute for me not to ask."

Simple as that. *She* hadn't had scruples. I raised my glass to him. He nodded, smiled.

Rose went down the bar and I swallowed the rest of my Jim Beam.

"I'd sure like to dance with your lady, if she will," said a voice behind me.

"Ask her," said Brody.

I turned. A tall cowboy, with a square face and a crew cut that displayed a perfect widow's peak, wearing a pink western shirt, loomed over me.

"Sure," I said, the smash hit, belle of the bar.

It was kind of like dancing with an ironing board, he was so tall and spare and hard. He never said a word to me. We swayed back and forth like the rest of the people, dancing to "Blue Eyes Crying in the Rain." He kept his eyes closed, so I closed mine, too, and life was sad and bittersweet, and somehow with all that sadness wonderful things could happen. I wanted to cry.

I opened my eyes and caught Doc's over at the bar, watching. He didn't look like a Valley man, more like a rich rancher—the ones who get out their shotguns when the hippie-environmentalists arrive to tell them their cattle can't graze anymore where they always have.

The cowboy led me back, keeping his hand flat on my back as if I needed guidance, and maybe I did. Brody had saved my seat. How was I ever going to make this up to him? Well, later for that. "You're my pal," I whispered with abandon in his ear. "My *good* buddy."

There was a shot of Jim Beam waiting for me.

"Doc wants to know if you got a request," said Rose.

"Like what?" I said, sipping.

"Jukebox," said Rose.

I looked down the bar. "George Strait," I called. I knew they would have it. I leaned down the bar, mouthing my words, "The one about the cowboy."

Rose looked at me, her blue eyes direct, almost warning. "Now, I don't know about that."

Brody took my arm. "Forget it. It's time to go."

Down the bar Doc nodded at me; even far away I could tell we were on the same wavelength. He got up.

I shook off Brody's hand. Later for that. Right now I was all for honesty, truth, and the direct expression of the emotions. It was all we had. "Not *yet*," I said.

Life, with death in the midst of it. Suns sinking like hearts. Beside me the man who'd been sitting so quietly slid down slowly on his seat, bending at the waist till his head rested on the bar.

"Chloe . . ." began Brody.

Doc was beside me as the music started.

"Dance?" he said.

"I knew—the stakes—were high—right from the start."

He was tall with a gallant air. We went out to the floor. I leaned into him, having a little trouble with my balance, though my heart was certainly in the right place. He crooked his arm up, leaning into me, half bowing.

"You like this son, hm?" he said, his voice tickling my ear.

I looked up into his chestnut eyes. I loved the bolo that kept the two dark green cords of his tie together, the turquoise chunk veined with baser minerals.

"Yes, I do," I said.

"Somebody else did too, from what I hear."

From the fog of Jim Beam–induced emotion overwhelming

me, I caught something. A casualness that wasn't really casual. For a moment, I was sober. "Who's that?" I asked.

We did a little twirl. "Come on, I know you know."

I suddenly realized no one else was dancing, they were all standing on the sidelines watching. "I've seen you before," I said. "At Safeway."

"Hey, you know, I think you did. At the frozen foods, am I right?"

"I've seen you around town here too. You're not, um, local?" I asked nervously.

"Just passing through."

How could anyone be just passing through the Junction? I thought with drunken cunning; all the roads either led toward it or away, it wasn't on the way to anywhere else.

And then Brody was taking my arm. "Come on, Chloe," he said. "We're going, if I have to carry you out."

"Here," said Doc, shoving something down in the right front pocket of my black jeans.

"For heaven's sake," I protested to Brody. "I'm *perfectly* sober."

We exited into the parking lot. I did feel almost sober. I walked carefully to emphasize my nearly sober feeling.

24

It was cool outside, and despite the fact that inside the bar there was loud music and people drinking and carrying on, out here the desert took over. The sky was filled with stars; every cloud had gone, passed on. Tomorrow would be hot. You could smell the greasewood, feel the void, as if the bar were just a tiny meaningless outpost in some essential emptiness.

"Well, it's nice out here," I said brightly to Brody.

He didn't answer, say anything. Incommunicado. His back was to me, set and straight, little-boy-like. Well, I'd dragged him, a staunch nondrinker, a recovering alcoholic, out to a bar and gotten drunk. It had seemed important to go, hang out with the natives when they were acting natural. Maybe now would be a good time to rant on about his insensitivity to my needs, but I kept thinking how a good part of human existence seemed to be giving and receiving pain. Right now I was on the giving end.

He got into his red '56 Ford truck and I climbed in the passenger side, so high up it was like mountain climbing.

I slumped in my seat while Brody drove the long straight roads that cut through fields of ocotillo and mesquite and yucca, through ranches and chili farms and pecan orchards. Neither of us spoke for miles and miles. My window was open, our speed making wind of the night air. It rushed in, blowing my hair, sobering me up.

We reached the turnoff for Highway 80, which led into Dudley. I needed to do something to save this relationship.

"What's wrong?" I asked.

He looked down the road to the left, far down as if trying to see if there was anyone he knew in Douglas. "Nothing."

"Come on."

Brody turned onto Highway 80. "You made a fool of yourself in there."

"Everybody was making a fool of themselves but you, Brody. Everyone but you was too drunk to notice me." Except at the end when they all stood on the sidelines watching me dance with Doc.

"Asking that guy to play that song."

"Well, he played it." It was a relief to have Brody mention Doc; I was beginning to wonder if anyone had seen him but me. Maybe they'd stood around and stared because I'd been dancing alone, carrying on a conversation with someone who wasn't even there.

"He's a fool too."

"He's a *doctor*." But I didn't believe it.

"*Sure*."

I'd seen Brody frequently until—two months ago. I'd told him nothing about what was going on in my life now, about the fact that almost exactly a week ago I'd seen an old boyfriend, with the top of his head blown off, and was now wondering if someone hadn't murdered him. Why hadn't I mentioned any of this to him?

We caught the curve round the pit, and the pickup rode it easily, strong silent Brody at the wheel.

*   *   *

Brewery Gulch was full of people lounging around in front of the bars, which were just closing. I knew what it would be like farther down the street, guys coming out of the St. Elmo's, revving up their pickups, throwing up in the parking lot, drunken couples groping each other in the alleyways, a fight or two. I felt even worse than I had coming round the pit.

A scene like this came to my mind, but in reverse, me driving and Logan beside me, saying banal things in a slurred voice and separated from me by an invisible and impenetrable wall, until the night I realized it was hopeless.

Forever and ever hopeless.

As usual, tourists blocked the street going up past the Copper Queen. Normal people, no doubt, at home, but here transformed into flocks of slow-moving sheep. Brody honked impatiently and they clutched each other in terror, stepping away in the wrong directions. Finally he got past them and drove the hill up to my house and stopped the truck in the street.

"See you," he said.

"You're not coming *in*?"

He shook his head.

I got out of the truck and stuck my head in the window. "Why not?" I asked as if I needed to. "I'm not drunk anymore."

He waved his hand in disgust and backed down the hill. Slowly I walked into the carport. I was maybe a little tipsy still. Tipsy. What a silly euphemism, making something disgusting sound cute.

Inside I almost tripped over Big Foot, my nemesis, my personal burden, as he nudged at my ankles. His food bowl was totally empty, and I'd taken the cat food bag from the top of the refrigerator and put it in a cupboard. I should have left him a can of beans, like hard-drinking people I knew did with their children, and a can opener, so he could fix his own dinner.

This struck me as terribly funny. I knelt, shaking with laughter, and tried to give him a hug, but he slipped away, with the quiet dignity of the sober.

I filled his bowl, went into my bedroom, undressed, and collapsed on the bed, which was a tiny rowboat on very rocky seas. The ceiling spun round and round over my head. I seemed to hear music still, people talking, as if the whole bar were congregated there in the bedroom, partying over my lifeless body.

But I was aware of something else too, an undercurrent of anxiety. I thought, *I should try to find Starry.*

Tainted with Jim Beam, my dreams were wild, chaotic. I inhabited several places all at once, my parents' house, the bar, my New York apartment, my house in Dudley, the bar, the road, Brody's shop, the bar—the bar kept coming back over and over. Brody and I were dancing in the bar, though Brody didn't dance.

And of course, because Brody didn't dance, people kept cutting in, but mostly Doc, whose mouth and nose were like malleable rubber, constantly changing. I was trying to get a fix on his face when Brody cut in again, but I pushed him away.

"Don't worry about me, about me, about me," I said. "We'll talk later." My voice had a funny echo as if it were at the end of a long tunnel. "Later, later, later."

Doc had his back to me, standing by the jukebox. I went over and grabbed his arm. "Aren't you a Sigma Chi?" I asked him.

"No, I'm with the students," he said, punching all the buttons on the jukebox at once.

I woke up suddenly, sweating under too many covers. A *Sigma Chi*. Hardly. I had no idea who he was. My pocket, he'd put something in my pocket. I got out of bed and found my white Western shirt and black jeans in a heap on the floor. I fumbled in the jeans pocket and pulled something out, a card. It said in one corner, PRESCOTT, ARIZONA, and a phone number, and under that:

ELLIOT KILDARE
Private Investigator

25

I sat at my kitchen counter waiting for the coffee water to drip through, staring at Elliot Kildare's card. Prescott. It was up north, an old historic town in the mountains. It brought home to me the fact that I knew nothing, nothing about Randall. Why would someone up in Prescott be interested in his death? Then through my kitchen window I saw Kyle Barnett coming up to the door.

He wore aviator shades, new stiff jeans, running shoes. There was something endearing and reliable about his walk, the walk of an Eagle Scout on his way to the podium to receive his one hundredth merit badge.

Hurriedly I went to the bookcase and tucked Elliot Kildare's card into *The Big Nowhere*, next to *Julio-Claudian Building Programs* and *AD 33: A Keynesian Depression?*, books written by my parents. Then I opened the door. Outside the sun was shining.

He'd shaved off his beard, but up close I could see he hadn't shaved this morning. For someone as neat as Kyle Barnett, he almost looked disheveled, as if he'd dressed hurriedly and not noticed what he was doing. The collar of his pale blue shirt was rucked up in back, giving him a hip fifties look he'd have hated.

"Kyle," I said, "are you OK?"

He looked startled. "What?"

I'd never seen anyone so impervious to his own feelings. He could have a nervous breakdown and not even notice.

"Never mind. Come on in."

He came in, his jaw clenched. "I don't understand what it was about this Leroy makes women nuts. We got two of 'em now standing up in public and practically saying, hey, shoot me next. And then Fern, calling me up all the time. Somewhere in the years she sure has changed. Used to be real quiet."

Standing in my kitchen, he looked stranded, washed up on foreign soil by the waves of women's emotions. He ran his fingers through his hair.

"Coffee?" I offered, in a soothing voice.

He nodded and sat down at the counter, removing his aviators. There were bags under his eyes as if he'd spent a couple of nights without sleep, and a small cut on his chin from shaving. "Bobbie Jean ever get hold of you?"

I set a cup of coffee in front of him. He stared down at it as if uncertain what it was there for.

"No, she didn't." I sat across from him, blocking his view of the dining area so he wouldn't see the dust on the rug, the spiderwebs in the corners, not that he would probably notice.

"She's real mad at you. She says you went and saw Starry Noel all by yourself. You're supposed to go with a partner. You could have endangered yourself and gotten the county attorney's office in hot water."

"No one was available." I took a sip of coffee. It was thick and bitter and maybe the worst cup of coffee I'd ever made. "All this bureaucratic stuff—how can anyone get anything done?"

"You think you got it bad?" He stared over my shoulder

at nothing. Then suddenly he grinned. "And here all along I was thinking you were a New York liberal."

"I am!" I protested hotly.

"Forget Bobbie Jean, you know she'd of done the same as you. I went and talked to Starry myself and she acted to me like she thought it was law enforcement that did it. She's that prejudiced. She tell you about the letter?"

"Yes."

He gave me a probing look. "Did she tell you anything else?"

I shrugged. "No, not really."

"Starry's out of town again or I'd ask her about that bar scene. Not that I'd trust anything she told me. She's crazy, got no credibility."

"None?"

"Well, some. We didn't find a cut-up letter at Leroy's, but yeah, the note looked like it was cut out of something." He paused and said in a different voice, "Is that what you called me about?"

"Partly. I also wanted you to know that Frank Gresham told me it wasn't Mrs. O'Hara who made the call about the gunshots."

"I already knew it wasn't Mrs. O'Hara. Went and talked to her." He took a sip of coffee and made a face. "Where'd you get this stuff? Drain it out of your car?"

"No, I just made it double strong," I said modestly. "I needed a boost this morning. So who called?"

"Got no idea, except it was a woman. And right now there's not a damn bit of concrete evidence he didn't do it to himself. He's got gunshot residue on his hands, all that forensic stuff worked out."

"It did?" I was disappointed.

He shot me a look. "Boy, you're sure interested in this case."

"I saw the body," I said, and added, inspired, "Smelled the blood."

He nodded. "And for a minute there, you thought it was someone you knew."

I held my breath.

He picked up his cup, then set it down again. "What was it you called him?"

There should have been a loud crash as my two separate worlds collided right there in my kitchen. But it was so quiet, I could hear the faucet drip-dripping into the sink.

"*Kyle.*" I forced myself to look him straight in the eye. "Please don't remind me." I shuddered and went on hurriedly, "That call, didn't it get taped? And can't you tell where the call was made from?"

For a moment he didn't answer. The faucet drip-dripped; from my bedroom I heard the digital clock click over a minute.

"It got taped," he said finally, "but we don't have the technology for the other. I've played that tape over and over, but I don't recognize the voice. That don't mean it's not a voice I've heard, though. You know fear will constrict the throat muscles, makes the voice kind of thick. And the breathing was off too."

I thought of a woman, late at night, dialing the number for the Cochise County sheriff—what she knew so lethal, it restricted her breathing, choked her.

"It's *shit,*" he said vehemently, "useless speculation, without concrete evidence. Even if we knew who did it. It's the worst thing about law enforcement. I knew a cop once, had a little stash of coke and a gun you couldn't trace he kept at his house, just waiting for the day some real real bad guy got off, then he figured he'd go after him on the highway, shoot him, put the gun in his hand, and plant the dope real conspicuously in his car, say he was resisting arrest."

It wasn't a new story, but suddenly I had the absolute conviction the cop he was talking about was himself. I made my voice light. "Your basic Smith and Wesson jury, huh?" My hands started to shake and I hid them under the counter. "Did . . . did he ever *do* it?"

Kyle smiled at me sadly. "Naw. He never did. It was just some kind of mental insurance, to keep himself sane." He cleared his throat. "Nothing I've said to you goes beyond this room. Right?"

"Right."

He stood up to go. "Thanks for the coffee."

"Wait." I stood up, too, and walked around the counter. "Didi's story, about the visitor that came late at night. Did anything come of that?"

He shrugged and put on his aviators. "Hell, it was two weeks before it happened. Could have been anybody."

But I caught a glibness in his voice; I knew he'd have checked it out, talked to people. "That's *all* you're going to tell me?"

We stood facing each other two feet apart in the kitchen.

The day came back again when I got the claim forms from the supply room. He'd followed and stood at the door. *The claim forms had slipped from the shelf, I knelt to pick them up, and he was behind me when I turned, so I ran right into him. Neither of us had moved for several seconds; I felt the grain of his oxford cloth shirt, saw every little square of the weave. I put my hand on his shoulder and he still didn't move. Then he'd stepped back, said, "Maybe you should just mail it."*

"I already told you too much anyway," he said now.

After he left I stood for a minute, in a daze, then went to the counter, picked up the two coffee cups, and carried them to the sink, which was full of dirty dishes. But I didn't put the cups in the sink. I held on to them for a while, staring out the back window. Big Foot walked by on the wall outside, tail high, picking his way across the ivy. I turned my back to the sink and threw the cups across the room as hard as I could.

They bounced off the refrigerator and one of them shattered. *Good.*

Shaky, I sat down at the counter and waited until I got my breathing under control. My mind was clear and blank as if I'd been born two minutes ago.

Life goes on.

I got Elliot Kildare's card from the bookcase and dialed the phone number on it and an answering machine informed me I had reached the number I'd dialed and to leave a message at the tone. I hung up and called Roxanne.

"There seems to be a private investigator on this case," I said. "I met him last night. He hasn't told me that, it's just a hunch. I've got his card and I'll keep trying to reach him."

"God, *no*," said Roxanne. "Do you think he knows who Randall is?" Her voice changed, got sugary. "Thank you so much, Janet, for calling, and please get back to me about the flowers, all right?"

Harry must have come in. She wasn't good for any more conversation. I hung up and almost immediately the phone rang.

"Hello?" said a prim little voice I didn't recognize. "Is this Chloe?"

"Yes."

"This is Violet."

My mind drew a blank. "Who?"

"Violet Wilson? I'm calling for my mom?"

"Fern's little girl, *of course*," I said.

"She doesn't feel too good, so I stayed home from church with her, but she wondered if you might be coming out to the Valley today."

I hesitated, deciding on the spot. "Yes, I'll be coming out to check on Starry."

"Could you stop in maybe before? She wants to talk to you."

26

Fern wore a dress printed with big pink and blue roses, with a lace collar, a style they were selling this year at Kmart, and on Fern it looked better than Kmart, but there was a strain in her clear blue eyes, as if she were looking at something a little too far away to make out what it was. Then she smiled, but her eyes were still tense.

"Chloe," she said. "How are you? Come in."

Violet stood in one corner of the kitchen, in a pink T-shirt and denim miniskirt, ironing a pair of jeans. Her hair was long and straight and thick as butter, except for the little fluffy topknot, and her eyes as blue as her mother's, but she was not beautiful. Pretty certainly.

She saluted me with the iron. "Mom got all dressed up for church, but she couldn't make it. She's got one of her sick headaches and she thinks she's going to die when she gets them, they're so awful. Mom, you sit and I'll get Chloe a cup of coffee."

Fern sat abruptly and held her head in her hands.

Violet poured a cup of coffee and handed it to me. Then

she stood by the table and stroked her mother's hair. "My poor little mother," she said.

Fern closed her eyes.

Violet went back to the ironing board. She held up the jeans she'd been ironing to check the crease.

Fern said suddenly, "Leroy gave me a letter, that day when I picked up Didi."

"Oh!" I said.

She opened her eyes. "I had to tell someone."

"I already knew. Didi told me. She saw Leroy give it to you, a manila envelope?"

"Yes. The letter was inside, in a regular envelope all sealed up. Did she tell the police about it too?"

"No. Just me."

Fern's eyes clouded with pain, but she went on slowly. "It was addressed to Didi in New York. If anything ever happened to him, he said I was to put it in the mail and not tell anyone."

So that was what he'd meant by getting in touch. "Is that all he said—in case anything ever happened to him?"

"That's it. It was that word 'ever.' It didn't sound like soon, particularly."

"Did you read the letter, after . . . ?"

Fern looked startled. "No. Course not. And he'd said to mail it, so I did."

Of course, it might say nothing about the murder, but it might be about Leroy, who he really was, why he wasn't Randall anymore. I had to talk to Roxanne. "When did you mail it?"

"I waited till Didi left. In case her mother . . . You know, some mothers open their kids' mail to read it first, and I didn't think that would be *right*." Her eyelids fluttered at the thought of Roxanne, someone maybe not right for Leroy. "I mailed it Friday, from Dudley 'cause I was there shopping. She wouldn't have it yet, not probably till Tuesday."

Tuesday. The day after tomorrow.

"But then I got to thinking, Leroy was a good man," Fern went on, "but sometimes he didn't understand about . . . children, and then when they get to be Didi's age, I see it in Violet, they're kind of crazy."

"Mom!" said Violet.

"That's why I decided to tell you. I thought maybe her mother should know, in case it slips by her, Didi getting something in the mail like that."

"She probably should."

Fern looked worried. "He said not to tell anyone. Do you think I should of mentioned it to Kyle?"

I wondered if Fern not telling constituted withholding evidence. "Why don't we let Didi and her mother decide that," I said.

It was hot outside and dry, even after all the rains. Something about the desert dirt seems to repel moisture. Unable to accept what it really needs.

Fern and I watched Violet ride away on Brown Beauty, going to her grandmother's for Sunday dinner. She was wearing the jeans she'd ironed so carefully, boots, her long blond hair streaming down her back. She looked young and free, and from the back just as Fern must once have looked, years ago when she'd been a Rodeo Princess. The way Fern stood and watched her, it might have been herself she saw riding away, then she turned, forehead furrowed.

"Fern," I said gently, not wanting to say anything at all, not wanting to ask her the question I was about to. "Didi told me Homer went out that Saturday night on a . . . a beer run. I keep thinking the police might be asking about that, if someone saw him. . . ."

The blue of her eyes was shot with pain. "There's not a think to ask, 'cause he didn't." Her voice quavered. "Didi was mistaken. He was at home with me, the whole time."

She wrung her hands.

"Leroy and I were close, but we never . . ." she

whispered, "we never, Leroy and I . . . we never *did* anything. We *talked*. And once . . . once he kissed me." From
the look in her eyes now he might have stabbed her with a
knife.

For a minute she was silent, then she said, "I know he
had a *past*, a sad one."

I stared at her, but she was looking beyond me at the
mountains far away.

"He said I didn't have a past like he did, a past that was
gone forever. I lived here, just always did. So whatever happened to me, I had to live with every minute. But he said
there's worse things than that."

Bereft as she was, her hair was molten gold in the sun.
"He said once, you know, *flattering*, 'Fernie, you're the
only beautiful woman I ever met whose beauty didn't
damage her soul.' But you know, sometimes I'm not even
sure anymore if I got one."

I suddenly felt her loss of Leroy as something total and
devastating, like the absence of rain in a parched land.
Behind her was the house with its bright zinnias, its
watered grass, but out here beyond the fence was the
desert; the hot sun shining relentlessly on the mesquite
and the pepper grass and the bare red unforgiving dirt.

27

The blue chair still lay on its side under the cottonwood in Starry's backyard; already little weeds were poking up with the petunias in the galvanized buckets. I went up the back steps. The kitchen door was half glass with plain white curtains. I knocked, then tried the door, but it was locked. I peered through a gap in the curtains and saw a cup on the kitchen counter, and beyond that a green bowl with two peaches rotting in it and then the corner of an open door that led to the living room.

One side of the house and the back looked out on open desert and the mountains beyond, but on the other side, down a way, was another house, also cinder block, painted green, a big sprawling garden growing at the side. There'd been a neighbor who looked after her plants. I took a walk down the road.

In the front yard of the green house, a little girl, maybe five, with fine pale brown hair, wearing a pink dress, white ankle socks with violets embroidered on them, and white

Mary Janes, was riding a tricycle round and round in the driveway.

"Hi," I said brightly. "Is your mom around?"

But the little girl was too busy to hear me, bent over the steering bar of the tricycle, like a tired racer on the last stretch of the Tour de France taking a curve at top speed. Her tongue was sticking out as if it were somehow connected to the steering.

"Louella!" someone called from behind the screen door inside the house. "Get in here and change your clothes."

Louella stopped and then backpedaled almost to the end of the driveway where it wasn't so easy to hear the voice.

"Louella," I said to her because she seemed like a little girl with possibilities, "do you know Starry Noel?"

Louella stopped pedaling, rolled her eyes back in her head, and smacked her forehead with an open palm.

"Lou!" A woman came out the door and down the driveway, too stout for jeans, wearing black sweatpants and a chartreuse and black block print top. Her features were heavy and exaggerated even more by makeup, her hair a stunning shade of cherry red. She stared at me.

"I was looking for Starry Noel," I said, and introduced myself. "I'm a Victim Witness volunteer, and I wanted to check on her, see how she was doing. She doesn't have a phone."

"No, she got no phone." The woman still stared at me, but her voice was friendly. "I'm Irene, Irene Carpenter. She left Friday, real upset, asked me to look after her plants, the ones out back, but we had rain and all, so I haven't been over there. She was supposed to be back yesterday."

"I guess she changed her plans," I said.

Irene frowned. "She never changed her plans yet," she said, "not in two years. She's not real friendly, but she is sure reliable."

"Camping," I said. "Is that where she is?"

"Yep. That's what we told the other one, the one who

called. It was right after she left, they almost caught her. And she just got back from camping. Spends half her life doing that."

"Who was that?"

"Louella got the phone," said Irene. "I was cooking at the stove and couldn't get away. They never said, did they, Lou? Told her they needed to get hold of Starry urgent and I yelled out to Lou where Starry always went."

"Was it a man or a woman?" I asked.

"It was Ronald McDonald," said Louella.

"Louella, don't you go lying now. And Ronald McDonald's a man."

"He's a thing," said Louella illogically. "And it *was* him." She stamped her foot. "They said in this funny voice, hi, little girl, this is Ronald McDonald."

"Louella," I said, "don't you know really who it was that called? Could it have been Rose?"

She shook her head indignantly, turned her tricycle around, and rode down the driveway in disgust, feet pushing down slowly on the pedals as if some tremendous force were preventing them from moving.

"Not Rose," said her mother. "Rose would have asked for me, she's a talker. I'm kind of worried. Camping and all, who knows."

"Irene, you yelled out to Louella to tell them where Starry went."

"She always goes the same place. Up in the Chirica-huas," said Irene. "Backpacks, you know. She parks close to the visitor center, then she follows the stream about a mile and goes up that trail. It forks somewhere and she takes the hard one, though they both go to the same place. I used to go there when I was younger with Louella's dad." She sighed. "When I was young and spry. I didn't always used to be this . . . big. Not till I quit smoking."

She rubbed her arms. "Not a day goes by I don't miss smoking. Plus when I gained all that weight I lost Louella's dad too."

*   *   *

On my tape player George Strait had to get to Amarillo by morning, as I headed for the Chiricahuas, the mountains Starry saw behind her house, the ones she said the vigilantes rode down from. The desert was greening up around me, falsely inviting. Maybe at this point I should have called Kyle, but I kept thinking of the fear in Starry's eyes when I'd mentioned Randall's name. Was there something in that fear that might damage Didi, Roxanne?

She might be fine and I needed another chance to talk to her.

It was two when I drove past the tiny cluster of houses and the store that was Sunizona, two-fifteen when I turned down Kansas Settlement Road and almost three when I reached the entrance to the Coronado National Forest. I drove in slowly and parked near the visitor center. I didn't see Starry's Volkswagen anywhere.

It was cooler here, and smelled of pine, even drier than in the Valley as if the rains hadn't made it this far. Birds called in the trees. To one side was a small dirt road and I went down that, and there parked to one side was Starry's Volkswagen. The hood was littered with leaves from the trees overhead.

Suddenly I felt as though I'd been running for days. I got out, leaned against my car, and looked around me.

Here I was in Nature. Hard not to think of it with a capital *N*, since it had had so little part in my life, despite my childhood, when my father took my two brothers and me for nature walks, naming the birds and the flowers and the trees. At the time it had seemed like important information.

Back then shredded wheat came in rows of three divided by cardboard inserts with nature lore about grizzly bears and how to make a canoe out of bark, how to make Indian deerskin moccasins: James had carefully saved them all, punching holes into the cardboard and tying them into a little book with lengths of leather, but they hadn't saved him.

James was thin as a bird at the end, spirit-thin, Hal shining with compassion. I hadn't seen James die, Hal had called me when it happened, but I'd seen the light leaving Hal's eyes, the blood rushing from the hole in his throat, drowning him. I'd *seen* it and if I didn't get control of myself, the videotape would start, the scene would replay, and I would be forced to relive it.

With all that had been going on, it had been a while since I had. I swallowed hard, focused on the path under my feet, the little pebbles in the dust, the white crepe-papery prickle poppies that grew in a cluster on the path's edge, and walked back to the visitor center.

Inside it was bare, cool, and all new. A deeply tanned blond woman in pale gray shirt, dark green pants, big cordovan cop shoes sat behind a desk, looking like she wished she were outdoors cutting down a tree or putting out a fire.

"Hi," I said. "A friend of mine's camping out somewhere around here and she was supposed to be home on Saturday. Her car's parked down the road, a blue Volkswagen?"

"Hmm," said the woman. Her name tag said Katie McCullough, a nice Irish woman, maybe a little older than me. "Supposed to be? Like how, something important she missed?"

"She just told her neighbor. But the neighbor says she always comes home when she says she will." I pulled out one of my cards. "Actually I volunteer for Victim Witness, but I'm kind of looking for her on my own now. She had a shock recently, so I've been a little worried about her. I'm going to go look for her now, but I thought I'd check in with you when I leave. If I don't, say by nightfall, then something might be wrong."

She looked at me, dead serious and nodded. "I probably wouldn't have worried about the car until after the weekend. You stop back in here then before you leave, and don't forget."

I wasn't prepared for any strenuous hiking, I'd really just wanted some assurance that Starry was where she was supposed to be, but I began to walk anyway, going down a little hill at the end of the parking lot, where there was the stream. Irene had said she went down the stream. I stood on the edge and took off my shoes. The trees met overhead and formed a golden hall, down which I walked in the water. The rocks were slippery, but the bottom was sand.

After a mile or so, I saw the trail leading off, so I waded out, dried my feet with grass, and put on my shoes. Then I went up the slope, to the trail.

"Starry," I called as I ascended, and the absurdity of the name came over me. "Starry Noel!"

I was sweating as the path narrowed and I reached the place where it forked, one path easy, the other hard. The hard one was obvious, very narrow and the rocks had fallen over it, greasewood bushes overgrown and neglected. I hadn't passed any other hikers.

I should have brought a hat, should have worn hiking shoes, my Keds weren't good enough. Yet to my left, as I went higher, I could see clear across to the other mountains beyond, all purple and gray and hazy and making it irrelevant whether or not Starry was a killer or a victim.

"Starry!" I yelled. "Starry Noel!"

My voice drifted out to the empty valley below and faded, vanished, not even an echo. The path here was crumbly, though fairly safe if you stayed close to the big rocks on the near side as it curved. I stopped for a minute and sat on one of them. A lizard joined me and I saw in the cleft of the valley a hawk floating on the current.

"Starry!"

Like the hawk, I floated too, giddy, in some weird combination of the ephemeral and the eternal, the mountains eternal yet crumbling, wearing away all the time; even now pieces of the mountain were crumbling away right below where I sat, large pieces, in fact, rocks and stones skipping and falling.

Wait. This wasn't natural. Something was making them fall. I got up and went to the edge. Dizzy, I lay down on my stomach and peered down and saw below, rocks and earth falling, and just at the edge of what I could see was an arm, pushing them out.

28

The helicopter's pounding whir grew louder, irritating as a bumblebee, then we could see it coming through the cleft where I had seen the hawk only, what, forty minutes ago? However long it had taken me to climb back down, wade through the stream, Keds still on, back to Katie McCullough at the visitor center. She'd taken over from there.

Now the helicopter hovered over the space farther up the trail, almost twelve by twelve, that two rangers had cleared out of brush and rocks, and began to descend. Below me but above two more rangers on the ledge, a silver metal basket rose gently on the ropes, bobbing against the rock face, then swinging clear. It seemed to take forever to make it to the trail where I stood with the brush-clearing rangers, then it was there.

I looked down at the woman in the basket, inert, almost lifeless. Her face was gray with pain and streaked with dirt, cobwebs in her hair. Her eyes were closed. "It's Starry, all right," I said. "Starry Noel."

The helicopter had landed, its wind rending the air, the

blowing grasses urgent. Medics were getting out. When they reached all of us I stepped back to let them do what they had to do and couldn't see Starry anymore. I was hot, sweaty from my fast trip back down to the visitor center, and my Keds squelched with every step, but it was cool here, cooler than it would be down in the valley. One of the rangers came over to me, older, wearing steel-rimmed glasses, a mustache going gray.

"Friday," he said, "that's when she left to go camping?"

"That's what her neighbor said. Supposed to be back yesterday."

"I'm trying to figure out what happened. I mean she just decided to go down the mountain here or what? No sign of the trail crumbling away. Just the very edge, but she'd have to be awful close to go over. She an experienced hiker?"

"Her neighbor said she hikes on this trail a lot."

"She must have had water. She's one lucky lady to have you for a friend, coming to look for her."

And I wasn't even her friend, hardly knew her. If it hadn't been for me, would anyone have come looking? They had Starry halfway to the helicopter.

"Can I go with her?" I asked.

"Just the medics," said the ranger. "Don't worry, she won't notice who she's with. Starry Noel, unusual name. She'll be at TMC, you can call. You're Victim Witness, huh? Well, get to work, let the relatives know."

"The relatives," I said. "All the Easters and the Thanksgivings and the Fourth of Julys."

The ranger laughed. "Something funny about the whole thing, but we'll talk to her. You forgot a holiday."

"What?"

He pointed behind me to a bush; on the bush was a length of thick orange yarn. "Looks like it's from some damn costume. Halloween. You forgot Halloween."

I stared at the length of yarn, something tickling at my memory, but the helicopter was lifting off, grasses blowing harder in the wind. We watched until it was out of sight.

"My God," I said suddenly.

"What?" said the ranger.

"Ronald McDonald," I said. "That's Ronald McDonald hair."

He snorted.

"Listen," I said, "she may be in danger. You need to call Kyle Barnett at the county sheriff's."

Ronald McDonald hair? It gave me the creeps. OK, someone pretending to be Ronald McDonald had called Irene's house, talked to Louella. And left Ronald McDonald hair at the scene like a calling card.

But Starry was *alive*. Eventually she could tell us.

I'd told the ranger everything I knew, but I didn't mention the Ronald McDonald hair when I called Irene from the visitor center. Let whoever would be investigating talk to Irene, decide what to tell her. Irene promised to look after Starry's plants, but she didn't know anything about relatives.

"She never mentioned anybody, a mother, a sister, never had any out-of-town guests. I guess Rose would be as likely to know about that as anybody. She don't have a phone, though. She lives in a little old trailer on Ocotillo."

I told her I knew where Rose lived.

I drove back through Kansas Settlement, Sunizona, and into the Junction. I was hot, tired, but wired too, with adrenaline. Somehow I hadn't really felt a sense of danger before, but this was an unmistakably clear signal, someone dangerous was out there. Not just dangerous, but strange—calling up Irene and pretending to be Ronald McDonald to her daughter, wearing that costume. There was an element of . . . creepiness, flamboyance, about the whole thing. Someone pretty nuts. Or somebody pretending to be.

I turned down the dirt road. Rose's oleander bushes were in full bloom, their deep magenta almost vengeful. A neighbor with black greasy hair and a shapeless garment

printed with faded flowers sat out on the stoop of her per-
manently rooted trailer watching me.

She let me go up to Rose's trailer, knock on the door
and call out Rose's name, then she waited until I had given
up and was almost to my car to get pen and paper for a
note before she said, "Rosie ain't home."

I faked surprise. "Oh?"

She brushed colorless hair off her forehead with an arm
purple with bruises. "She went off to some big car show in
Tucson with Lance Eubanks." Her mouth turned up in a
semisnarl, or maybe she was smiling. "She got men coming
round here all the time, sometimes they even sneak over
late at night, no telling who they might belong to. She's
head over heels in love with Lance this week."

"That's nice," I said cheerfully. "It's always fun to be in
love." I pulled out a notebook from my purse and wrote a
quick note to Rose—*Starry in hospital, call Chiricahua
National Monument visitor center for more details* and my
name and number. I didn't want to make it any clearer
where Starry was in case the wrong person read it.

"Something wrong?" asked the woman, hopefully.

I looked noncommittal. "I'll just leave her a note."

She watched me with little eyes, as I went back to the
trailer and wedged the paper in the slit between the door
and the jamb. She watched me walk back to her car. I gave
her a friendly wave and drove off. I figured she would get
up and come over and read it the minute I left, but what
could you do.

*She got men coming round here all the time, sometimes
they even sneak over late at night, no telling who they might
belong to.*

Oh, give it a break, I told myself as I drove to Randall's. I
parked, nervously glancing over in the distance at Frank
Gresham's house. His pickup wasn't there. At least out
here I could see him coming for miles and miles. The sun
had begun to set as I walked Randall's forty acres: scrub

oak, mesquite, grasses along the wash. The colors of the sky were as improbable, as unreal, as polyester, as unreal as Randall, left winger from New York, being a cowboy. But isn't that what this country's all about? Self-invention?

The monsoons had left little rain ponds everywhere, tadpoles swimming in them, and on the edges, tiny black frogs. As a child I'd taken tadpoles home in jars of water and watched them grow—get front, then back legs, shed their tails. Somehow I always seemed to miss the moment when they left their water-jar world for good; one morning they would just be gone, hopped away to their death in the unnatural world of heating ducts, couch legs, caves under the carpet.

I tried to pace forty acres, but I wasn't sure what direction they extended, if the house was on one end or in the middle. There wasn't much way to tell either except I could see a wire fence away a way, and then farther the house and outlying buildings that belonged to Frank Gresham. Still no pickup parked, nor one coming down the road. Back behind that even farther away was another house, bigger but too far to make out architectural details, that might be the O'Haras'.

I stopped by the windmill, its blades still in the airless desert, and got a drink of water from a tin cup. Then I walked to the edge of the wash, where the grasses grew tall, some feathery, some bushy, some delicate as a spider's web. A lizard with a blue throat sunned itself on a rock. Across the wash things glittered in the dirt.

I went down and up the other bank. Beer cans not yet rusted littered the ground, a lot of them, and bullets. Someone had been shooting at them, and not all that long ago. I looked across the wash, eyeballed where the shots would have come from, and walked back. There I found shell casings.

Randall had been shooting at beer cans, probably shortly before he'd died. The day he'd died maybe? Didi had said he was loading his gun. Wouldn't that account for gunshot residue on his hands? I'd have to ask Kyle.

Just because I'd been in love with Randall more than twenty years before didn't give me any special privileges, any rights to him; he'd left me behind long ago and I'd eventually left him behind too. But still we were alike, different from Fern or Homer or Kyle or Bobbie, Randall and I; we never stuck with our histories, we got bored or couldn't take it, left things behind over and over and moved on.

I was thinking about this as I walked back towards the house when I saw the silver Ford Bronco, tooling down the road.

I jumped up and down, waving my arms. "Wait!" I yelled. "Stop!" I began to run.

My car tires squealed as I peeled out down the dirt road from Randall's and onto the blacktop. The Bronco was maybe a mile ahead but easy to see; I pursued for miles and miles, then the Bronco finally turned at Double Adobe on the road towards Dudley and I followed along out to the Douglas highway. It turned towards Dudley, but instead of going round the pit, stayed on the traffic circle to the road that headed out towards Safeway, and Palominas, and Hereford.

My gas gauge was nearly on empty. If he started going out to Hereford, I'd have to turn around, I couldn't get much past the Safeway. But suddenly he slowed, signaled a turn, and pulled into a parking lot next to a little pink stucco building that said LILLIE'S CAFE in faded letters over the door.

I pulled in and parked a little way away from the Bronco. He got out. I got out of my car. He wore a fawn-colored cowboy hat, kind of Western Mountie style, and a blue and white plaid shirt, turquoise bolo, black string tie, jeans, ostrich-skin boots. He was just about as handsome as a man can get without extensive plastic surgery.

He walked towards me.

"Hi," I started to say as he came closer. "Remember—"

But before I could finish he reached over and took my arm, smiling into my face with the casual air of an old friend.

"Hi there, Chloe," he said. "You're going to love Lillie's food. It's just about as good as what my mama used to make. Hope you're hungry."

29

A large orange cat slept in the tangle of plants in the window of Lillie's Cafe. The place was about three-quarters full of mostly blond blue-eyed families, all at least slightly overweight including the children. A woman sat behind a counter, resting on arms as big around as elephants' legs, dimpled with the kind of fat you get from eating pork chops, spare ribs, and pure lard.

"Evenin', Lillie, what you got tonight that's good?" asked Doc in passing as he steered me to a vacant corner.

"Ha!" said Lillie.

We sat at a table. Doc set his hat on an empty chair. I'd eaten nothing all day except for cereal in the morning, and here I was transported suddenly to a land of plenty. I looked at Doc. In more ways than one.

Lillie hefted herself up out of her chair, came out from behind the counter, and walked to our table. She walked slowly, enormous hips swaying from side to side, like saddle-bags equipped with provisions for a whole army. In her tightly curled gray hair was a little pink bow.

"We got nothing tonight that ain't good." She smiled flirtatiously at Doc and touched the bow. "How about the chicken-fried steak with home fries and milk gravy?" She glanced at me. "Be good for the scrawny one."

"It does sound good," I said politely, wanting to impress Doc. "And iced tea."

"How 'bout you, Doc? Maybe you'd like something a little lighter. I got some fine catfish. Catfish with hush puppies."

"Oh, boy," said Doc.

Lillie looked down at him fondly, though he wasn't even a local. Not a local local, but it seemed pretty clear he was at least not from one of the coasts, not some refugee from New York or New Jersey.

"I'll try that catfish," he said. "That's provided you caught it yourself."

She simpered. "Well, course I did."

They began bantering together and, left out, I stared, a little nervous, at a painting of a cactus, a road runner, and a sun setting on the wall beside me. Underneath it said, *This painting was done by Alvin P. Slater, who lost the use of his arms January 1979, may the good Lord bless and keep him.*

"Think it's funny, don't you?" Lillie had gone and Doc was grinning at me. Without his hat, the hair fell across his forehead boyishly, thick and straight and dark chestnut in color.

"What?" I said.

"Alvin Slater's artwork."

"Sad, I guess."

"It's bullshit," said Doc. "One of Lillie's sons did it and hung it up for a joke and it's been fooling people ever since. Be careful not to misjudge the peasants."

"Listen," I said, "I don't know who you're working for or what you're doing here exactly, but things are getting serious. I just found Leroy Harris' girlfriend, Starry Noel, up in the Chiricahuas. It looks like she was pushed off the side of a mountain."

"Good Lord!" said Doc. "That's awful. She's dead?"

"Alive but just barely."

"Hell of a thing," said Doc. "You two good friends?"

"I just met her once."

"You're sure taking an interest. Trouble's just fascinating to some people. Where you from, Pennsylvania?"

"New York."

Lillie set down a red plastic bread basket that held what looked like a whole loaf of Wonder bread and put a large glass of iced tea in front of me, coffee in front of Doc.

I sipped the tea, the real thing, not some herbal blend, with a bite that could take the enamel off your teeth. "I think you should tell me who you're working for and why they're interested in Leroy Harris."

Doc didn't seem to hear me. He went on, "Had a roommate at the U. of A. from back east like you—Pennsylvania. I don't recall him having morbid interests, though. We both majored in animal husbandry. I was supposed to take over my daddy's ranch, but instead I sold everything and became a dilettante. At least that's according to my third wife."

He grinned again, a gold tooth flashing from somewhere in his molars. Next he would clamp a cigar between his teeth and start to lay down cards on the table, one by one.

I wished he would. "Want to tell me what's going on?"

"I should be asking you," he said.

Lillie set a large plate in front of me, with maybe a two-pound slab of breaded fried steak and piles and piles of generously peppered golden brown potatoes, everything ecstatically drowning in white gravy. A tiny sprig of parsley rested on the edge of the plate, representing the vegetable.

Doc smiled up at Lillie from his plate of golden food: catfish, hush puppies and fries. "This looks fantastic," he said.

"I don't know if I can eat all this," I said when Lillie had gone.

"Try."

I took a bite of the steak and gravy. It was delicious,

greasy and savory with a spike of pepper, the way food used to be when it was innocent, before we all got taught it could kill you.

"Look," said Doc, forking a couple of hush puppies, "you should know I got client confidentiality to think about. It's not my choice to tell you or not. Who'd hire me if I told all to every pretty woman comes my way?"

"I'm good at confidentiality," I said. "We can pool our resources, ever think about that? I might know things you don't."

"Shoot," said Doc, skewering me with his chestnut eyes. "Go ahead, tell me something I don't know."

I stared back at him. "How can I tell what you know and what you don't?"

He ate three fries, poker faced. "What's *your* interest in all this?"

"I'm a Victim Witness volunteer. I saw Leroy's body. I've talked to his daughter and to his daughter's mother. I guess I got a little involved. And suicide gives me the creeps. I'm wondering what was going on before he died, why he would kill himself."

"There's no more to it than that?"

"That's it."

Doc put a big chunk of catfish in his mouth and chewed. He wiped his mouth. "Not enough," he said. "There's more, isn't there? Let me guess."

He leaned across the table, over his catfish and hush puppies. "You were in love with him. He was kind of a romantic type, Leroy, am I right? Full of a lot of idealistic stuff, so he didn't have time to love anybody back. But that's OK 'cause he was going to save the world, right?"

Suddenly I was certain that Doc knew Leroy was really Randall. He must be telling me this because he thought I knew something and he wanted to know what. I could learn things if I played it right. Let him think it was safe to tell me things. Maybe we were on the same side. The same side of what? I had to give him something.

"OK," I said. "This is confidential. I knew Leroy a long time ago."

"OK," said Doc. "So did my client. And that's confidential too. When was it you knew him?"

"In college."

Doc raised his eyebrows. "That long ago?"

"Don't make a big thing of it." I could feel myself blushing. I ate several greasy delicious home fries to hide the blush.

"Must have been pretty bad, being there with the body. You still love the guy maybe a little bit for old times' sake, still think maybe if he'd had a chance, he just *might've* saved the world."

"It was too many years ago. I'm not even sure now what world there is to be saved."

"Anybody else know you knew him before?"

"No." I hesitated for a moment. "I didn't know him by the name Leroy."

Doc leaned across the table to me. "And neither did my client."

I took a deep breath. "Let me give you one initial," I said. "Maybe first name, maybe last. *R.*"

But he shook his head. "That's not it. Not first and not last."

I felt terribly disappointed. Was he playing straight with me?

"Then what name did your client know him by?"

But Doc shrugged.

"When did your client know him exactly?" I persisted.

"Look," said Doc, his mouth full. He'd finished the last of the catfish and was eating his fries, dipping them in the tartar sauce. He swallowed, then rolled up the right sleeve of his pink shirt. He rolled it high; on the upper biceps was a scar, puckered, maybe two inches long.

"What happened?" I asked.

"I got shot. Could have been a whole lot worse."

"That's an old scar," I said.

"It's old 'cause I learned. I don't get shot at anymore. But you, you haven't learned anything yet. You're sure you never told the cops all this stuff?"

"I'm sure."

"I wouldn't. You care about this guy, you won't say anything. I'll figure this out, let them know just what they need and no more. You can find out the best way—read it in the papers. What happened Saturday night, us dancing together, you playing that song, it wasn't smart."

"Don't go all paternal on me," I said. "You were there too."

"So I was dumb too. Two wrongs don't make a right."

"I'll do what I want."

"Shit." Doc exhaled, looking annoyed. Lillie sailed over, like an ocean liner, full lifeboats hanging over the edges. "Want some dessert? Lemon meringue pie? Strawberry shortcake?"

I stared at him aghast. "No, thanks."

"Guess not," said Doc to Lillie. "Eats like a bird."

She sailed off.

Doc took a toothpick out of his shirt pocket and rolled it around between his thumb and his finger. "What you're doing, asking around about Leroy, it's dangerous. I'd tell anyone that, man or woman both, so don't take it personal. You don't know what you're getting into, and the less you know the better."

"The *more* I know the better," I said. "Look, if you're frank with me, I'll be frank with you. And I already told you stuff. This is a cop-out."

"Interesting term," said Doc. "Sixties."

I made a face at him.

"After all," he said, "why should anyone trust anyone?"

I felt tired, fat and greasy. I wanted to wash my face in cool water, let it run over my wrists. I looked around for the rest room.

"Back to your right," said Doc.

The rest room was tiny and cramped, with no mirror. I washed my hands and face and put on a little eyeliner and a considerable amount of blusher using the minuscule mirror that came with the blush. I came back out. The restaurant had emptied out around us as Doc and I talked, and now there was no one at our table either.

"Hey there, honey," called Lillie from her spot by the register. "Doc had to get going, but don't you worry, he paid the bill."

"Had to get going?" I asked stupidly. I glanced at the table, already cleared as if we had never been there at all, except for a five-dollar bill under the sugar. A big tipper. Naturally.

I went up to the register. "Did he leave a . . . a note or anything?"

"Nope, he just told me to tell you, if you asked, that he had an appointment."

"At this time of night?"

"That's what he said—grinned when he said it like it was a joke, maybe you'll get it—'appointment,' he said, 'in Samarra.' "

30

Appointment in Samarra, very funny. God, I thought, as I stopped at a Circle K and filled my tank with gas, I'll never eat again. The mountains to my right looked sensational—deep indigo, outlined in neon pink, backlit by a silver sky. Unconnected to all this spectacle, I drove home through the desert evening, feeling leaden, trying to remember what the last thing was that Doc had said to me. *Back to your right,* no, before that. *Why should anyone trust anyone?* Why indeed.

Actually, I was attracted to Doc, had been instinctively right from the beginning, and God knows, I needed a distraction from my obsessive thinking about Kyle. But my job had made me wary. I started to think about Wilma, case No. 92–87, next to Jolene, my favorite victim; Wilma had gone all over the country with her abusive lover till he'd pushed her out of their van, going sixty miles an hour, because she'd handed him mustard to put on his hot dog instead of ketchup ("I can only blame myself, I knew he hated mustard.")

*And I knew the minute I laid eyes on him that we were meant
to be together, there's some things you just can't explain, kind of
like it's already written somewhere.*

When I got home it was nearly nine and the air inside
my house felt as though it had been leavened, kneaded
and baked like the big doughy inside of a loaf of bread. I
opened every single window in the house. Dishes lay in the
sink, though I couldn't remember eating much at home
lately. A thin delicate line of tiny ants made their way from
outside across the floor, up onto the counter into a bowl
where I'd had cereal after talking to Violet, and from there
to the sugar bowl where they swarmed inside in big black
ecstatic clots.

If I didn't start cleaning more, my house would be taken
over by nature. I dumped the sugar and ants into the toilet
and flushed, then I washed all the dishes, stacked them
high in the drainer where the breeze from the open
window over the sink could dry them better than I would,
cleaned the counters, swept the floor.

I put cat food in Big Foot's dish, though Big Foot was
nowhere to be seen. Moved out maybe, gone to someplace
where they appreciated a big hungry cat. Pine needles fell
from my clothes when I undressed to take a shower, the
way sand does when you've gone to the beach. In the
mirror my cheeks were bright bright pink, blusher on top
of sunburn I'd gotten up in the mountains looking for
Starry. I felt as though I'd been on a vacation and had just
returned, everything a little different.

After I showered I called Tucson Medical Center and
asked for Starry Noel. The women who answered left the
phone for a moment, then came back and asked guard-
edly, "Who's calling?"

At least they were keeping some kind of watch. I explained
that I'd found her, that I worked for Victim Witness.

"There's a broken collarbone," said the nurse severely,

"and a broken leg. Not to mention the effects of exposure. She can't talk. She's resting."

I hung up and started to call Roxanne to tell her something from Leroy was coming in the mail for Didi. Then I remembered it was midnight, New York time. How would she explain that to the judge? I could call in the morning.

It got cool and I closed and locked the French doors and lay down on the couch, thinking of Starry lying out on the mountainside alone and not even having anyone to come look for her; her aloneness felt lonely as death.

The dark outside deepened and my obsessions returned, the little nightmares woke up in my mind and I began to think again of James, and Hal and Randall, until I could feel their deaths inside me, their deaths in my bones, permanent dead parts of me I would carry around for the rest of my life.

Finally I fell sleep.

I woke up. Suddenly. To the sound of a creak or a crack. The moon shone through the skylight over my head, nearly full, looking down at me, spying, like a cold white eye. I was wide-awake, but I stayed still and tense as a rabbit. Had I dreamed the noise? I knew every sound that was normal in my house and I listened now for all of them: the drip of the faucet from the kitchen, slow and not serious yet except to worrywarts like Brody; the rustle of the cancer tree next to the house, rubbing one corner of the skylight; a truck far away on the highway, on its way to El Paso, Dallas, Baton Rouge, downshifting in the night.

I listened. Nothing. Then why was my mouth so dry, my heart on hold? Big Foot? He'd been known to break through the French doors, which never fastened right even when locked. They were wide open right now. Hadn't I locked them? I swung my legs over the couch and onto the floor. I eased myself up slowly. Damn the moon, it made things too light, and I didn't need the light, I knew the

house by heart. My gun was in the drawer in my bedroom.
Was it even loaded?

Yes. Yes, it *was* loaded, I was pretty sure.

Then I heard a new sound, a sliding whisper, so faint,
unless your ears were straining you wouldn't notice it, the
subtle sound that the muscles make when they move the
legs forward.

I would make that noise too if I moved again. But my
gun, loaded, was in the bedroom—for all the good that did
me, it might just as well have been in Samarra with Doc.

I turned my head slowly, could see nothing behind me,
nothing in front, no shadow, large and looming, in the
opening where the French doors should have been closed
and locked. I made myself get up and move slowly to the
edge of the room.

Then suddenly something was around my neck, pressing on my throat, something cold and round against my
forehead.

A gun.

"What . . ." I tried to say, but I couldn't seem to speak. I
reacted fast, without thought, using all my strength to
push away the gun and wrench my arm free. In the moonlight I had a horrifying glimpse, of a familiar face—freckled,
red, leering at me.

Ronald McDonald.

I hesitated a fraction of a second and then the arm was
around my throat, pressing harder this time.

"You're *dead*," said a voice, muffled behind what I now
realized was a mask. "Do that again and you're dead."

I strained at the sound of the voice, almost familiar but
too deep, artificially deep.

There was a loud series of crashes from the kitchen—as
if someone were breaking in to rescue me. The hold on my
throat loosened.

I wrenched again, broke away, and this time I screamed.
I screamed as loud as I could, because after all, this was a

neighborhood, not the middle of the desert with no one around, not New York City where no one would come. At the same time that I screamed I felt something wham on the back of my skull, and as I dropped, heard the sound of footsteps running out of the kitchen door.

The phone began to ring.

31

I lay in the space by the counter between the dining area and the kitchen and the phone kept on ringing. Time was slowed down, everything taking too long, someone had broken in, no—crashed into the kitchen, but where were they? I heard a police siren coming up my hill. I dragged myself up and found the phone on the counter. Slumping down onto a stool, I picked up the receiver and the ringing stopped.

My head hurt a lot, like a bad headache; the kind that you know—before you even take them—that aspirin won't help, but you take the aspirin anyway because you'll do anything to stop the pain and then you call some friends to see if anybody has some codeine.

"Hello," I said.

I could hear the police car, pulling into my carport.

"Chloe, it's Lourdes. I called the police."

"Thanks. You did right. They're here now." It hurt to talk. I hung up.

I went to the door.

Soto stood outside, dark and sincere and handsome, hair graying around the ears in a most distinguished way. He was a Dudley cop, not Cochise County Sheriff's deputy like Kyle. I'd first met him more than a year ago when my younger brother Danny's girlfriend had been found dead of what looked like a drug overdose. Danny was long gone, to the Buddhist colony in Vermont; now it was me, carrying on the family penchant for problems.

Soto appeared not to remember me, but other things had happened with that case and I bet he did. "You OK?" he asked.

"Someone was in my house," I said. "They held a gun on me, then there was this big—"

The phone rang again, shrilling through my brain. I picked up the receiver. "What?" I said.

They hung up.

I touched the back of my head, where it was beginning to swell. "Look." I turned my head so Soto could see the bump, though it was pretty dark in the kitchen. I hadn't thought to turn on the light. "There was . . . some kind of crash that startled them and I got away and I screamed and they hit me."

Soto walked over to the switch and turned on the light.

Dishes lay on the floor, a couple broken, most not, a glass, a cup. Big Foot stood by his bowl, eyes big with a message—food, food, food.

"The *cat*." I went over and got his food from the cupboard, though his bowl was full. "It was the cat. I left the window over the sink open and I guess he came in that way—he's clumsy. See, he knocked the dishes out of the dish drainer."

"Good goin', kitty cat," said Soto. "No pound for you today."

Big Foot licked his tongue clean round his black-spotted lips and looked at Soto with contempt. He sniffed his food but didn't eat.

Soto looked at me. "Who's mad at you?"

"What?"

"You fighting with someone? Boyfriend maybe?"

"No," I said. "Listen, you know I work for Victim Witness." My voice began to rise, even though raising it made it feel like a thousand insane monkeys were hammering inside my head. "This isn't a *domestic*." It hurt to talk, and in the tradition of the inarticulate everywhere, to make Soto understand, I banged my fist on the counter.

"*Chloe!*" Lourdes, my neighbor, walked in the door, looking gorgeous. "You shouldn't get upset like that." She was wearing a silky nightgown, a sweater over it, and had a pot in her hand. I was amazed she'd had the presence of mind to put on lipstick and earrings. "Bill Soto, don't you get her upset."

"*Lourdes,*" said Soto, his face getting pink.

Lourdes touched the side wing of her hair ever so gently. "I brought Chloe some *menudo*, I just made it last night. It won't keep too good, so I'll put it in the fridge, unless you'd like some now?"

I shook my head.

"What happened?" she asked.

I was clearer now. "Someone in a Ronald McDonald mask held a gun to my forehead and got me in a choke hold."

Lourdes backstepped, her fist to her mouth, her eyes round. "That's terrible. Teenagers, that's what it sounds like." Her eyes veered to Soto. "You better catch them." Her voice was severe.

"I'm trying, I got to talk to Chloe here first," he said, but he kept his eyes on Lourdes.

"Bill used to be my boyfriend," said Lourdes, "in eighth grade. Guess I should go. You *call* me, Chloe, if you need *anything*."

"She looks good," said Soto when she left. "Just got an old nightgown on, not even trying. And she brought *menudo*." His voice was reverent.

I cleared my throat to remind him of my existence; surely I'd earned the right to be the center of attention. "For heaven's sake, this is a small town, you must have seen her a million times since the eighth grade."

"Sure I have," said Soto, "but I usually was ready."

"Anyway," I said firmly. "He put a gun to my forehead and got me in a choke hold. He must have come in through the French doors in the living room."

Soto looked businesslike. "I'll check them out. You got any idea who it was?"

"None."

"Then a description maybe?"

"They had on a mask, a Ronald McDonald mask. It was the same person who knocked a woman over the edge of a cliff. The same person who . . . A murderer, that's who it was. Talk to Kyle Barnett, he's working on the case."

"Barnett's with the *county sheriff*," said Soto, with dignity. "This happened in Dudley, we've got jurisdiction. . . ."

And Starry wouldn't be Kyle's case either, it would be the ranger's. "The hell with jurisdiction," I said vehemently. "It's all connected."

"You're saying the hell with jurisdiction to a *cop*?"

Soto and I turned.

Bobbie stood in the half-open door, wearing her Victim Witness clothes, the shoes you could run in, no jeans because cops didn't like little ladies to wear jeans, and she had her clipboard in her hand. No partner, though. "I heard it on the scanner," she said. "The address. I didn't wait to get called. Are you OK?"

"Tell him I'm not crazy," I said to her. "Tell him women aren't hysterical creatures with no brains, the guy had on a Ronald McDonald mask. So did the guy who pushed Starry over the cliff. And I don't have any idea who he was."

Bobbie came around and put her hand on the back of my head.

"Look," I babbled, "a lot of things have happened. How's Starry? Has Kyle talked to her yet? Where *is* Kyle?"

"Boy," said Bobbie, "you got a bump there. Let's take a drive to the emergency room. You can tell me all about it on the way. Then Bill can look around and get a full report later." She took my arm.

I shook her off. "No. I just work *part-time*."

"What's that mean?" asked Bobbie. "Come on, Ruth's on call, but I didn't wake her up 'cause I thought you'd be easy to handle."

"I don't have any *insurance*." I was astounded that, even in my somewhat disoriented state, I could still be thrifty.

Bobbie laughed. "You don't have to worry about insurance, Chloe. You're a crime victim. You can apply for victim compensation. I might have the claim form in my car."

By the time we got to the emergency room, a bruise on my throat was starting to show up. In the doctor's office I sat in a kind of fog and stared at the posters of the Heimlich maneuver and larger-than-life-size blowups of various kinds of skin cancers, which all resembled various spots on my body, till the doctor came in. He was short and chubby and rosy cheeked.

He clucked and peered in my eyes, and did various things and then he said, "Well, I wouldn't do anything too strenuous and I wouldn't go to sleep for a while. If you start vomiting, or anything changes, then you come back here."

"What about brain damage?" I asked him.

"Brains are pretty well protected," he said. "But I couldn't tell you for sure." He gave me a big smile. "One thing that won't help is worrying."

The Copper Queen Hospital was over in New Dudley, where the responsible people with good family values lived. The sun was coming up, bringing with it a hot wind, as we drove the traffic circle back to Old Dudley. The hot wind tickled the tamarisk, bent the paloverde, and made the vast pit a dusty wound in the middle of the desert.

We reached the turnoff for Old Dudley and Bobbie put on her right turn signal. "This brought back memories of working for old EMT tonight: funny, I don't miss it exactly, but boy, you're never bored."

"How long ago was that?" I rolled up my window because finally I couldn't stand the hot wind whipping my hair into my face.

"Oh, a real long time ago now. Before Jim and I got married. I quit right after the DUI with his arms cut off. I don't know, it got to me, that one. Al, Alvin Slater."

I closed my eyes.

After Bobbie dropped me off, I sat for a while, without moving, at the stool at the counter in the kitchen. The wind was still blowing, though. Leaves and bits of things kept hitting the skylights and everything rattled. What was that Dylan song? "Idiot Wind."

My already haunted house was becoming more so, but not by the wind. Someone had come in last night and maybe tried to kill me, and I didn't see how I could close my eyes tonight and sleep in my own bed unless I found out who that was. Doc knew something, but he'd run out on me. I had to find him, but first I would have to talk to Starry. She *owed* me.

I had to call Roxanne and tell her about the letter coming for Didi, about Starry. I had a lot to tell her. The phone only rang twice, then I got an answering machine.

"This is the Steinberg residence. If you're calling for the judge, call 555-1720. Anything else, please leave a message."

I left my number only, not my name in case the judge got to the machine first.

God, my head really hurt. I didn't want to be doing much anymore unless I had my gun beside me.

That was where I'd been going when Ronald McDonald put the choke hold on me, heading for my gun, my trusty .38, my sweet little snubby. I went into the bedroom to the dresser, pulled out a drawer and found the gun underneath my black winter leggings. I released the catch, peered into five empty chambers.

32

As I drove in the hot wind down the I-10 to Tucson I made plans about changing my life, that thing that had just been given back to me, but the pain in my head made it hard to focus. Exercise regularly. Make food from scratch and freeze. Have my annual Pap smear, way overdue. Have Brody to dinner because I owed him. Play more music.

Meanwhile the dead, the dead were coming back, James, Hal. They had been last in my thoughts before I fell asleep last night, before Ronald McDonald. Their ghosts were separate beings from their reality—they didn't nourish me the way the living James and Hal had. They were more like discarded lovers turned stalkers, phoning late at night, lurking outside convenience stores, nagging and insistent. I'm *tired* of you, I thought to their ghosts. Go away and leave me alone. Get a death.

I giggled shakily. I'd never been so rude to them before.

My hands trembled on the steering wheel. Guilt and a sense of betrayal mingled with a momentarily overpowering sense of relief. Play more music. That was the answer.

Play more music, a good substitute for life, love, tears, and sorrow.

I popped in a tape and, driving down the I-10 to Tucson, the temperature rising a degree every three miles, over my headache I sang "The Heart that You Own" out loud with Dwight Yoakum. It was a wonderful song, full of pain and resignation, but sexy too.

And all the lines felt so perfect, as if they could bring rest to my own heart, but all the time I was just plain scared. I had to figure out what was going on, who this guy was—or was it a guy?—before they got to me first.

Starry Noel, who owed me, lay on her hospital bed with her hair spread out around her, thick strands of brown mingled with gray. Her eyes were half-open, so I knew she saw me, but she didn't look happy or excited, not that I'd expected that. But gratitude, maybe just a little, hadn't anyone told her who found her? Instead, a look of scorn came over her face, as if to say, not Chloe Newcomb from Victim Witness *again*.

"What happened to you?" she said, looking at the bruise on my neck.

"The same thing that happened to you." I rubbed my arms to warm them. I was freezing in my sleeveless black T-shirt with the air-conditioning on full blast here in the hospital. "Want to tell me about it?"

Starry turned her head, looked out the window, though all you could see from the bed was the flat cloudless blue sky. "If it happened to you too, why should I have to?"

Bitch.

"They wore a mask," I said.

"Raggedy Andy."

"Ronald McDonald actually."

Her blank expression told me she was above such small cultural nitpicking.

"Did Kyle Barnett talk to you?" I asked.

"Yes. That's what I told him *and* the rangers and the

damn nurses; they were wearing a Raggedy Andy mask. They were waiting for me. That's all I have to say."

I pulled up a chair and sat down, though Starry hadn't invited me to. "Listen," I said, "you made a big scene at the bar, told everyone you knew who it was."

Starry sighed. She was still looking out the window, not at me. After what seemed like a long time she said without turning her head, "I just wanted to get it over with."

"Get what over with? Starry, help me out here. You think it's OK for people to go around attacking people?"

She didn't answer.

I got up and went to the window. Standing there, eleven stories up, I could see the mountains, and closer, a bunch of palm trees, stucco houses with red roofs, streets snarled with traffic. My head hurt and I felt very tired.

Starry said in a dull voice, "I feel like Big Blonde in that Dorothy Parker story, you know the one where she tries to kill herself and they bring her back to life?"

"Starry," I said accusingly, "where you're living I bet you don't know a single person who's read that story. What are you doing here, in Arizona, in the middle of the desert? At least Randall had some kind of philosophical justification."

"Randall?" asked Starry. Her voice was as hard and smooth as a big river stone.

"Come *on*."

"He didn't have the guts to live without them."

"Without what?"

"Reasons." She closed her eyes. "There was a time when I had them. I lived by them more than most people do. Most people are cowards, they don't live anything out. Now I don't have them, and I intend to live that out too."

There were people down below, too tiny from here to make out any features. It did take guts to live without reasons. And that was what Starry must have been doing for a long long time. So long, maybe she couldn't break out of it. Maybe almost everyone looked to her all the time like they did to me from here, eleven stories up.

I sat down to try again. "What was going on with you and Randall before you moved here? You knew him already, didn't you?"

"Randall who?"

"Starry, what do you have against me? I just want to know what happened, the truth, I want to catch whoever it was that killed Randall, who tried to kill you and me."

"You want to know the truth, the honest truth."

"Yes."

"The truth is I don't know."

"Great."

"Randall," said Starry, turning her head and looking at me directly. "Did he mean anything to you ever? I mean, were you in love with him?"

"Once. A long time ago."

"Well then, why don't you stop nosing around? He's dead. Let him lie in peace."

"Tell me why and maybe I will."

"No."

Suddenly I was sick of the whole thing. "Want to explain why you're so damn superior? Don't you have human feelings? What goes on in your head? Doesn't it ever occur to you you're missing out on being alive when you don't have to, when you could try to relate, try to understand how humans are just human and most of us are just going ahead blind, trying to do our best? I know people like you, I used to know a lot of them back in the sixties, but now it's about time you grew up and recognized we're all in this together, Starry or whatever your name is."

She turned her head away again, and punched the bell to ring the nurse. "I want you to leave."

"Look . . ." I started to protest, but a nurse strode into the room.

She had a snub nose and blue Nazi eyes that looked at me accusingly, coming into her nice tidy hospital room and disturbing her innocent patients.

Starry half rose on her elbows, though it was obviously an effort. Tears were streaming down her face. "Get her out of here," she croaked.

"Why is she in such a *bad* mood?" I whispered shamelessly, like a detecting machine, to the nurse in the hall. "Is she going to be *OK*?"

"Collarbones, legs, aren't that serious and she's recovering nicely from the exposure. She's a very strong person," said the nurse. She was maybe forty, forty-five, with deep lines around her mouth. She looked at me a little suspiciously. "Now, that friend that came to visit, she made her laugh. The blonde."

"Rose," I said. "It must have been Rose, she's a riot."

"Rose, that's right."

33

I drove straight out to the Valley in a haze of golden sun, the hot wind blowing, the grasses that edged the road bending and bowing like waves on the water, as if I were traveling on a bridge over a shimmering sea. Maybe it was my head injury that made me take the wind so personally, convinced that it had started up to tease, to irritate me. It nibbled at the edges of my thoughts with Randall, with Didi, with Doc. Damn.

I wished I'd been able to reach Roxanne.

The wind blew just as hard in the Junction as I drove down the dirt road to Rose's trailer. This time a big ugly maroon Eldorado spattered with rust spots was parked next to an equally battered mud-colored Ford pickup. The wind bent the oleander bush next to the green double-wide so its deep magenta flowers touched the ground, and it snapped and twisted at the clothes on the clothesline in the side yard where Rose was hanging up the last of a long line of bright, skimpy garments.

She had on a blue gingham halter top and shorts made

of old jeans, cut high. Lance danced slightly pigeon-toed beside her, holding his hat on with one hand, clamping a clothespin onto a black strapless bra with the other.

"Rose?" I called from the road.

She turned. Her pale hair blew in her face. "Hi there. Hey, thanks for leaving me that note."

I got out of my car and walked over to the clothesline. Bikini underpants in kelly green and fuchsia and cobalt snapped, a minidress of orange and black flowers danced.

Lance smiled a quick cocky smile at me, the smile of a spoiled kid who gets away with things, his cheeks, creasing in a thousand wrinkles, his Roy Rogers eyes getting extra squinty. "Windy enough for you?" he asked.

"Your neck," Rose said. "What happened?"

"Don't ask," I said. That was what she would have answered, wasn't it? "Could I talk to you in private?"

"Sure." She looked at Lance and made shooing motions with her hands was if he were a big chicken. "Get home now."

A box fan whirred gently and uselessly in one corner of the trailer, a pale relative of the wind outside that *tick-tacked* against the loose trailer windows. Rose sat on the couch on a pile of clothes and propped her bare feet on the fifties veneer coffee table littered with empty beer cans, a full ashtray, and a book, *Rock Star*, by Jackie Collins.

She gestured to a big armchair. "Have a seat. I can't talk too long. I got the early shift." She lit up a Kool.

"You went and saw Starry." I removed a towel, a hair-brush, and a dog's leash, though no dog was in sight, and sat down. "Rose, someone attacked me last night, the same person, I'm pretty sure, he was wearing a Ronald McDonald mask like he was with Starry."

"Jesus Christ," said Rose. *"Ronald McDonald."*

"What did Starry say to you?"

"She didn't tell me a damn thing. I know her better than to ask, too. You know Shawn ran away from home?"

"He did?" I stared at her.

"Yeah. It's not the first time." She stubbed out the Kool on the edge of a beer can and dropped it in. "He's got a place he goes to, he told me about it."

She went over to a tall chest and pulled out a drawer. She dumped a deck of cards, a tin of shoe polish, a knee-high stocking, and a pair of pliers onto the floor and took out a film can. She opened it and began to roll a joint.

"Lots of people confide in you, Rose, don't they? Even Leroy."

"Leroy." She shrugged. "It's 'cause they know it won't go no farther. This is a gossipy little town. But I never broke a trust."

"He came to see you the week before he died, Lance said."

"Sure Leroy came over. We smoked a number together, is all. He didn't want to do it in front of Didi, but sometimes you got to do something for the tension, you know?"

"He was tense?"

"Hey, life is tense. There's times I can't face going to work without a buzz on." She grinned. "Times I *can* face it, but I get a buzz on anyway." She lit up, took a toke, and held it out to me.

I hadn't smoked in years. I shook my head, then reconsidered. Turn down marijuana, with a headache like this? "I'll take a toke," I said.

I took a good one and a stillness came into my mind. I almost imagined the wind was dying down outside the window. Rose took the joint back.

"Got to change," she said, and carried it with her into the other room.

"Why did Shawn run away?" I called out to her, the light in the room suddenly more transparent as if all this were something I was dreaming.

"You mean you got to ask?"

"I guess his father's pretty bad."

"You said it. My dad was too. I left home when I was

thirteen." Rose slammed a drawer shut. "Never looked back. Course, I blew it for a while. I was young and dumb and I met this guy, good looking and, you know, wild, and he persuaded me to go into this car lot and sign my name along with his on the credit papers for a truck. Well, it ended up he got the truck and he got away, they never did catch him, and I got six months. Not even suspended."

Rose came out of the room in tight jeans and a black halter top, full chains. Her mouth was dark red, her eyes freshly mascaraed, and the joint nearly gone. She grinned at me.

"Fraud," she said.

She was so tough and so easily bruised all at once. Maybe someday women will learn to avoid the wild, good-looking ones, but I still think it's a choice, not so very different from the choice made by people who take up skydiving, or who sail tiny boats solo across the ocean.

Rose went on, "Starry always said she respected my being in prison, like it hadn't really been my fault, but the fault of the government. If I told her once, I told her a hundred times, 'Starry, it didn't have a thing to do with the government, it was just plain hormones.' "

"Rose," I said, "how come you and Starry are friends? I mean how did you meet?"

"That I can tell you exactly, 'cause it was Christmas eve—two Christmases ago. George Baxter owns the Watering Hole, I was working there then too, and the asshole stays open Christmas eve. I mean he closes early, at ten, but still . . . And then people do show up, so maybe it's OK 'cause if you got to go to a bar on Christmas eve, then you really *need* to go to a bar."

She lit another Kool and sat down. "The place was fixed up for Christmas, you know, a little tree, and lights turning on and off, and Leroy was the only one in the place, Leroy and me. Leroy was drinking the way he did, which is not much, but making it look like a lot. And she walks in. I'd never seen her before in my life and she walks into this bar in the middle of nowhere like she's been coming in there all her life."

Rose got up. "Christmas! Here we are talking about Christmas and the damn fan isn't doing shit."

She went to a window and opened it. Dried leaves flew in and she brushed them aside. "This wind keeps up, the mountains will burn right up."

She grabbed her purse. "Got to go."

I walked out of the trailer behind her and she paused in the yard, where the clothes whipped on the line and the oleander still bent its flowery branches to the ground. Somewhere there actually *was* a smell of burning.

"Yeah," Rose said. "She walks up to the bar. Leroy looks at her. She looks at Leroy. These are two of the coolest people you've ever seen in your whole life. All at once it was clear to me it was no accident, Leroy being there and her walking in. I'm real friendly, I mean don't work in a bar if you're not, especially on Christmas eve, so I said, 'Hi, I'm Rose. Merry Christmas.'

"She stands there for a minute looking around, there's the little tree in the corner, glitter on the branches and the lights blinking on and off and there's mostly phony Christmas presents underneath, but some of them are real, and then she looks back at me and says, 'Hi, I'm Starry. Starry Noel.' "

Rose dropped her cigarette on the ground and twisted it out with her foot. " 'Hi, *Starry*,' I said."

34

I drove back to Dudley through the red dirt desert slowly, my headache still there but better. The heat would soon be turning the silver-green grasses to gold and the little frogs on the edges of the rain ponds at Randall's would be dead, little dried-up husks, after all that lying watery promise. The air still smelled burnt, but I couldn't see flames, smoke, anywhere, more like the air itself was not air at all but colorless fire.

I had to find Doc. That nice Ford Bronco wasn't a car you'd use for camping out, and besides, he was clearly the type that enjoyed a little comfort. So where would he be staying? Considering his style, the Copper Queen was the logical place.

I turned up the street that led past the hotel and found a parking space by the Presbyterian church. It was more sheltered here and the oleanders that grew in a thick hedge, white and deep purple, were still. The steps and the outdoor dining area of the Queen were lined with boxes of marigolds, alyssum, and pink petunias, and its upstairs windows opened onto balconies. I took a deep breath.

Inside, the red plush and dark wood were palmy cool and the world suddenly became negotiable again.

I went to the desk and there was Shirley—two months ago she'd been a waitress at El Chapparal where Brody and I sometimes went for fajitas.

She wore her hair pinned up on top of her head and someone had gone wild on the frosting, painting it on with big strokes. As if to emphasize that she was a blonde by choice, she'd painted blue eyeshadow clear up to her eyebrows. Her blouse was pink and frilly and optimistic.

"Hey," she said, with a big smile. "How you guys doing?" *You guys* meaning me and Brody. "Great!" I lied. "Shirley, listen, I'm trying to find this guy, Elliot, Elliot Kildare? Is he checked in here?"

Shirley put her hand to her mouth, took it away, and looked behind her and to either side elaborately. Then she leaned over the dark wood counter towards me. "The cops were here looking for him," she said breathlessly.

"The cops?" I couldn't think why.

"Well, just one, a *detective*. I don't think Mr. Kildare wanted to talk to him because when I told him, he checked out." She fluttered her eyelashes innocently.

The eyelash flutter was definitely for Doc.

"A Dudley detective?"

"County sheriff," said Shirley. "He came back later, too, and I told him the gentleman had already checked out. His name was Kyle and he was very nice. He asked me if I knew where Mr. Kildare went."

Kyle was looking for Doc? Just how much did Kyle know?

"Course, I had no idea where Mr. Kildare went," Shirley went on. "People don't tell me that kind of stuff."

"Shoot," I said. "You know, Mr. Kildare had a car Brody was interested in. Up in Prescott. Brody really wanted to buy the car and Mr. Kildare acted like he needed the money. You're sure you don't know where he went?"

"I think maybe," said Shirley, "Douglas. Earlier he was asking me about that hotel, you know the Gadsden. Course, I don't know he went there, I mean I'm not sure enough to tell the police. You don't think it was about anything serious, do you?"

"Who knows? Probably not."

"No, probably not," echoed Shirley. " 'Cause the thing is, I kind of thought about it and then I told the detective, he went back up to Prescott. Probably find his name in the phone book there." She gave a shuddery little laugh.

I drove away feeling smug, smarter than the cops. But not that much smarter. Why would Kyle be looking for Doc?

My house was still, Big Foot snoozing on the porch, the wind at last had died down. But it wasn't the house I was used to; like a woman raped, my house had been violated. I could feel what had happened last night in every corner. I got my .38, my snubbie, out of my purse and opened the catch, checked to see that it was still loaded. I knew it was, I'd loaded it this morning, each bullet slipping into its spot, five bullets.

I could kill five people. I could cause massive damage to flesh, tear through it to bone, wipe out memory, destroy the child that lived on in the adult, change a life forever or just plain end it. I could be my very own Smith & Wesson jury, I could be God.

I called Roxanne and she still wasn't home or had been when I wasn't. I left my number again. "Call me right away," I said. "It's urgent."

Then I went into the living room and lay down on the couch, set the gun on the coffee table. I turned on my stereo and put in a George Strait tape. His cool elegant twang made me dream of other times, of ranches and campfires under the stars, spunky cowgirls and horses fording streams shaded by cottonwoods; different times, when orange groves gleamed in the Arizona moonlight and everyone was safe at home.

Or had we ever been?

Anyway, the room cooled down and after a while it got to be dusk. I took a shower and changed to black leggings, long black tank top. The bruise on my neck made me look like one of my poor battered clients. I folded a pink bandana over and over, and tied it on to cover the bruise—it looked good with the black tank top. There was room under the top to put the gun in the waistband of the leggings, but I was afraid I'd shoot myself in the leg, so I put it in my purse instead.

The hardest things can be done easily if they're done step by step. I wasn't thinking, as I got in my car and drove down the hill from my house. The sky was that dark purple-blue it gets just after the sun has set, a neon color, inhuman.

I started thinking about a Keats poem I knew—*And for many a time, I have been half in love with easeful death*. Little goose bumps rose on the back of my neck. I stopped and filled my tank with gas, though Douglas was only a quarter tank round trip.

35

Faded to the soft sadness of a town that had seen better days, and is not yet capitalizing on that, Douglas sits right on the Mexican border next to its sister city in Mexico, Aqua Prieta. And though the chamber of commerce may not bring it up, its principal import is marijuana. Conveniently a prison opened up there recently, but it used to be a mining town until the smelter closed down. I drove through an underpass, past palm trees onto G Avenue.

Two-story brick and frame buildings in the frontier style now housed factory outlets, with signs in the window saying ¡HOY! ¡ESPECIAL! in big red letters and tables and bins of chrome-bright useless things made of polyester and plastic.

It was a weeknight, but people, mostly Hispanic, were still on the street, the women gloriously dressed and looking like the tropical flowers that grow from dust and adobe.

The Gadsden loomed ahead like a rich dowager among the upstart outlets. I turned just beyond the hotel and drove down a side street that led to the parking lot. It was right there in plain sight, the silver Ford Bronco. I felt a little sick. I parked down from the Bronco, then changed my mind and drove out to the street and around a corner to park.

The night was balmy, somewhere mariachi music played, and from across the border down South came a smell, a hint of rain.

Inside the Gadsden enormous columns, decorated with gold leaf, held up the vaulted ceiling, and a broad white marble staircase led to a mezzanine and a forty-five-foot Tiffany stained-glass mural of a cactus, coyotes, and mountains. Big brown leather sofas stood in a quartet facing each other over a low table. I found my way to the desk.

A woman, maybe sixty, with white hair and fancy silver glasses set with turquoises sat reading Danielle Steele. She had on a blue ruffled prairie dress and brown boots and an armload of silver bracelets.

"Hello," I said.

She looked up, blind for a moment, coming back slowly from a world where she was a beautiful heiress and dashing handsome rich men were continually pursuing her, blinked, and there she was at the desk of the Gadsden Hotel. She didn't seem to mind. Her smile was bright. "Hi there!"

"Hi!" I said back. "A friend of mine is staying here. I just got into town. His name's Elliot, Elliot Kildare?"

"Sure," she said. "I remember him. Checked in real recent. Let me ring his room, it's 204."

She rang a couple of times, then shook her head. "He must of stepped out. You could try the Saddle and Spur."

"The what?"

"That's our lounge." She gestured with her head.

The door of the lounge had an overhead stained-glass insert of a cowboy on a bucking bronco, and inside it was dark and cool, with cattle brands burned into the walls. Two elderly gentlemen in cowboy hats sat at the bar and

one young blond bartender with a scanty mustache made
desultory wiping motions with a cloth and stared off into
space. He almost jumped when I came up to him.

"Hi there!" he said. "You looking at our brands? We got
two hundred of them here. See those musical notes?" He
paused and then said triumphantly, "Gene Autry's Melody
Ranch!"

"*Really,*" I said. "I wish I had time to look at them all,
but I'm trying to find a friend who's staying here." I
described Doc.

"Yeah, sure, he came in." The bartender lowered his
voice. "Not much action here, if you know what I mean. I
recommended the Warehouse or the Boot Heel. Warehouse is rock and roll, Boot Heel's country western. But
it's a weeknight, so not much is really going on anywhere."
He suddenly focused on me. "I mean," he said, "if you're
his old lady or something, he didn't ask about the action, I
just meant . . ."

I found him at the Boot Heel after drifting down G Avenue and onto a side street, a *gringa*, one to reckon with in
tight black leggings, pink bandanna, and a .38 in her
purse. Cars slung low to the ground and pickups on giant
inflated tires drove by, full of teenagers; marijuana smoke
hung lazily in the air, mingling with the smell of stale beer.

The Boot Heel was a cinder-block rectangle, neon beer
signs in the windows, with a big wooden door and a faint
smell of urine entangled in the bushes just outside. I
walked in to the sound of Randy Travis protesting that his
heart cracked, but it did not break. It wasn't full, just two
couples dancing in the dim gold light, a couple of men at
the bar, and Doc, sitting at a table in the far corner,
smoking a cigar.

I walked over and sat down.

There was a beer in front of him and a stack of quarters.
He had on a Navajo-striped pearl-studded cowboy shirt
and his chestnut hair gleamed even in the sleazy bar light.

He took the cigar out of his mouth and rested it carefully on one corner of the ashtray advertising Dos Equis beer.

"Hey there," he said, as if he'd been expecting me. "What's up?"

"What do you mean, *what's up?*" I said scathingly. "Let's pretend this guy we both know isn't dead, let's pretend we don't both think someone killed him. You must have driven your mother nuts."

"Didn't have time to." Doc picked up the stack of quarters and let them fall one by one onto the table. "My mama got run over by a threshing machine when I was three—tore her all to pieces, arms and legs coming out everywhere."

"Bullshit."

He grinned.

"Doc, just tell me what I want to know."

"What you *want* to know?" He raised his eyebrows. "Let's dance."

Somebody must have fed a whole bunch of quarters into the jukebox, someone who loved Randy Travis, maybe even Doc himself, and now he was singing, "It's Just a Matter of Time," a song older than the singer, while Doc and I slow-danced.

"Leroy's girlfriend," I said, "that fell off a mountain maybe, except it turns out she was pushed?"

"I believe you mentioned it last night," said Doc. "At dinner."

"That was last night?" I was astonished. "Anyway," I said after a moment, "the guy wore a Ronald McDonald mask."

"Now, that," said Doc, "you didn't mention. Colorful."

I took a deep breath, inhaled cigar and soap. His whiskery chin prickled and tickled my cheek. His earlobe was pink and downed with fine hairs. Some other time we could have danced all night.

I spoke into his clean Navajo-striped pearl-studded

shirt. "And somebody came into my house last night and attacked me."

"No *kidding*?" Doc took a step backward and looked me in the eye. He seemed perturbed. "I told you, I *told* you."

"See?" I took his hand, put it on the bump on my head, stepped back and undid the pink bandanna, so he could see the bruises on my throat. I didn't like to play on my weakness too much, but then again, whatever works. "I don't know what's going on, but I need some help."

"OK," said Doc. "Let's go back to the hotel. We need to talk in private."

We returned to the table. Doc got his cowboy hat but left the quarters and the cigar. "I want to stop at the bar," he said. "Pick up a bottle of Jim Beam."

I sighed. "Well, *I'm* not drinking."

"Well, I am," he said. "I been lying to you, for one thing."

"Lying to me?"

"Fibbing. Like about being a private detective. Just had that card made up at one of those cheap printer's. So if I'm going to tell you what I guess I got to, I'll want a few shots."

36

"So it was you all along, not some client," I said, as I walked beside Doc down the street, "that knew Randall a long time ago."

"Eighteen years. Course, people change in that long a time and he had a little bit, but not much. I recognized him right away when I saw him on the street in the Junction. I braked my car so damn fast, I almost went through the windshield. Couldn't believe it."

Lightning flashed in the distance, somewhere over in Aqua Prieta. Maybe it would start to rain again; the desert always fooled you. Dark men in cowboy hats clustered in groups on corners, laughing in the summer night and drinking beer.

"I drive down to Mexico every now and then," said Doc. "Go to Kino Bay. Coming back sometimes I'm not in any hurry, so I'll drive up through the Valley, through the Junction. I'd of thought he'd have gone about as far as possible from the state of Arizona." He laughed. "Course, the border's pretty close."

6226Betsy Thornton

It certainly was. The border was walking, running, tunneling, flying, dope dealing distance away. You could feel the border in the air, in the architecture, in the flourishes on the buildings; feel all the people on the other side, across the line, wanting to get across.

"The kid was with him," Doc went on. "I parked and watched them go into a store. I waited till they came out. Got a good look at him then and I was sure. I followed them back to where he lived."

We passed the cheap bright stores, the ¡HOY! ¡ESPECIALS!, and reached the Gadsden, walked in past the leather couches on the Persian rugs, past old cowboys talking, past the woman in the ruffled prairie dress and the turquoise and silver glasses.

"We could sit here," I said, "in the lobby."

We looked at each other. Doc had dark circles under his eyes, lines I hadn't noticed before around his mouth. "Don't know if they'll let me drink Jim Beam in their lobby," he said.

I was kind of counting on that Jim Beam to loosen him up, and me cold sober. Plus I had the .38. I didn't feel scared of him anyway; he looked too tired, vulnerable for the first time, like someone that needed to be taken care of. We went up the white marble stairs.

"After you found out where he lived," I said, "you didn't go see him right away. You waited till it was late at night and the little girl would be asleep. She knew someone came to visit him, but she didn't know who."

Doc didn't respond. I followed him up where the stairs narrowed at the next floor and walked down a narrow red-carpeted hall, old-fashioned light fixtures like candles. The door to room 204 was elaborately carved wood. Doc unlocked it and we went in.

What I wanted to see was dim red carpeting, bed with iron bedstead, white chenille spread, dresser with spotty mirror, washstand next to it. Instead I saw pale blue wall-to-wall sculptured carpeting, machine-made quilt on the modern bed, thrift-store fake antique wing chair by the window, fake oil painting scene of cows in green English meadows over the bed, fake Rembrandt on the opposite wall.

Bedecked with bright blue ruffled curtains, the window was open and looked out onto a fire escape. I saw on the fake antique wing chair and looked down at the parking lot, which looked real enough.

Doc sat down heavily on the bed. For a moment he stared past me, out the window, then he rubbed his face. "I came back down here 'cause of the guilt," he said.

"The guilt?"

"I read about him dying and it got to me. I couldn't get it out of my mind, thinking maybe it was me, maybe if I hadn't gone to see him, none of it would have happened, he'd still be alive."

"Well, I guess I got to trust somebody sometime." Doc lay flat on his back on the narrow bed, head on the pillow, arms behind his head. "Might as well be somebody cute."

"Always the best bet." I was tickled pink at the compliment, but not wanting to show it. I sat in the armchair, pushed over by the window, a paper cup in my hand, with an inch or so of Jim Beam, but I didn't want any, just the smell of it coming from the cup was sickening.

Doc took a big swallow of his and lay back again. "You might not believe it, but I wasn't always a regular kind of guy like I am now."

"What do you mean, *regular*?"

He sighed. "If you have to ask, then forget it. I grew up here in Arizona, up north, and when I turned eighteen I went off to college and took a bunch of agricultural courses, graduated, worked a little with my dad. But I couldn't hack it. Had this long hair, so none of the cowboys wanted to have anything to do with me. Went off to California, L.A. for a while, just kind of did nothing and everything."

I leaned back in the armchair, put my feet on the radiator.

"Tell you the truth, I never was really like the people I met in California, there was always something in me, sitting back and watching it all. So I left there and started wandering—I'd been hitching in Colorado coming down from Aspen and this couple in a red Dodge van picked me up on the New Mexico border." Doc laughed. "They asked me where I was going and I said nowhere and they said they were going nowhere too. We were like that then, you know?"

"Yes," I said.

"They both had short hair, really short hair, but it didn't look like it'd been cut, just lopped off. They were both wearing jeans and flannel shirts and they kind of giggled and said her name was May and his was Charlie."

"Charlie?"

"It was your boyfriend. He was calling himself Charlie."

"Charlie *Pomeroy*." I sat up straight and spilled a little Jim Beam. "That was Randall's best friend. In college." Poor Charlie. Was he already dead in the snow then? I tried to think, but matching dates eluded me.

Doc waved his hand. "She was kind of snotty, but I liked him. I helped out with the driving and while she was sleeping in back Charlie and I shared a joint and talked. He asked me a lot of questions about growing up in Arizona, ranching, stuff like that. By now we've driven clear across New Mexico, and we're in Arizona, passing through Holbrook on Interstate 40 headed for Flag and it's nighttime late."

I took a tiny sip of Jim Beam. "And you were all still going nowhere?"

"Well, there was talk of Mexico. He told me he and May had been on the road for a month. He said they were doing a grass-roots thing but it wasn't working out. Nobody was around the way they used to be, and besides, they were running out of money. I kind of sensed he was burnt-out—sick of driving around the country in a red Dodge van and sick of doing it with May."

"Starry?" I said. "Could May have been Starry? Tall, strong, determined?"

"I got no idea. I never met Starry."

"Well, if she *is* May, she's not telling anybody anything. She's a hostile person. Or maybe just very very frightened."

"If she is May," said Doc, "I got no desire in the world to see that woman ever again. 'Cause in a lot of ways, she's to blame."

"For what?"

"I'm trying to tell you. Anyway, we traded off driving and eventually it got to be May's turn, so I got in back and went to sleep. I woke up after a while and they're arguing. She's saying they need to get hold of a credit card and he's saying hell, why not just rob some store, be up front and honest about it. If he robs a store, the guy's insurance will cover it, so nobody loses but the insurance company and it probably deserves to be ripped off."

Doc paused.

"Well, lots of people talked that way back then," I said.

"Sure, they did and he was wired, burnt-out. But worst of all, he's got her with him. 'You know,' she says, 'I'd like to see you do that, I'd like to see you carry out your convictions all the way through to the end, just once, I'd like to see that.' "

I shuddered. *Most people are cowards, they don't live anything out.* Starry had said that.

Doc continued. "I sat up then and saw him open the glove compartment and pull out this gun, a .22.

" 'Hey,' I said, 'leave that behind or it'll be armed robbery. That's a few more years in Florence.'

"May says, 'Don't worry, he's just talk, he's always been good at talking.' "

"I wanted her to shut up and not challenge him and she did for a while and I fell back to sleep, and then I woke up. Charlie's driving now and damned if they're not arguing again. Then I felt the van slow and we're exiting the freeway just outside Phoenix and passing some all-night convenience store and then Charlie's pulling into an alleyway and parking. He pulls the .22 out of the glove compartment and gets out. So I got out too."

Doc paused. He took a sip of Jim Beam, stretched his legs.

I looked out the window. Thunder rumbled over in Mexico, heat lightning flashed in the sky. A breeze drifted in, blew the curtains.

"So," I asked, "did you *stop* him?"

"No," said Doc.

There was a silence. Doc looked doubly tired now, lying there clutching the bottle of Jim Beam, not dangerous or dashing, just a man.

"So Randall robbed a store?" I said. "Armed robbery. And he's been on the run ever since?"

"He never made it to the store," said Doc. He patted the bed, a spot beside him.

"Why don't you come over and sit, hold my hand, and make it easy while I tell you about it. It wasn't armed robbery, it was murder. What your old boyfriend did was, he killed a cop."

37

"No," I said. I thought suddenly of Didi and felt immeasurably sad.

I took my feet off the radiator, got up and went over to the bed. I sat down and took his hand. His palm was warm, callused. I put my palm on his, folded his fingers over, more for my own comfort than for his, but his too.

"I can still see it," he said, "this very minute, like it was the night it happened."

Noises, faint but distinct, drifted up from the parking lot. Two men shouting at each other, car doors slamming. A woman laughing, low pitched, mocking.

"We were in the alleyway." Doc took a sip of whiskey. "There was parking in front of the store, but I guess he figured this was the best place to make a getaway from. May stayed in the van."

I squeezed his hand.

"I walked behind him. I couldn't really believe, you see, that the guy was going to go hold up a Circle K. What I thought was that we were going to go around the corner where May couldn't see us and fake it. I mean this guy was just some . . . some college kid. But he was keyed up, pissed at May, he had the gun right out there, one of them .22s you don't do nothing to but fire. We turned the corner and I started to say something and that's when the cop showed up."

Doc let go of my hand. "He stepped right out of a doorway, like he'd been waiting, and I guess he must have seen the van park down the alleyway and wondered why. Just a rookie probably, trying a little too hard, 'cause this guy, he's young, younger than me—I can see that even in the dark."

"I jumped 'cause I wasn't expecting anybody and that's when Charlie shot him—he shot him right in the face."

I drew in a long breath.

"Twice, bam, bam," said Doc, his voice low. "It wasn't intentional, more like an involuntary reflex. It was fucking horrible."

Doc sat up and swung his feet off the bed. He went to the window and said without looking at me, "The guy didn't just drop dead, he kind of screamed and then, then he . . . he called out for his mom, for his mother."

He crumpled the paper cup the Jim Beam had been in and tossed it out the window. "It's another country," he said. "You don't know a thing about it till you've been there."

He came back to the bed, stood above me, looking down, and took a swig of Jim Beam out of the bottle.

"Charlie was white as a corpse himself and he looked sick, but he didn't lose his head. 'Now I'm going to shoot you,' he said, 'then I'll leave. If you're shot, then you're off the hook, like you got shot trying to stop me.'

"I held out my right arm, I'm left-handed. 'Right here,' I said. So he did. Then he took off running."

Doc lay down. The fake quilt was puffy and soft. His arm went around me, the arm with the old wound he'd showed me at Lillie's Cafe, and I put my head on his chest.

He went on. "I stood there for just a minute, then I walked as fast as I could, bleeding like a pig, to the convenience store and told the clerk that a man had been shot. Everybody came real fast, but no one could save him. And there I was wounded, too, and a nice Arizona boy from a good family. Still I didn't think they'd get away, but they must have made it to Phoenix, dumped the van, and then who knows. May and Charlie. For a while the cops'd call me in to look at mug shots, but nothing ever came of it.

"William Hodges," said Doc. "The boy that got killed. That was his name, but his friends probably called him Bill. Or maybe Will. I could have grabbed that gun away from Leroy back at the van, or even in the alleyway."

With my head on his chest I could feel Doc's breathing up and down, up and down, as if it were me; smell cigar smoke, Jim Beam. "I could have done that," he said. "Anyone could see how wound up he was."

In a false dream that women have, I imagined my presence could draw the memory out of him and take it on as my own. I turned and lay full length against him, closed my eyes.

I woke up in the dark and I was alone on the bed. I heard sounds in the distance, as if the earth were turning over, and then I realized it was thunder. Where was Doc? Then I saw him, at the window. "Looks like it's going to rain," he said, though I hadn't spoken.

"I never did turn him in." He held the bottle of Jim Beam to his lips, upended, but it was empty, then he set it down. "I never told the cops very much, 'cause I saw how it happened, how it came about, and the law doesn't care about that."

"What happened when you went to see him?"

"We talked. We went out on the porch where the kid couldn't hear us and we walked around on his land. He did most of the talking. He said a day hadn't gone by that he didn't think about what he'd done. He asked me if I

knew much about the cop that died and I said no, that I
hadn't exactly wanted to, I'd really wanted to forget if I
could."

Doc shrugged. "He said he knew he could never make
up for it and if I wanted to turn him in, would I just wait
till his little girl left. I was kind of insulted. 'Who do you
think I am?' I said. Then he laughed and said, 'I can think
of a few people who wouldn't mind, someone turning me
in. They'd do it themselves if they could think of a
reason.' "

"Doc," I said, "did he say *who*?"

"I wouldn't have known them if he did. Now I wish I'd
asked. But I didn't. I said I wasn't going to turn him in, I'd
just wanted to see what had happened to him. He stopped
then and stared at me. 'You mean just idle curiosity?' *'Idle
curiosity?'* I said. 'Hell, no, it's not *idle*.' "

Doc came back to the bed and lay down beside me.
"What I was thinking, I drove him to suicide coming to
him out of the past."

"Maybe," I said, "you led someone to him."

There was a silence. I could have bitten my tongue.

"I hope to hell I didn't," said Doc fervently.

I said after a moment, "Someone who wanted all of us to
think it was suicide."

"Someone," said Doc.

I walked up the hill to Hal's house, my house now. It
had been newly renovated and its paint gleamed in the
sunlight, a sunlight so bright, I had to close my eyes
against it. I felt my way into the house and then suddenly
it was raining, drops pelting on the roof, and I opened my
eyes. Hal stood, his back to me, cooking something on the
stove.

"Oh, Hal," I cried. "Oh, Hal, thank goodness, you're
alive. I was so worried."

Then he turned and it wasn't Hal, it was Randall. Blood

flowed from his mouth, his eyes, blood flowed down his body and dripped onto the floor and made little splashes like the rain. "I'm dead," he said, "I'm still dead, Chloe, still dead, Chloe, still dead, Chloe."

Then I was awake, opening my eyes onto the room in the Gadsden. It was raining for real, the curtain billowing out and rain coming in. I got out of bed and went to the window. Outside I could see it was day, but dark from the storm. I closed the window. Doc lay sound asleep, probably due to all the whiskey he'd drunk.

I thought we should get to know each other better, some other time, sometime when the world wasn't so gray, so I scribbled him a note on the brown paper bag the Jim Beam had been in, *get in touch before you leave town*, and my phone number. Then I left the room, walked down the dim red hall, down the white marble stairs, and out to the rainy street; dread followed me all the way.

38

The road back was slick and black and the sky like beaten silver, brushed with a gray soft as the wings of the doves who cooed in the trees here all summer. It was so ridiculously beautiful that it was easy to believe in some Presence out here, divine and arrogant, crazed with beauty and contemptuous of human beings and the ugly little messes they made down here on the ground.

The nightmare had left me sick with anxiety, a kind of post-traumatic stress disorder for dreamers. Not that being awake was much less stressful, not with what Doc had told me. I was wide-awake and utterly exhausted trying to fit what he'd said with everything else.

I pulled into my carport at nine-thirty; the Arizona cypress by my house smelled rich and musty, water trickled down the drainage ditch next to the driveway, and water had puddled in the carport because I hadn't cleaned out the drainage spout as Brody had told me to do a thousand times.

Big Foot stood stolidly by the door, looking at me with

chilly green eyes. Lourdes' door opened, she leaned out. "Chloe, are you OK? Did you go on a call-out?"

"No." My voice quavered. "I'm fine."

"You're sure?"

"Absolutely." I could hardly get the word out. "I just need a shower."

But first I had to call Roxanne, today was a *red-letter* day. I giggled as I punched in Roxanne's number and got the answering machine. "*Call* me," I croaked, and banged down the phone.

That was it, a long shower, then I'd get dressed in clean clothes and what? The shower was easy, finding clothes was hard, I put on my nightgown finally and lay down on the bed. I slept for hours.

The telephone screamed me awake and I sat up abruptly, not knowing which room which house which state I was in and certainly not knowing where the phone was. I found it as usual on the kitchen counter.

"Hello?"

It was Roxanne, her voice tight, hurried.

"What?" I asked. "What's happened?"

"I called you this morning at *six o'clock* and you weren't there. I . . . I had this premonition, Didi's been acting so strange, so I called Jennifer's, they'll never forgive me. . . . Anyway, I've been going everywhere looking. . . ."

"What's the matter?"

"Didi's gone, she's run away. She was supposed to be at Jennifer's house. I wasn't thinking when I let her go. It just hit me early this morning, I sat up straight in bed. Harry's on an overnighter. But she wasn't. At Jennifer's, I mean. She . . . she ran away once before when her dog got killed and went to the beach house, but she wasn't there this time. She left a note in her bedroom. All she says is that I'm not to worry. Don't worry, Roxanne, I love you and I'll be back soon." She laughed wildly.

"OK," I said. "Calm down." I added, with false assurance, "We'll find her."

"Harry. He's going to blame me, he's not going to forgive me for this. God, I don't know if I can forgive myself. I said to Jennifer, well, what did you think was going on? They're so stupid at that age and they all band together. She got a letter. . . ."

"I know, I know, from Leroy . . . Fern sent it on Friday."

Roxanne rushed on. "It's on the end table by her bed, the envelope, addressed to her, postmarked Dudley. *Thursday*, not Friday."

"Fern told me . . ." But that didn't matter now. "Look," I said, "she could be at a friend's house. Maybe she went somewhere to be alone, because the letter upset her. You don't know. . . ."

"She's in Arizona."

"How do you know that?"

"She took the limo, the one that goes to the airport. When she wasn't at the beach house I drove to the limo place. The driver remembers her, she was all dressed up so she'd look older. The last trip they made out last night. She's already in Arizona. I'm sure."

So that was where she'd been when I called her this morning, out frantically looking for Didi.

"Shawn," I said. "Shawn ran away from home. Rose knows where he goes. He must have met her. She's got to be with Shawn."

"I hope to God she is," said Roxanne. "I knew I could count on you. When you weren't home this morning I was so panicky I did something else and I probably shouldn't have. . . . Oh, never mind. Would you just go get her?"

"It's not that easy," I said, "but I'll figure it out. OK?"

Everything was getting blurry, merging together as I drove to the Valley, to the Junction, to Rose's trailer. The storm clouds were building up again and all her clothes were still on the line, a little sodden, so it must have rained out here and would probably rain again later this afternoon. Her Eldorado was parked in front, one tire pretty flat.

She had to be home, had to be there to take the clothes off the line, had to be there to tell me where Shawn was.

Like some personal nemesis, the woman from next door was out in a faded muumuu, pink flowers this time, trimmed with green and gold ricrac. Something about the smug way she looked at me told me Rose wouldn't be there, but she let me go to the door again, knock.

"Not home, right?" I called over to her.

Her mouth turned down and she scratched her arm.

"Any idea where she might be?"

The woman shrugged. "She went off with Lance. Hell, I don't know, I ain't her keeper."

"What do you mean went off with Lance? You mean she's not working tonight?"

"She wouldn't go off with him if she was. She's not *rich*, you know."

"Where does she *usually* go with Lance? I mean is she in *town*? Where does Lance live?" I heard my voice, out of patience and contemptuous, getting me nowhere.

"Lance, he lives over by the feed store, that little shed place in back, worse place to live than here even, probably that's what he saw in Rose."

"The feed store," I said, "the one on the main road?"

She sighed, looking at me a long time in silence, and during that time I seemed to see her whole life pass in front of me: minor accidents in parking lots, washing machines that overflowed, cars that overheated, TV sets that turned the picture over and over—just nothing working out the way it should ever ever ever and someone had to pay.

Finally she scratched her arm again and said, "Well, there ain't but one feed store in town."

Thunder rolled as I jumped into my car. The horizon was deep gray, lit up with streaks of lightning. Yet the rain might never reach here, the monsoon was always unpredictable. I tore over to the feed store. Behind it I could see a little shed, like a miniature house, with a miniature porch in front and a big fat dog sleeping in the dirt yard. Or was he dead? He lay motionless as I walked up to the door, knocked, waited, knocked; as I passed him again I heard him sigh, and his eyelids flickered. Probably just drunk.

A dirty white pickup drove by slow. A white-haired man, with doggie jowls, chewing a toothpick, leaned out. His eyes were sky blue and seemed to be focused on distant hills. "You looking for Lance?"

"I'm looking for Rose. It's an emergency."

He sat there in his pickup for a little bit, thoroughly digesting what I'd said, then he said, slowly, "You know, I think they went into town."

"Dudley?"

He considered. "Uh, yeah, Dudley. To see Lance's big brother. Yeah, I think Lance said something about that to me."

"Where does his brother live?"

"Damn, where does that boy live? Saginaw? Naw, maybe Bakerville."

"That's OK, his last name's Eubanks?"

The man looked sad. "You know, I think it ain't. They had a different dad. What the hell was . . . *Damn*."

"Thanks anyway."

"It looks like it's sure going to rain. Now, you have yourself a real good day," the man called after me as I drove off, heading for Fern's.

Fern, I thought, Fern knows everyone in town, she's related to everyone.

She was in her kitchen putting cosmetics—bath oil, lipsticks, compacts—into little white bags, being the Avon lady, or was it Mary Kay? She gave a little start when she saw me and gestured for me to come in. "Oh, Chloe, I'm

so glad you're here. I got to tell you this right now before I
lose my nerve. I keep thinking someone saw me. Saw me
when I went to Leroy's that night."

"What night?" I asked sharply.

"The night he was killed. I just slipped out, the envelope
he gave me had got me worried. I wanted to ask . . . I
should have told Kyle Barnett. I can trust Kyle, don't you
think? It would kill Homer to know. . . . He'd think . . .
But if someone saw me . . ."

"Fern. Did you see anything? Was anyone else there?"

"I heard the shot. I went back to the Junction, but I had
to wait to call the police until Homer . . . I was so scared.
Then later I called Kyle. But it was all too late."

She put a lipstick and a pink sponge into a bag and
folded it over twice. Her hands were shaking.

Oh, God. So it was Fern who'd gone out that night, not
Homer. "Fern," I said, "it's important what you told me,
but right now something else is more important." And I
told her.

"You know," she said, "I did mail that envelope out on
Thursday. I don't know why I told you Friday, except I was
thinking, it won't go out till Friday, but that's here in the
Junction. In Dudley, I think they have a late pickup."

"It doesn't matter now," I said. "I just need to know
where Shawn is."

Fern unfolded the bag she'd just folded. "I don't know
where he goes. I really don't." Her hands moved over the
table blindly.

"But Violet would, I bet."

"Well, she might, but she's over in Douglas, shopping
with her girlfriend. School's going to be starting. . . . I can
have her call you. It's almost three now, she should be
back soon. . . ." Her voice was low, baffled, as if she
weren't sure of the purpose of what she was saying. "Or
did they say they were going to have an early dinner
there?"

She folded the bag again, then picked up several others

and moved them over to the kitchen counter. It took two trips to get them all moved.

"Have her call me just in case, no matter what," I said. "What's Lance's brother's last name, isn't he related to you?"

"Lance is, by marriage. He used to be married to my niece, Hazel, but all Lance ever thought about was having a good time." As she talked she lined the bags up in a row, very very neatly, and her voice got louder and faster. "I mean, he was kind of handy with cars, but who isn't, but he sure liked to drink and then Hazel got this real good offer of a job over in Yuma. . . ."

She was losing it fast. She would have to find it again by herself, I didn't have time to counsel. "Fern," I said, "*Fern.*"

A bag fell to the floor. She put her face in her hands. "I should have looked, I should have checked to make sure it wasn't . . . wasn't something dangerous. I should have remembered right what day I mailed it. Maybe he said something in it. . . . Oh, Chloe, I got to tell you this. Vi— Violet must of said something about the letter."

"What do you mean?"

"Marge from the cafe came up to me on the street and asked me right out, you think he told her who done it?"

"It's OK," I said to reassure her, but I didn't think it was OK at all. "We don't know he told her anything."

"But people are thinking he might of. That's all it would take."

"People," I said. "Who? Who would know? Where did Marge hear it?"

"It don't matter. Don't you understand?" Fern's voice was anguished. "Living out here, people know things like it's in the air, in the wind. Even if you think no one can tell, they sense it, they smell it. . . . It's like your chest is torn open and there's your heart . . . just . . . bleeding and they all see it." She stopped suddenly, wringing her hands.

But I didn't have time for that now. "Think," I said. "Who would know where Shawn is?"

"Bobbie," she said, suddenly, "you got to go find Bobbie. She knows everyone in Dudley. She'd know Lance's brother. And when you find out where Shawn is from Rose, Bobbie will know how to get there."

39

Bobbie's house was on the outskirts of New Dudley, a rectangular stuccoed structure, freshly painted white and planted round the edges with marigolds. Next door a woman in a pink jogging suit was unloading groceries in front of an equally well-kept house. As I pulled up a big red-brown rottweiler galloped out of nowhere and began to bark at me fiercely.

"Sheriff!" the woman yelled. "You shut up!"

Sheriff waved his tail frantically, belly to the ground.

"Don't worry," the woman said to me. "He won't bite."

I got out of the car. Behind the house, the yard sloped to an arroyo; the clouds had parted to show a brief moment of sun and the shadows of the rocks and bushes were lengthening—it must have been nearly six o'clock and I was no closer to finding Didi.

"If you're looking for Bobbie, she's still at work, you know, over at the hardware store."

"This is urgent," I said. "Victim Witness."

"You can go inside and call. She never locks up—go in

the front door and the phone'll be right there by the divan. Number's 5301."

I stood in Bobbie's living room on the wall-to-wall carpeting in front of a line of photographs on the bookcase, staring into Kyle Barnett's eyes, a younger Kyle, hair shorter and wearing a huntsman plaid jacket, jeans. He looked determined, vigorous; proudly holding a shotgun, or was it a rifle, like in those pictures you see in the newspapers of survivalists, snapshots taken by wives or girlfriends, a couple of weeks before they finally snap.

I backed away, sat on the couch, mauve and blue plaid, a glass-topped coffee table in front of it. Across the room was a fireplace, a couple of shotguns or were they rifles displayed above the mantel. The phone was on an end table next to a philodendron plant and another cluster of photographs. I punched in the number and listened to the phone ring and looked at the pictures.

Bobbie, maybe thirteen, Kyle, and an adolescent boy stood in a field, Kyle holding a football. The boy looked just like Bobbie; her brother, it must be, Hedge. Must be one of those Kentucky family names. Hedge, who was killed in Vietnam, standing in the sunshine, death just around the corner.

"True Value Hardware." It was Bobbie's voice.

"Bobbie," I said in relief. "We have a big problem. Leroy sent Didi a letter, we don't know what about, but it might tell us who killed him. And now she's run away to Arizona."

"To *Arizona*?"

"She's got to be with Shawn. And Rose knows where he is, she's here in Dudley, with Lance's brother. You know his name?"

"Sure, Delmore French," said Bobbie. "I can call his house, but they're probably all at the Hitching Post by now getting drunker than skunks. That's all anyone does in that whole family."

"Should I call Kyle?"

"He's off, went to Tucson," she said. There was a silence. "We don't want some asshole handling this. Look, I'm on my way out the door. I'll find Rose. Then you go home and wait so I know where to find you. I'll come pick you up, we'll go find Shawn and Didi."

"Great," I said, "that's fantastic, I really appreciate this, Bobbie."

"Appreciate it?" Bobbie snorted. "I wouldn't miss this for anything."

"I was wondering. . . ." I glanced at the guns over the mantel. "I've got a .38."

"It's against *all* the rules," said Bobbie. "But so's the rest, probably. Bring it."

The clouds had closed in completely, and it was raining as I drove round the pit, evening coming on fast. I kept the car in second gear, the gray rain impeding me all the way as I half drove, half hydroplaned on the slick highway, until I exited at Dudley. I roared past the Lyric, past the Copper Queen, and up the hill to my house.

Rain was pouring down, puddling even worse in the carport than usual. I stepped round it, my shoes soaking by now, and pushed open the kitchen door. He was waiting there all along, knowing I would come in from the carport, wet and unwary. Waiting there all the time just behind the door. Ronald McDonald.

He came at me, I opened my mouth, and something wet, smelling medicinal, covered my face. I inhaled and entered a magic dreamy land, where all things were momentarily to be explained. Then everything was dark.

40

Someone was holding poppers under my nose—I'd never liked poppers, never wanted to do them, not even in my wild experimental youth, thought they were one of the grosser forms of drug abuse, along with drinking cough syrup for the codeine.

"No," I said. "No way." I was aware of a strange smell, tingly, medicinal, not the popper smell.

"Chloe. Hey, come on, wake up."

"She looks maybe a little better."

I opened my eyes. Bobbie was kneeling on the floor beside me, Lourdes peering over her shoulder.

"What's going on?" I said, then I remembered. "Ronald," I said, "Ronald McDonald."

"You scared the shit out of me." Bobbie stood up. "I drove up, the kitchen door was wide open, and I could see you inside lying on the floor. And now you're babbling."

"I'm not babbling." I sat up. "What's that *smell*?"

"Ether, something like that."

"The French doors were open," said Lourdes excitedly.

"I just checked. Chloe, you got to *fix* those doors. Bobbie, somebody tried to get her and they tried once before. We should get Bill Soto over here."

"No," I said. "Not that. They put something on my face—to knock me out. Not *kill* me."

"Well, thank goodness for that," said Bobbie sarcastically. "I found out where Shawn's place is from Rose."

"Where?" I said.

"It doesn't matter," said Bobbie. "I don't want you going there. I'll go by myself. It's not that far. You should be resting. And after that, call the cops. About the break-in. Sleep at Lourdes' tonight."

Lourdes looked around my kitchen, then opened a drawer in the stove and pulled out a pot. "Look, I'll make you some tea."

I said to Bobbie, "I don't want you in danger. What if someone tries to follow you?"

"Hey," said Bobbie, "I can tell if I'm being tailed. Don't worry. Like I said, I got a lot of connections in this community."

"That's the truth." Lourdes rummaged through some shelves, opened cupboards. "Where do you keep your tea?"

"I don't drink tea."

"Want to get up?" said Bobbie. "Lourdes and I will help. We'll get you to the bed, or would you prefer the couch?"

"Why don't you want tea? All these new people, they drink tea," said Lourdes. "All kinds of tea, peppermint, chamomile, even that stuff my granny used to make, echinacia. Ugh."

"Bobbie, I'm fine, I have to go with you. It's my ca—responsibility too."

"All I'm gonna do," said Bobbie, "is go get her, bring her back here. To your house. Then we'll all sit and talk. You won't miss out on too much fun."

I stood up, sat down again. "Couch," I groaned.

*   *   *

Lourdes and I locked the door and pushed a chair in front of the French doors. From the couch I could hear the rain falling outside, falling on the skylight above me, see it streaking the windows by the French door, except the window to my left, which was open, the curtain blowing. Big Foot leapt in and landed with a big thud on the floor.

"There's that big boy," said Lourdes fondly, looking in from the kitchen where she was reluctantly making coffee instead of tea.

"Could you feed him?" I called. "His food's on top of the refrigerator."

"He's got a lot of food in his dish."

"He only eats it straight from the bag," I told her. "He likes to watch you give it to him—it makes him feel powerful." I should call Roxanne, just to report in, but not with Lourdes there. "Lourdes, did Bobbie tell you just where she was going?"

"No, I didn't ask her. Don't worry about Bobbie, she's smart and she's a very tough lady too. You want something in this coffee?"

"Everything." I sat up. The room around me, the rain on the roof, seemed unreal, oddly enlarged, as if I were Jack in the giant's castle. "What if something happens to her?" I called plaintively. "If she turns up missing or . . . We won't even be able to tell the police where she was headed."

"Chloe, you're making me nervous. Why don't we call Bill?" Lourdes said wistfully, coming in with a cup of coffee and handing it to me.

She closed the open window and sat on the rocking chair.

"What can he do?" I said. "Bobbie will be out of his jurisdiction. Maybe Violet will call. She's supposed to when she gets home. She'll know."

Lourdes sighed. She must have had her hair done recently, it was styled like a chrysanthemum, and she was wearing the deep rose-colored pants and a matching deep rose top decorated with flowers made from rhinestones and faux pearls she told me she'd bought in Douglas at La Parisian. She'd managed to find earrings that almost exactly matched the flowers and little velvet ballet shoes in the same rose shade as the pants and top.

"Do you know Lance Eubanks' brother?" I asked.

"Sure, that's Delmore, Delmore French. They had different fathers. Their mother had three or four husbands. She was just a drunk and she got killed, one of her boyfriends backed her very own pickup truck on her, some people said it was on purpose 'cause she was going out on him."

The rain gusted, blowing on the skylight. Lourdes paused till it died down. "Lance's mom was nice, though, when she was sober. Lance just doted on her."

"And Lance married Fern's cousin," I said. "Fern from out in the Valley. Her cousin Hazel, but Lance drank too much and Hazel got a good job in Yuma and left him." I was proud I was learning the history.

"That's right," said Lourdes. "Estelle was Hazel's mom's name. No one thought it would work out. I remember that Fern, she was just beautiful. Lance was good to Hazel too, except he couldn't keep a job. We went to high school together all of us or we played football games, basketball, against each other, but so many of those boys are dead now. Course, there was Vietnam, but other things too."

Rain gusted again and Lourdes shivered.

"It was hard on Bobbie, I guess," I said, "having her brother killed in Vietnam."

"It was terrible," said Lourdes, "just terrible. Hedge, they used to call him because their last name was Hodges. Hedge Hodges. That's a joke, a hedgehog is a porcupine. His real name was William, he was the sweetest boy, but he wasn't killed in Vietnam. It would have been better if it was the war, then at least Bobbie could have gone to Washington, gone to the Memorial there and looked up his name."

William Hodges. I *knew* that name.

"It was the war," I said. "Fern told me about it. Along with somebody Kilmer and Henry Stone."

"Well, they were killed in Vietnam. But not Hedge."

I couldn't remember the conversation exactly, but Fern had mentioned Bobbie's brother a little later. I'd just assumed. "Then some drunk shot him, or what happened?"

Lourdes shook her finger at me. "Don't you tell *me*. It could have been a drunk, though. Hedge was a cop up north—just a rookie and someone shot him right in the *face*. It was so horrible, and they never even caught the guy who did it."

I screamed then; it was involuntary. I couldn't help it.

41

I took the forty-five-mile-an-hour stretch around the pit at seventy. I hadn't wanted to explain anything to Lourdes and I'd had to push past her to get away; luckily her fancy shoes didn't give her much traction. If Randall's killer thought Didi might know who he was, then Didi was in danger, but it was worse than that now.

Kyle. An experienced cop, but this had never been just another case for him. Had he kept an eye on Doc all those years until finally he led him to Randall? Had the story about the other cop, the one with the little stash of coke and the mental insurance plan, been a symbolic confession?

But Randall hadn't been a real real bad guy. Not really. All that chemistry between Kyle and me, making it easier for me to trick him and him to trick me. The man who'd conducted the investigation into Randall's death—a primary suspect.

Even Bobbie was a possible suspect.

The parking lot at the Hitching Post was full of cars and

trucks, including, thank God, Lance's mud-colored pick-up. Inside the bar the place was packed as if in celebration of the weather, everybody nice and dry and drunk inside. To my right was the long bar and a couple of game machines, and to my left, a big dance floor with tables all around. A few couples were dancing close, though it was early for that sort of thing, but maybe because it was Clint Black, telling someone they were the lock made to fit his key.

Or the rain outside hissing sex, sex, sex.

I spotted Lance and Rose dancing over in a corner, Lance bending over Rose, his arm pumping up and down in a style I associate with Club Dance on the Nashville Network or junior high. They were dancing pretty close, but love would have to wait.

I pushed my way through and tapped Rose on the shoulder.

"Chloe," she said, looking surprised, "what are you doin' in this decadent place?"

"Didi may be in danger," I said. "I need to know where Shawn is."

"I just told Bobbie," said Rose. "You mean she didn't get ahold of you?"

"Hi there, Chloe." Lance lurched, giving me an enormous squinty smile. His cowboy hat was pulled down low so his eyebrows were concealed. "Come on, you can dance with us." He held one arm out, almost losing his balance.

Rose pushed his arm down, looking at me worriedly. "What's wrong?"

"I've got to get to where Shawn's hiding out right away. Please, Rose, it's urgent."

Her face hardened and her eye glittered, the eyes of a woman made for crisis, for danger. It was the in-between times that hung heavy. "Let's go then."

She broke away from Lance and headed across the floor. Lance and I followed her out the door.

It had stopped raining and in the parking lot Rose and Lance argued. "Look, I got to show Chloe where this place is, Lance. It's easier to go along than try and tell her, in the dark and the rain and all. It's important."

"I know it is, Rosie Rosebud." Lance stood on the verge of a large puddle, staring down at his boots, his voice intensely serious. He teetered back and forth just a little. "And that's why I want to be there for you. So I'm asking one thing." He raised a finger. "Just one. I take you both, you two fine ladies, in my truck."

Rose stamped her foot. "Lance, you goddamn drunken *shit*-head, could I just do this without this bullshit?"

Lance looked hurt. "Drunk don't have a thing to do with it. I want to take care of you, Rosie Rosebud. Hey, come on, sweetie, can't you at least try to understand?"

"OK, OK." Rose looked at me in exasperation. "We'll leave your car and just take his damn truck. If we don't, he'll follow us and probably get into an accident. I'm driving and you're getting in back, Lance, you hear me? Chloe and I have things to talk about."

We clambered into the truck, which smelled of three-day-old french fries and beer. Beer cans clanked together on the floor under my feet, and as I settled in, a spring dug into my back. "Whereabout are we going?"

"San Pedro, around Palominas, Hereford. A friend of Shawn's mom's got a little place there Frank don't know about."

We took off with a jerk, skidded out of the parking lot, slid down the road and onto the traffic circle to the Hereford-Palominas highway.

We didn't speak as we plowed down the dark slippery road, Rose hunched over the steering wheel, clanging through the gears. It sounded like the transmission didn't have much longer to live. Finally she said, "You want to explain?"

The pickup swayed, tires probably not aligned, suspension

shot; terms I'd picked up from Brody. Behind me I could just make out Lance, lying on his back on a mattress, no doubt kept there for happier times.

"No," I said. "In case I'm wrong. OK, Rose? I just don't know if I can trust Bobbie. Let's leave it at that."

"Yeah? I don't know, I think I would. Trust Bobbie, I mean. Shit, there's too damn much play in this steering wheel. Hang on, we're hitting a curve."

We turned in to black space, headlights cutting a narrow long wedge into nothing. It began to rain again, rain falling on the windshield, and Rose turned on the wipers; they moved slowly, too slowly, just like the truck.

"How much farther?" I asked impatiently.

"I can go faster, but it's harder to steer then." Rose stomped on the accelerator as if to make her point and we swerved. "At least another ten minutes just to the dirt road." She glanced at the rearview mirror. "That dumb Lance's just sitting in the rain. He's got a tarp back there."

There was a thumping on the window behind me, and I turned; Lance had his nose pressed against the window.

"Just wave," said Rose, "then don't pay any attention. Shit, that guy behind us is traveling. Must be going eighty. On a wet road. *Asshole*."

I peered around and saw lights a way away, but gaining rapidly. I sat silent as lights came up from behind, filling the cab. I heard honking then, but I couldn't see what kind of vehicle it was, its lights blinding me.

"*OK, OK.*" Rose hit the brakes lightly a couple of times. "I'm going to slow and let this sucker pass."

I took a deep breath and said, after a minute, "What's he doing?"

"Not a damn thing. Shit. What's he trying to do, run us off the road? Got to be drunk."

"Maybe not," I said. "Rose, I've got a .38 in my purse. I'm going to get it out, just in case."

"There's a .22 somewhere in this trunk, loaded and all; why don't you look in the glove compartment."

The truck was jouncing badly and my hands shook, but I got the glove compartment open, rummaged through, and found the gun.

"OK," said Rose. "Hang on, I'm going to signal a turn, then speed up this curve. Hope they don't know the road too good."

More thumping. Lance had his mouth open, yelling, I could just hear him.

". . . pee!" he was shouting.

"What's he saying?" Rose took a slow curve fast. What did she care about what he was saying? I certainly didn't, hanging on to the seat, my heart beating fast, my mouth dry. Suddenly the lights behind us went away.

I turned to look back and couldn't see the car behind us anymore. "Gone!" I said.

Rose let out a whoop. "All right! They must have gone off the road. Goddamn, we did it. The turn's coming up if we can make it before he catches up again."

"He—?" I said. "Did you get a look at the car and the driver?"

"It was one of those white compacts half the people in America own. Probably some drunk."

"It's pretty early for people to be—" Lance banged on the window hard. "Maybe not," I said.

"What's with him?"

"I think he has to pee."

"Goddamn it," said Rose. "He can pee in the damn truck. He hauls manure in it all the time, what's the difference? Keep your eyes out the back just in case."

I turned and looked past Lance's bleary agonized eyes, into the blackness behind, but now I couldn't see any lights.

"Nothing," I said, relieved.

"OK, this is the dirt road, coming up."

"No one's behind us."

"OK, then we're safe." She turned onto dirt, cut the

lights, and the truck bounced and jounced some more. But we were safe. No, what was I thinking?

We drove slowly down the road in the dark. It wasn't raining anymore, but I heard splashing, maybe water dripping from the trees. No, it was Lance taking a leak over the side of the truck. He shook himself and lay down on the mattress.

"Still no one behind us?"

"All clear," I said.

Rose slowed down. "We're here. I'm not going to get too close to the house. I'll park and we'll walk." Her voice was dutiful as if she were humoring me. "I mean since you're worried . . . about Bobbie."

"I just don't know," I said. "Why take a chance?"

She stopped the truck. I handed her the .22, and she checked to see if it was loaded. I knew my .38 was.

I whispered, "The guns are just in case. We're going to go up there and check it out, see if cars are there, look in the windows, see what's going on. Let's go."

"Shawn's car is an old Chevy Malibu," Rose whispered. "He was keeping it at a friend's house so his dad wouldn't know he had it."

We got out of the truck.

Lance lay on his back on the mattress, arms crossed over his chest, hat over his face, snoring. In the middle of nowhere, and with a lot more pressing things on my mind, I had a flash, a satori, that this was what a cowboy really was, drunk half the time, and on top of that, a clear picture of Brody coming towards me, smiling, wearing a T-shirt that said on it THIS BODY IS MADE FROM USED PARTS.

What had I done? I'd gone to a bar with a man who'd given up drinking, a man I was proud of because he'd done that, gotten drunk in front of him, and flirted with another man. All caught up with Randall and before that with my memories and obsessions about James and Hal, and there was nothing I could do about the dead; I could at least try to be halfway decent to the living. Suddenly the past seemed to recede, replaced by a just possible present. But there were other things at stake at the moment.

" 'Bye, Lance," whispered Rose. She giggled. Rose was taking this seriously and yet she wasn't. It annoyed me.

A light breeze had come up. Above, over the cotton-woods, the moon was about half-full and clouds raced over it. It would maybe clear up by morning if the wind kept up. We walked a little way down the dirt road to where it curved and we could see the river. Back east we wouldn't have called it that, you could walk across it without having to even swim, but it had water in it most of the time.

Now the moon shone on the water, the cottonwoods rustled overhead, the breeze dappled its surface, and it was as magic as anything can ever be. Involuntarily we both stopped.

"Look," said Rose in the silence, "I kind of lied to you back at my trailer. About when Leroy came over to get stoned that last week? I never seen him so upset before. He, um, well, he did tell me something."

"He did?"

We could see a house ahead in a clearing, smoke coming from the chimney, a flickering light in the front window. They must have a fire going in the fireplace. A Chevy Malibu, Shawn's car, was parked in front, but I couldn't see Bobbie's.

Rose looked at me uncertainly, her face as white as the moon. "I mean," she said, "he said things in confidence."

I wanted to know whatever he'd told her, if she was willing to tell me, but right now there were more pressing things. "Do you think Bobbie's even here?" I whispered. "God, I hope. . . ."

"Her car could be around the side." Rose looked down at her .22, then shrugged her shoulders and said in a rush, "Look. I know a few things, like that Leroy maybe had something to do with Bobbie's brother getting killed."

I stared at her. "*Maybe* had something to do with? That's putting it mildly."

"Is that what this is all about?" whispered Rose. "But Bobbie doesn't know. Neither does Kyle. Leroy said . . . I mean you really don't think that Bobbie . . ."

Suddenly my mind focused for the first time since I'd talked to Lourdes. "None of this makes sense," I said, "and Leroy didn't even know Bobbie."

"He never met her," said Rose, "but he knew her, all about her, and about Kyle. When he came back to this country he went to some library in Phoenix and he researched. . . ." Her voice sank again to a whisper. "But how do you know anything about Leroy? You never met him *either*."

"Rose," I said urgently, "we really need to sit down and—"

Suddenly a branch snapped behind us, and something else, a rifle being pumped. A voice said, "I've got a gun on you two and I'm prepared to use it."

We both turned. Bobbie.

42

"Don't *move*," said Bobbie, the gun jerking.

"It's just us," said Rose. "For Christ's sake."

Bobbie lowered the gun. "Chloe. Rose," she said in surprise. "What are you guys doing here? You scared the hell out of me."

Rose glanced at me a little uncertainly. She said to Bobbie, "Well, Chloe wanted to get up here fast, so I brought her. She'd never have found this place by herself."

"You should be home resting," Bobbie said sternly to me. "You didn't have to show up here. What? You don't think I can handle things? I've been a Victim Witness volunteer for years before you ever even heard of it."

"It's only been in existence about five years," I quibbled. "And they have it in New York, you know."

"Well, I was an EMT before that."

Were we going to stand here and have a petty argument, when I was afraid Kyle might have killed Leroy, tried to kill Starry? Might even come up here now to kill Didi and Shawn? Bobbie's brother whom she loved passionately, the only one she had left now after Randall killed Hedge. I'd even entertained the thought that Bobbie herself might . . . But she seemed so ordinary, so Bobbie, standing there.

I suddenly felt hopeful. No one would have to kill Shawn and Didi unless Randall had written his daughter something incriminating. And maybe he hadn't.

Rose looked from me to Bobbie and back again. "Shit, you guys." She let her gun fall so it was pointing at the ground. When you thought about it, why should Rose trust me, when Bobbie was an old-timer, a long-term genuine local? "Cut it out. What are you doing with a gun anyway, Bobbie?"

"I brought it with me because Chloe was worried. . . ." She let her voice trail off. "Anyway, I heard your truck and there's no good reason why anyone would be coming up here, so I came outside to check. We're about to leave. Shawn's doing a few things inside and seeing about the fire. Maybe five minutes. I got Didi to agree to stay at Fern's. I had to explain to Shawn things like, well, the law. It's lucky for him he's under eighteen."

Inside the cabin, on a card table, a kerosene lamp flickered on raw wood and mortar. Didi, wearing running shoes, jeans, and a big cowboy shirt that was probably Shawn's was sitting on a straight-backed chair by the table. Her short hair was tousled, and on her the big shirt looked French and chic and pretend. She was biting her thumbnail and staring at nothing when she looked over and saw me.

Her mouth widened into a polite smile. "Hi, Chloe."

"Hi, Didi," I said, annoyed but not mentioning that she had run away from home and caused people pain and worry and forced them to send other people to find her and those people might have earned more than a polite smile.

Shawn was over by the fireplace, doing something about the ashes, his shoulders hunched and tense. You could feel the warmth from the fire still in the room, but it was fading fast. And I had a sense of something else going out of the room, some loss, above and beyond losses already sustained.

My annoyance with Didi faded. "Want to talk?" I asked her.

She shrugged, nodded.

We walked to the door.

We went across the clearing and over to Shawn's car. We stood leaning against the hood. The clouds were still racing across the moon, but there was more sky now, fewer clouds, millions of stars.

"I've talked to your mother," I said. "She's very worried."

"I told her not to be." She looked exasperated. "She doesn't have any faith in me."

"Maybe she just doesn't have faith in the world," I said. "In its basic benevolence towards young girls."

She shrugged, bit her lip. "Le Roi wrote me a letter, but he wasn't straight with me. It was a letter like a parent would write, telling me to finish school, to be kind to people, books I should read." She sighed. "He didn't even know how to be a father. I was hoping he wouldn't just write me a letter like a father would."

"What do you mean?" But I knew.

There was a silence.

"I was hoping he'd tell me why," she finally said.

Did that mean then that she'd decided he did kill himself, that she'd accepted it? I felt sad, I was hoping for more, from a daughter.

As if she read my mind Didi added, "Or who. But I promised Shawn I'd let it go." She looked meditative. "I guess I didn't mean it, though. Are you going to keep looking?"

"Yes," I said, but it was a chilling thought now that I knew about Bobbie and Kyle's brother. I wasn't sure I would like what I might find, just as I wasn't sure Didi needed to know what her father had done eighteen years ago, what he'd been trying to make up for ever since.

. . . went to some library in Phoenix and he researched . . . A newspaper library probably, and I knew what he had researched, everything he could find out about the cop he'd killed, and then he'd moved down here to where the cop was from. A way to never forget. Maybe Didi did need to know, but I would have to think long and hard before I told her.

She bit her lip again. "I guess I ran away partly to come back and think about Leroy but partly, 'cause back at home I didn't think I could live without Shawn."

"And you can? Live without Shawn?"

Her face got set and polite. "I like Shawn a lot, but you know, he doesn't even think I have to go to college 'cause he thinks I'm already twice as smart as him. He doesn't even think it matters if I do anything at all. But if I don't, I'll be like Fern—always sad 'cause I don't have enough interesting things to think about."

It was cruel, but I knew she didn't know better, didn't know that sadness can sometimes swallow up all the interesting things in the world.

She sighed. "So I guess I'll go home in the morning."

Didi and I walked back inside. Shawn looked over at us, his eyes mournful and hurt. Didi went over to him, smiled, and he put his arm round her shoulders, but he couldn't quite manage a smile back. What was it Fern had said— *looking for his mother now in every girl he sees.*

Didi stepped back and walked to the window. "Here comes someone *else,*" she said. "How many people did you get to come after us, Chloe?"

Headlights flashed into the window.

"Shit," said Rose.

"Didi, Shawn, get back from the windows," I said.

"Lie down, you two." Bobbie raised her rifle.

Shawn snorted. "You shittin' me?" He went up to Rose and grabbed at her .22. Rose jerked it away.

"I ain't a damn kid," he said in a hollow voice.

"Chlooeeeee?" came a voice from outside. A voice I knew.

"It's *Lourdes*," I said. "It's OK." What was Lourdes doing here? I went to the door and opened it.

A white compact was parked outside, its lights still on. Lourdes was always terrible about leaving her lights on. She was standing in the clearing, looking forlorn, mud on her rose-colored shoes. Someone else was still in the car.

Lourdes saw me. "Did you find Didi?"

"Yes, but what . . . ?"

Then the car door opened and a woman got out; a tall woman in jeans, down vest, and flannel shirt. I knew her and I didn't know her—I couldn't see her well, until she stepped into the headlights.

It was Helen, Helen Hartman, Randall's mother.

"I'm here to get my granddaughter," she said, looking just as bossy and determined as ever.

43

Didi walked out the door and into the clearing.

Helen watched her until Didi got close, then Helen took out a handkerchief and blew her nose. "Diandra? I'm your grandmother. Randall's mother."

Didi looked at her wide-eyed. "Who's Randall?"

I held my breath. Everyone was watching, listening.

"Leroy. Excuse me, I mean Leroy."

Didi hesitated, looked over at me.

I nodded.

Helen wiped her eyes. "You look exactly like him. And both of you got my lousy hair." She looked at the rest of us. "Excuse me, Diandra and I need to talk."

"Come on, Shawn," said Bobbie loudly, "let's load up your car."

"I'll help," Rose said.

Helen and Didi walked a little way into the dark. I foresaw strong wills battling each other, somewhere in the future. But some good too.

"Helen said Didi's mom called her this morning,"

Lourdes whispered to me. "Told her everything. What did she mean? How can she be her grandmother if she's never even met her?"

"It's a long story." I could hear Roxanne's voice saying, *I was so panicky I did something else and I'm not sure . . .*

"She's a very strong lady," Lourdes said with awe. "She showed up at your house and I was looking out my door and . . . well, you know. We called Fern. Violet was there and she knew where you would be going. Then we even caught up to you. . . . We were honking and honking."

"We heard you."

"Why didn't you stop? We ran off the road, then we got lost for a little while."

"It turned out OK, didn't it?"

Shawn came out of the house, opened the back door of his car, and put in a small duffel bag. Rose and Bobbie followed.

And then Helen was beside me. She took my arm. "I'll take my granddaughter with me," she said commandingly. "Back to where she belongs. Could we talk for a moment?"

We walked away from the others under the starry sky. The moon winked at us. "One letter from Randall, long ago, saying I'm all right, but don't try to find me," Helen said, "postmarked Aqua Prieta, Mexico. I never heard from him again, not for years and years. After a while I thought he must either be dead for have betrayed me in some terrible way, not to write or call. And his father was sick—I had to say Randall was dead to explain. I suppose I thought death was better than this betrayal. Could you tell me just what happened?"

I took her hand. It was warm, callused on the fingertips. "When I know," I said. "And if."

"It will always stay just between you and me."

"I'll write you a letter."

Helen squeezed my hand. "Thank you," she said, and we walked back to the others. "I'll call Roxanne right away."

Bobbie looked inquiringly at me, but her voice was businesslike. "Everything's squared away? I'll give Lourdes a ride home, Chloe, since you left your car at the Hitching Post and Rose'll have to take you there. Didi can go with her . . . grandmother. Chloe, what the fuck is going on here?"

"It's a long story," I said. "I'll explain later."

I didn't know Leroy's parents were even alive," said Rose, as we walked down the road to the pickup.

"I hope Lance is," I said. After all the excitement the reality of the thing was settling down on me like a shroud. I wanted to change the subject.

"He hasn't been exactly alive in years," said Rose, "more like pickled."

"What was it Leroy told you?" I asked her. "All of it."

"No," said Rose. "I already told you too much. Not much more than what I said, though. But I shouldn't have said anything. It was a secret and I got my scruples about betraying the dead."

"You never discussed it with Bobbie?"

Rose stared at me wide-eyed. "Are you *kidding*? People don't talk to Bobbie about her brother. She can't handle it."

"What about Kyle?"

Rose shuddered. "Never."

That didn't mean he didn't know. And there was no doubt in my mind he was capable of doing something about it.

Lance lay on his back in the pickup, the tarp pulled up to his chin, still snoring. We got in the truck and Rose started it up.

"Leroy was a funny guy," said Rose. "I liked him a lot. I asked him once why he was living out here in the middle of nothing, him being so educated and all, and he said it was penance. He wasn't even a Catholic, but he thought about things like doing penance, and sins and stuff. I know it don't make much sense."

"Yes, it does," I said.

"But how do you know so much about him?"

"You can have your secrets and I'll have mine."

We bounced and jounced over the road until we hit blacktop.

Once the ride got smooth I glanced over and asked, "You didn't tell any other cops anything about it?"

She looked indignant. "You think Leroy'd of told me if I was the kind who'd go to the cops? Anyway, Leroy's dead, it doesn't have anything to do with now. Why even bring it up?"

I nodded. "You're right."

"I mean," she said, "it wasn't like Leroy actually killed him or anything."

I watched the road go by, watched the fields, visible now in the moonlight. I rolled down my window a little. *It wasn't like he actually killed him or anything.*

I could smell the greasewood and the rich fecund smell of the soil. It had smelled that way at Leroy's the night he was shot and I thought of the peacock vainly strutting and spreading its wings as Bobbie and I walked up to the porch.

Maybe it was that peacock image that did it, but suddenly the whole thing came to me, and I finally knew what had happened at Leroy's that night.

44

I called him up. "I was afraid you'd be gone," I said.

"Soon," he said.

"We should see each other again before you go," I said, sugar-sweet and wistful. "I know a great place, halfway between you and me on Highway Eighty. It has a bar and the ribs are sensational."

"And so are you." His voice was so confident, so quick on the draw.

"Thank you," I said modestly.

I got there first. I was wearing a long-sleeved black T-shirt, white leggings, and cowboy boots. The place had a couple of pickups parked in front and an old VW bus, with a bumper sticker saying VISUALIZE WHIRLED PEAS.

It was just dusk and somewhere in the distance coyotes were yapping like crazy children. The wind had cleared away all the clouds the night before, the day had warmed up, and now the evening was indigo blue, fringed with purple mountains, the half-moon hanging so perfect in the sky.

I went in. There were three men at the bar, lined up like regulars, a couple in the middle booth busily gnawing on the ribs that were the bar's specialty. I sat in the back booth, facing the door. Over the bar was a big oil painting of a stag, somewhere high on a cliff in a dreamland of snow-covered mountains. Next to that was a calendar with a Vargas-type bosomy rosy cowgirl in a short short skirt and fringed jacket with lariat, dated 1979.

The waitress came from behind the bar with a notepad, frizzy blond hair, pink camisole, silver earrings to her shoulders.

"I'm waiting for someone," I told her, and she retreated.

I flipped the jukebox selector. I didn't want George Strait tonight, I wanted someone with a little taste of the apple in their voice, I wanted k.d. lang singing "Western Stars." But I guess it was too straightforward a place to have k.d. lang.

Then the door opened and he came in, black cowboy hat, turquoise-studded concha hatband, purple, *purple* cowboy shirt, black bolo tie with turquoise bolo. The bartender nodded, the waitress perked up. He slid into the seat across from me, took off his cowboy hat, set it brim up on the table. His chestnut hair fell thick across his forehead and his crooked smile was gallant, reassuring, and knowing. Time hung suspended for a moment, me and this perfect man sitting in a booth in a bar.

Then he spoke, "Hi there, Miss Chloe."

"Can the cowboy shit," I said.

He kicked me in a friendly way under the table. "What did I do *now*?" he asked as if we were old longtime lovers. "I haven't even seen you." He looked over at the waitress. "Two regular orders of the ribs," he said, "extra sauce on the side, beans, slaw. Biscuits? Beer." He looked at me. "You want to have beer with that."

"Not Dr. Pepper?" I asked sarcastically.

"Couple of Coors," he said to the waitress. He turned back to me and took my hand. His hand felt warm and strong and competent. I liked being with him, liked the charge in the air between us, the sense that what was happening was unique, not a repetition of banal social formalities.

I said, "Did you pour the Jim Beam down his throat or did he drink it voluntarily?"

He glanced round the bar and then back at me. "Aw, honey," he said.

There was an extended silence. He rubbed his chin thoughtfully and flipped the jukebox selector. "Anything you'd like to hear?"

"You pick," I said brightly.

He dumped in change and pushed buttons. A country-western singer I didn't recognize began to sing in a low growly voice.

> *"Watch out for the sheriff, honey,*
> *The love sheriff.*
> *Better hide from the sheriff, honey,*
> *The love sheriff."*

Doc winked at me. The waitress brought our orders over, long lengths of ribs spilling over the edges of the thick white plates, sides of beans, swimming in pork grease, slaw rich with sweet pickles and Miracle Whip. The ribs smelled of mesquite and had crackling delicious bits of fat clinging to them that tripled the flavor.

> *"The sheriff got a big old gun,*
> *You seen him coming, better run."*

I wasn't so hungry.

> *"The love sheriff, the love sheriff."*

"OK," said Doc, "it was like I told you. Except . . ."

"Except *you* had the gun and you shot the cop."

"It was fucking awful—the kid stepped right in front of us, no warning, and I shot him. It was just me and your boyfriend, but I had the gun, see, 'cause I was the rancher's kid, the damn cowboy, I wanted to show that New York City boy. . . ."

I wish I could say he lost all of his attractiveness right then when he told me that, but he didn't—he was just as cute as ever. He reached his hand across the table and I took it.

"It was Charlie's .22, so I shot myself in the arm, I said to him, 'I'm a local boy—who are they going to believe, and even if they do believe you, you're going to be charged with something. If you leave right now, we'll all get off, I'll make sure they won't catch you.' "

He took a deep breath.

"Well," I said, "they never did."

I let go of his hand.

Doc looked at me apologetically. "When I went to see him that first time, we took a walk and he told me about his daughter, that he was thinking about turning himself in, getting cleared for her sake. I mean he'd had some involvement, it was conspiracy at least. I said hey, wait a minute, you want to think about that, and he said he understood that it would involve me a whole lot. And would I think about it, because he'd testify it was an accident."

I looked down at the ribs, I could see them for what they were, a whole section of a cow's skeleton.

"What do we have to talk about this for?" said Doc. "It's ruining our dinner."

"You killed two people and now you don't want to talk about it," I said between my teeth.

"Not at *dinner*." Doc sighed and set down his ribs. "Shit, I mean the guy's like some kind of a saint or something, but it's my ass. That's what I said when I went back, it's my ass, man. I thought I'd be able to persuade him to forget it, so long ago and all. I didn't understand the guy, why he was living here in the same damn state where the shit had happened."

"He had to," I said. "It was his penance, his way of making himself understand. He was a big pain in a lot of ways, but you had to respect him."

Doc wiped his mouth. "I parked way away and walked in from the mountains so no one would see my vehicle. Looked like the rain would take care of footprints. We sat at that table of his for a while, talking, me trying to persuade him, and there's this letter sticking out from a pile of stuff, the bottom part with the cowboy thing, and I kept thinking, that would make a hell of a suicide note."

"So you'd planned to kill him all along."

"I didn't plan shit, I just didn't want the guy ruining my life for some philosophical bullshit. I didn't plan it, but I brought the Jim Beam and we were drinking it and I wasn't getting anywhere, so I blew up, I grabbed the damn rifle he had right there and made him drink the rest of it. Then I dragged him over to the couch, stuck the gun in his throat and . . ."

I bit my thumbnail. "Why didn't you just go kill Starry too, that same night? Make it look like a double suicide?"

A look of distaste crossed Doc's face. "I didn't know she was there even, I left fast, and then came back a few days later and saw her in the damn bar. I didn't think she saw me, but I couldn't be sure."

"And me," I said. "You attacked me too. Twice."

"Not to hurt you," Doc said. "At least not that second time, 'cause I'd got fond of you. Just to scare you off so we wouldn't have to sit through a dinner like this."

I had a lump in my throat, my hands felt cold. "So," I said, "are you going to turn yourself in?"

Doc looked at me in surprise. "What the fuck for? Everything I just told you was total bullshit, Chloe; you wanted me to tell you some damn story like this, so I did. There's not one shred of what a cop would call real evidence."

"Starry," I said.

"A nut case. She didn't see anything anyway."

"Excuse me," I said. "I think I'm going to be sick."

I put my napkin on the table and got up. I walked down the long stretch of the bar past the painting of the mountain goat and the calendar of the rosy cowgirl. The waitress flashed me a smile and pointed to the ladies' room.

I went in. The walls were cinder block painted a pale green that was peeling off. There was just the sink and toilet crammed together and a spotted mirror that gave back a wavery image. Above me was a small window, open, showing the black star-spangled sky. I didn't feel sick anymore.

I pushed up the sleeves of my T-shirt, long so Doc wouldn't see the wire Kyle had put on me. I had a Nagra reel-to-reel tape recorder in one boot, transmitter strapped to my chest.

It was all uncomfortable and also useless—I could see how the whole thing would go in court, except I was pretty sure it would never get there. And I figured Kyle had listened to this whole thing, out where he'd parked, and would be thinking the same thing. There wasn't any evidence, just a tape of a guy telling a tall tale to a woman who'd asked for it.

I never trusted him, I thought. Never. Never. I mean, not totally. I opened my purse and took out eyeliner, lined the bottom of my eyes, took out blusher.

I knew he'd be gone by the time I came out, and he was. But he'd put some money in the jukebox, that same song again.

"The grass is blue, the sky is green.
I'm telling you he's mighty mean.
When he comes knocking at your door.
The sheriff, the love sheriff."

A large sack sat on the empty booth.

"He had me pack up everything for you, hon," said the

waitress. "Said you have a big appetite. Don't you worry, he paid."

"Thank goodness," I said.

I picked up the sack with the ribs and the slaw and the beans and went outside to my car. I heard the whine of a police car in the distance as I stood under the sky in the middle of nowhere. Someone said once the whole Valley was nothing but a corridor for the transportation of things that were illegal, be they guns or drugs or people, but of course, that wasn't true. People lived here, raised families, died, but their rules were maybe a little more flexible than some.

While I was thinking this it got very quiet, like the quiet you hear in the woods when a predator is near, so quiet I imagined I could hear sounds from miles and miles away, sounds from across the border, but I knew Doc didn't make it there because then in the middle of the quiet I heard the gunshot clearly, like it was speaking to me—and I knew right away what Kyle had done and should have known he would all along and maybe I did—heard the gunshot clearly, one juror, Smith. I waited for the second, for Wesson, but it was all quiet again.

Match wits with the best-selling

MYSTERY WRITERS

in the business!

SUSAN DUNLAP

"Dunlap's police procedurals have the authenticity of telling detail."
—The Washington Post Book World

☐ AS A FAVOR	20999-4	$4.99
☐ ROGUE WAVE	21197-2	$4.99
☐ DEATH AND TAXES	21406-8	$4.99
☐ HIGHFALL	21560-9	$5.50

SARA PARETSKY

"Paretsky's name always makes the top of the list when people talk about the new female operatives." —The New York Times Book Review

☐ BLOOD SHOT	20420-8	$6.99
☐ BURN MARKS	20845-9	$6.99
☐ INDEMNITY ONLY	21069-0	$6.99
☐ GUARDIAN ANGEL	21399-1	$6.99
☐ KILLING ORDERS	21528-5	$6.99
☐ DEADLOCK	21332-0	$6.99
☐ TUNNEL VISION	21752-0	$6.99

SISTER CAROL ANNE O'MARIE

"Move over Miss Marple..." —San Francisco Sunday Examiner & Chronicle

☐ ADVENT OF DYING	10052-6	$4.99
☐ THE MISSING MADONNA	20473-9	$4.99
☐ A NOVENA FOR MURDER	16469-9	$4.99
☐ MURDER IN ORDINARY TIME	21353-3	$4.99
☐ MURDER MAKES A PILGRIMAGE	21613-3	$4.99

LINDA BARNES

☐ COYOTE	21089-5	$4.99
☐ STEEL GUITAR	21268-5	$4.99
☐ BITTER FINISH	21606-0	$4.99
☐ SNAPSHOT	21220-0	$5.99

At your local bookstore or use this handy page for ordering:

DELL READERS SERVICE, DEPT. DIS

2451 South Wolf Road, Des Plaines, IL . 60018

Please send me the above title(s). I am enclosing $_____
(Please add $2.50 per order to cover shipping and handling.) Send check or money order—no cash or C.O.D.s please.

Dell

Ms./Mrs./Mr. _____

Address _____

City/State _____ Zip _____

DGM-8/96

Prices and availability subject to change without notice. Please allow four to six weeks for delivery.